MW00342929

PRETTY DIRTY SECRETS

Jeana E. Mann

Copyright © 2016 Jeana E. Mann

All rights reserved.

ISBN-10: 1-943938-08-3

ISBN-13: 978-1-943938-08-7

To the douche canoe who told me
my dreams were crazy
and I'd never do it.

Chapter 1

Beckett

AT EIGHT o'clock in the morning, I opened my eyes to bright sunshine and a disturbing case of amnesia. I blinked twice and tried to determine my location. New Orleans. At least I knew that much. With one hand on my forehead, I pushed aside the bedcovers. The silken threads of the hotel rug tickled the soles of my feet. Soreness taunted my thighs and lower back, the kind of pleasant pain that came from a night of fucking. *Serious* fucking.

Tangled sheets twisted across the bed and around my total nakedness. A pair of skimpy panties dangled from the lampshade. The sound of running water in the bathroom put my senses on high alert. I wasn't alone. Snippets of the previous night teased from the shadowy fringes of my brain. Shots. Lots and lots of them. Naked girls dancing on a stage and grinding against my lap. More shots. More girls. Rinse. Lather. Repeat. And then—*nothing*. Nothing but a blank wall until this very moment.

I tried to relax, but something seemed off, something I couldn't put a finger on. It wasn't the first time I'd brought a random girl back to my hotel room, and God willing, it wouldn't be the last. By the number of used condom wrappers littering the nightstand, it had been quite a night. A surge of smug male ego swelled my chest and mitigated my anxiety. I might not remember it, but apparently I'd had one hell of a good time at Sam's bachelor party.

1

The water shut off in the bathroom. I steeled myself for the awkward conversation of the morning after. I had plenty of experience in this area. I would offer to call her a cab, walk her to the hotel lobby, and—depending on how things went—exchange phone numbers. I wracked my brain for clues as to her identity and came up with nothing.

The bathroom door opened to reveal a long-legged girl clad in my white T-shirt. Glossy blond hair cascaded over her shoulders. My gaze swept along the smooth stretch of calf and thigh, over the swell of perfect breasts, up the creamy column of her neck, and stopped at the very blue, very turbulent eyes of my best friend's little sister. Venetia Victoria Seaforth.

"Fuck me," I said and rubbed the back of my neck. Her eyes narrowed. I stumbled backward and tripped over a pair of stiletto heels at the foot of the bed.

"Again?" One of her shapely eyebrows lifted, trademark smirk in place. Her shrewd gaze slid down my body before returning to my face.

My cock twitched in a traitorous show of agreement. "Jesus." I ripped a sheet from the bed and wrapped it around my waist. For the first time in my life, eloquence eluded me, and I stuttered like a fool. "Y-y-you and I? Last night?" She nodded. I sank to the bed and tried to calm my thundering pulse. "How did this happen?"

"You don't remember?" The full pout of her mouth twisted into a frown. I shook my head. "Any of it?"

"Nothing."

A knock rattled the door, and we both flinched. Sam's deep voice floated through the barrier of walnut and brass. "Beckett? You up?"

"Shit." I sprang from the bed and trundled Venetia toward the bathroom. I shoved her over the threshold and tossed her clothes into the room behind her.

"I'm not hiding from my brother." Her soprano voice trembled, a flush high on her cheeks.

"Sam will kick both our asses if he finds you here, and you know it," I growled.

"Don't you mean he'll kick *your* ass?" An adorable smile tilted the corners of her lips.

"Either way, I'm not into it." I remembered the way Sam had reacted when our buddy Tucker had taken her out on a date. *One* date. It had been hell for all parties involved.

"Don't be a drama queen." Her jaw tightened. "Sam will just have to deal."

"Sam won't have to deal, because Sam is never going to know."

Her mouth opened to form a retort.

Before she could continue, I slammed the door shut between us. "Just stay in there and be quiet while I get rid of him." Blood thundered through my veins. I was going to have a heart attack in the prime of life, all because my pecker couldn't behave himself. Stupid, horny bastard.

Sam knocked again, louder this time. "Beckett, get up, you lazy fucker."

I drew in a deep, calming breath, shoved a hand through my hair, and opened the door.

His gaze swept over me, taking in the sheet clutched at my waist, and shook his head. "Rough night?" Sam's eyebrow lifted in a gesture identical to the one his sister had bestowed upon me thirty seconds earlier.

"Uh, yeah." My focus flickered to the bathroom and back to Sam. Unease prickled along my skin. I prayed Venetia would have the common sense to remain hidden. "What's up?"

"We've got lunch at the plantation in an hour." Like his sister, Sam was tall and blond and brimming with self-confidence. He pushed through the door and into the room. I shifted from foot to foot, nerves on edge. "Have you talked to Tucker?"

"No. Why?" In spite of my best efforts, my gaze kept darting to the bathroom door.

"I tried his room and no answer." Sam's attention swept the room. When he

3

turned his back, I brushed the condom wrappers into the trash can beside the bed.

"Maybe he got lucky last night." My voice sounded too high, too thin for a thirty-year-old attorney.

"Probably." Sam walked to the lamp and took the panties from the lampshade. "Looks like he's not the only one." The scrap of blue silk hung suspended from his index finger. His eyes twinkled. "Very nice. Stripper?"

"No." Geez. Could this get any worse? If he knew those panties belonged to his baby sister, he'd annihilate me. My mouth went dry. At six feet seven and two hundred pounds, I didn't fear many men, but Samuel Seaforth was a corporate predator. He'd made a fortune through hostile takeovers and ruthless behavior. I might be able to overpower him with my physical size, but Sam could ruin my career forever with a few well-placed phone calls. Even worse, it would destroy our friendship, a bond I treasured more than my career.

A crash sounded in the bathroom, followed by a string of muffled profanities. I shifted into emergency mode with a calm buoyed by years of high-pressure courtroom experience. "Hey, man, I need to take care of this." I jerked my head toward the bathroom. "Let me get rid of her, and I'll meet you downstairs in fifteen."

"No need. I'm leaving now. Dakota and I have a few things to discuss this morning." His eyes brightened at the mention of his fiancée. "You can meet us there. Grab Tucker and Venetia on your way, will you?" He balled the panties in his fist and tossed them to me. "Don't be late."

The door had barely closed on Sam's back when Venetia bounded out of the bathroom, fully dressed and teeming with anger. If the situation had been less dire, I might have been inclined to stop and admire the sight of her. She'd piled her long hair into a messy bun atop her head. Tanned and toned, she exuded lithe sensuality. A white tank top and dark skinny jeans molded over the swell of perky breasts and slender thighs. I swallowed hard to dispel a vision of my hand inside the waistband of her pants. I blinked away the memory to find her standing in front of me, one hand outstretched, palm facing upward.

"Panties, please." Her delicate nostrils quivered with indignation.

"Sorry." I placed the scrap of silk into her hand and tried not to think of her going commando.

"Yes, you are." She turned and stomped toward the door. Her bottom swung inside the tight denim. I felt a traitorous twitch in my groin. "But not as sorry as me."

I closed my eyes and tried to quell the random thoughts bouncing around inside my head. I'd known Venetia since she was fourteen. I'd seen her awkward phase, plagued with braces and acne, saw her dyed hair and pierced nose during a rebellious phase, and watched her date teenaged jerks unworthy of her. During those years, I'd regarded her in turns as a nuisance, a burden, and an amusement. Never had I considered her to be a potential sex partner. Thoughts like that could only get a man in trouble. I rubbed the back of my neck. Shit. Who was I kidding? I *was* in trouble. Deep, deep trouble.

"Wait." I grabbed her arm and spun her to face me. "I really am sorry."

"You said that already."

"I mean it, V." The angry lines around her mouth softened the smallest amount. "I think we can both agree this was a mistake."

She snorted and crossed her arms over her chest. "You're telling me."

"Look. We just need to get through the rest of today and the wedding tonight without tipping anyone off. You can do that, right?"

Her eyes searched mine. An unfamiliar and heady thrill rocketed through me. For the space of a heartbeat, I forgot who we were and drowned in the bottomless pools of blue staring back at me.

The spell broke when she blinked and looked away. "Fine. If that's what you want."

Without another word, she opened the door and disappeared into the hallway. I shut the door behind her, leaned against my back against it, and blew out a sigh of relief.

Chapter 2

Venetia

BECKETT CLOSED the door. I waited by the elevator and wished the floor would swallow me whole. I'd never been so embarrassed, so humiliated, so mortified in all of my years. The way he'd trundled me into the bathroom, hidden away like some dirty secret, scraped over my pride and left it raw. It wasn't like I expected marriage or commitment or even a phone call afterward. This was Beckett, manwhore and eternal bachelor. I'd gone into the night knowing it was a one-off. What I hadn't expected was to be shoved out the door in a flurry of half-hearted apologies. *It's me, not you. We both know this was a mistake. We can still be friends.*

To make matters more uncomfortable, he didn't recall any of it while I remembered every heart-stopping moment, and it hurt. A night with Beckett had topped my wish list since I was old enough to recognize how hot he was. He hadn't disappointed in the sex department. It had been even better than my vivid imagination. The space between my legs ached, and a number of light bruises peppered the inside of my thighs. Good bruises. The kind that came from a marathon of sex.

The elevator doors slid open with a quiet swoosh. I glanced up to find the curious eyes of my brother staring down at me. Could this morning get any worse? Now I had a witness to my walk of shame. I steeled my nerves for a round of merciless teasing.

7

"I got off on the wrong floor," I offered before he could ask and hoped it would ward off the litany of questions certain to follow.

"Okay," he said. We stared at each other. Well, he stared at me, while I stared at the wall behind him, unable to meet his eyes.

Most people considered Samuel Seaforth to be the most intimidating son of a bitch to walk the earth—next to my father Maxwell. Tall, broad-shouldered, and serious, Sam exuded control and confidence. His exploits in the boardroom and bedroom were legendary. To my eyes, he was still the skinny snot-nosed brat who put plastic spiders in my bed and introduced me as Vagina to his friends.

"Oh, wait. I'm going up," I said, assuming he was on his way to the lobby, and slid a hand between the doors before they could close. "I'll catch the next one." Anything to avoid sharing a confined space with his overly curious mind.

"Me, too. I forgot something in the room." His gaze roamed over my smudged makeup and wrinkled clothing. "Late night or early morning?"

"Both." I pushed the button for my floor and stared at the tips of my toes.

"You were on Beckett's floor." Sam continued to stare, relentless. "Did you see him?"

Heat rushed into my cheeks. God, did he know? He couldn't possibly. Could he? "No." To cover my discomfort, I scowled at him. "Why would I?"

"I don't know." It was only two floors, but the ascent seemed to take an eternity. My brother knew me better than anyone. He could probably see the guilt on my face. "I stopped by there. He had a girl in his room," he continued, voice laden with amusement. "You know Beckett."

I did know Beckett, and one-nighters were his trademark. Shame on me for joining the cast. The elevator crawled to the next floor.

"For a second, I thought maybe it was you," he said. A bead of sweat broke out on my brow. "But that's ridiculous, isn't it? You and Beckett?"

"Yes. Ridiculous." Was it? Apparently Beckett thought so. The serious hotshot attorney and the socialite trust fund baby. Forget Sam. I didn't care what he thought. After all, he was marrying a girl I hated, and he didn't give a crap about my disapproval. I did, however, care what Beckett thought, for reasons I didn't want to analyze at this particular juncture.

"He's old enough to be your father," Sam continued. He knew I'd had a crush on Beckett since I was fourteen, a tidbit Sam loved to exploit every chance he got.

"Don't exaggerate," I snapped before I could stop myself. "Geez, Sam. I'm twenty-three, not twelve." No one knew how to push my buttons better than Sam. He'd spent a lifetime perfecting the skill. Somehow, no matter how old we became, we always reverted back to the habits of our childhood, teasing and taunting each other.

"Still just a baby." He was enjoying this entirely too much, but my pique lessened. My father always forgot my birthday, but Sam had never missed the date. In spite of his constant jibes, I knew he loved me, and the knowledge filled me with warmth.

"How's your backstabbing, money-grubbing fiancée?" I asked to change the subject. The tactic worked with spectacular success. A muscle jumped in Sam's jaw. The elevator dinged at my floor, and the doors opened.

"Don't start." Sam held the door and waited for me to disembark then followed. I hadn't realized we were on the same floor. He trailed on my heels, radiating irritation.

"So, it's okay for you to bug me about Beckett, but I can't touch your precious Dakota?"

"The difference, sweet V, is that Dakota's going to be my wife. Beckett's a crush. He barely knows you're alive." Sam teased me the way only a big brother knew how, provoking my temper for sheer entertainment value. "I want this weekend to be drama free. Promise."

I swiped the key card through the lock on my door then turned and flashed him an innocent smile. "What? I would never—"

"Everything for you is fun and games." With an arm on the doorsill, he

9

blocked my entrance to the room. "But I'm serious about this. It's important to me." The gravity in his voice gave me pause. A wave of guilt washed the smile from my face. "I want everything to be perfect for Dakota."

"Fine. I promise." At that particular moment, I would've said anything to get away from him. I shouldered past, eager for the privacy of my room and a few minutes to reconcile what had happened.

He stepped out of the way and continued down the hall. "Don't be late. I told Becks to pick you up. Better hurry. And bring Sydney along if you want."

Any illusions of time to regroup were quashed by the sight of six large Louis Vuitton suitcases stacked inside the door of my suite. Only my best friend packed an entire wardrobe for a two-day trip. I barely had time to close the door before a whirlwind of smiles and laughter barreled into me. Sydney—my best friend, reality TV star, and fellow trust fund baby—jumped into my arms and squeezed my neck with the force of someone twice her size.

"V! Oh my God!" She stepped back, holding my arms out to the side, and gave me the once over. A frown wrinkled her smooth brow. "You look like shit."

"Thanks," I replied. A genuine smile tugged the corners of my mouth. Sydney's bubbly personality was impossible to refute and highly contagious. "I'm so glad you're here."

"I would've been here last night, but we had to reshoot some scenes for the season finale, and the wrap party went long." She paused for a rapid breath before continuing. "It looks like you found something to do without me." Devilish light brightened her eyes. She took my hand in hers and tugged me toward the couch. "Come tell Auntie Syd all about it."

I met Sydney at private school when we were kids. She was the sole friendly face in a sea of aloof snobs, the first to introduce herself, and she became the

10

sister I always wanted. We remained friends through college, spent our spring breaks together, and survived a litany of broken hearts. To be honest, they were her broken hearts, not mine. Sydney had the tendency to fall in and out of love the way some people changed clothes. I existed on the opposite end of the spectrum and preferred to keep my heart locked in a steel-reinforced cage.

"Well, you'll never believe what happened." I paused for a dramatic breath. She flopped on the sofa beside me, one foot folded beneath her, large eyes wide with interest. "I can hardly believe it myself."

"You met a guy," she said. With a pink-polished fingertip, she touched the side of my neck. "You've got a muffler burn and stars in your eyes."

"Not just any guy," I said. "*The* guy. Beckett."

"No!" Her jaw dropped with an appropriate amount of shock. She shoved my shoulder. "No way."

"Yes way." If anyone understood the significance of what had happened, it was Sydney. She'd been at my house the first time Sam had brought Beckett home with him. We'd been awkward teenagers lounging around the swimming pool when he'd appeared, a vision of rippling abs, long legs, and smoldering hotness in a pair of blue board shorts. I'd never forget the easy grace of the way he moved, the water glistening in his black hair when he surfaced after a dive, or how his deep voice rumbled when he laughed. Of course, he'd barely noticed me beyond a polite nod following our introduction, but it hadn't stopped me from fantasizing about him for the rest of the following decade.

"Holy shit." She tucked a wayward strand of her sleek pageboy behind her ear. "This is epic, V. Epic, I tell you." Her voice lowered to a whisper. "How was it? Was it amazing? Is he hung like a stallion? Details, girl. I need them. Now."

I exhaled a long, tortured breath. "It was good. Amazing, but he doesn't remember any of it."

"What?" Her dismay lessened a little of my own. "That sucks." She tapped a finger to her lips. "Okay. Let's start at the beginning and try to work through it.

Tell me everything."

"I went to the hotel bar last night after my flight came in. He was down there and already smashed, I think." I rubbed my aching forehead. "He said Sam wouldn't go to a strip club, so he and Tucker went on their own. I said I didn't understand the appeal, that I'd never had a lap dance, and next thing I know, he and I are at a strip club down the street."

Laughter burst from Sydney's lips like a gunshot. "OMG. No way."

"Yes way," I replied gravely.

"I have to admit, I like Beckett's style." She snuggled deeper into the sofa and leaned forward. "Then what?"

"Then I got a lap dance."

"From a girl?" Her lips formed a perfect O.

"Yes. Don't judge."

"Not judging. You're doing great. Now get to the sex part." She twirled a finger in the air between us.

I collapsed against the couch and rubbed my temples, which were beginning to ache from the strain of recollection. On any other occasion, I would have regaled her with intimate details, but this time was different, too personal. I wanted to keep the sweet sting of the night tucked away, protected, to savor and lament in private. "Let's just say he rocked my world." I held up three fingers. "Over and over and over." I raised a fourth finger. "And over."

Sydney pursed her mouth. I could hear the gears of her brain working. "And you're sure he doesn't remember?" I rolled my eyes, and she patted my knee apologetically. "Of course. Why would he lie? So what did he have to say this morning?"

"Honestly, he seemed pissed." The vision of his clenched jaw returned the heat of mortification to my cheeks.

"Tell me what he said. Exactly."

I gave her the short version of the morning's events. A prickle of hurt stabbed

12

my pride. "Then Sam came to the door, and he shoved me into the bathroom like some common whore and told me to stay quiet."

"Oh, wow. That *is* bad." We fell silent for a long moment. "But you really can't blame him. You know how overprotective Sam is about you. And Beckett is his best friend. I'm pretty sure in Sam's eyes that would be a direction violation of the bro code."

"I know, it's just—" The prickle of tears returned to confuse me.

Sydney pulled me into her embrace. Her hand rubbed soothingly along my spine. "I know, honey. I know. You've been in love with him forever. That's gotta smart."

Chapter 3

Beckett

TO SAY the drive from our hotel to the plantation house was tense would be a gross understatement. Tucker, suffering from a hangover like my own, remained silent throughout the trip. I suspected his eyes were shut behind the protection of his sunglasses. Venetia sat between us in the back seat of the chauffeured car, cool and lovely in a pair of white shorts and a flowing blue halter top. Her hair cascaded loosely down her back. The occasional brush of her long locks over my bare forearm lit my skin on fire.

"Tucker, get off me." Venetia shoved Tucker's head from her shoulder.

"Sorry," he mumbled, straightening in his seat.

The movement stirred the scent of her shampoo, clean and floral. I drew in a lungful. She smelled good enough to eat. I leaned toward her and took another sniff then stiffened, appalled by my attraction. What the hell was I doing? She was too young, too off-limits. I'd already violated Sam's trust a hundred different ways by sleeping with her, a mistake I had no intension of repeating. On the other hand, every time her arm brushed against mine, my skin prickled with awareness—the sexual kind, the kind that made me wish I had no principles.

"Can you turn up the air?" she asked the driver. "It's hotter than Hades today."

"Supposed to pass a hundred this afternoon," the driver answered in his unique Creole accent. In the rearview mirror, his eyes lingered on Venetia's cleavage.

"How much farther?" I asked. The chauffeur's gaze met mine in the reflection. Irritation stiffened the hairs at the back of my neck, and I narrowed my eyes. He blinked away quickly.

"Almost there," he said.

"Not soon enough," she muttered, and I couldn't have agreed more.

In preparation for a day of casual outdoor camaraderie in the oppressive Louisiana humidity, I'd worn a pair of Bermuda shorts. A scant inch of space existed between Venetia's leg and mine. My skin prickled at the proximity. Tucker's head lolled onto her shoulder once more. She pushed him aside and slid against me with the effort. I twisted away, seeking to put distance between our bare flesh, but only succeeded in dragging my hairy thigh over her smooth one. A picture of her calves balanced on my shoulders as I pounded into her flashed through my head. The scene was too vivid, too detailed to be imagined. The muscles in my groin tightened. I passed a shaking hand over my eyes.

"Looking forward to the wedding?" I asked her, seeking to break the unbearable tension through a neutral topic.

"Don't talk to me." She lifted a hand into the air. I admired her forthright personality. A guy always knew where he stood with her, even if it was in the doghouse.

"You can't still be pissed." I groaned in relief when the cab turned onto the long, oak-lined driveway to the plantation, eager to get out of the confines of the car.

"I can and I am." After a growl of irritation, she crossed her arms over her chest and stared out the opposite window. "Don't pretend nothing happened, Beckett."

"Venetia." I glanced at Tucker. He remained silent. His chest lifted and fell in a quiet, even rhythm. Satisfied he was sleeping, I continued in a whisper, "We both agreed it was a mistake."

"You're a dick." She shifted her back to me, affording a view of her smooth shoulder. My fingers curled with the desire to stroke her unblemished skin. "Take my advice and shut up before you make it any worse."

Chapter 4

Venetia

THE WEDDING party sat at an oblong table on a veranda lined with white columns. Huge ceiling fans circulated the air above us and created a teasing breeze in the sweltering heat. The view beyond offered glimpses of ancient oaks and velvet lawns. An arched bridge traversed a small stream where water splashed across rocks. Over a crystal vase of fragrant hydrangea blossoms, I fought the urge to glare at Beckett and turned my attention instead to a plate heaped with fresh fruit and beignets.

"Hey, Vagina." Dakota's brother, Crockett, greeted me first. I hadn't seen him in years, but he hadn't changed much. He still dressed in head-to-toe black, his shaggy hair hanging over his forehead. When we were kids, he'd spent a lot of time at my house, doing chores while his mother cooked for my family, and thinking of ways to torment me. "Long time, no see."

The use of my childhood nickname resurrected deep-seated insecurities. "Hello, Crackhead." I lifted my chin and gave my haughtiest glare. He needed to know I wasn't a timid little girl anymore.

There were eight of us in all. Sam's friends, Tucker and Beckett, would serve as his groomsmen. Mrs. Atwell, his prospective mother-in-law, sat across the table, his driver Rockwell at his left, and Dakota at his right. I watched my brother interact with his bride-to-be and felt a swift surge of protective rage swell inside me. He'd been married before—to Dakota—and she'd fucked him over royally. Despite my father's best efforts, they were headed to the altar once again, and I could do nothing but watch helplessly from the sidelines.

"We missed you last night, Venetia," Dakota said. The hot Louisiana breeze lifted one of the long brown curls near her face.

Deceitful gold digger. My fingers tightened around the napkin in my lap until my knuckles ached. I refused to believe anything she said, no matter how sincere her expression.

"Where were you anyway?" Sam asked, at the exact second I placed a too-large bite of papaya into my mouth.

My gaze flicked to Beckett. Although his expression remained cool, a flush of scarlet colored his tanned throat. His deep brown eyes pleaded for my silence. I choked down the fruit and used the time to formulate an answer, reveling in the power of the moment. This could go one of two ways. Either I confessed to debauching Sam's best friend, or I swallowed the indiscretion along with the papaya and maintained the civility of breakfast. Beneath the table, a large foot nudged my toe.

"I was tired after the flight," I said. Beckett's broad shoulders lowered a notch and the pressure of his foot eased away. "I caught a cocktail in the hotel bar and went to sleep."

"Too bad," Tucker interjected in his lazy southern drawl. His black Wayfarers hide the collateral damage to his eyes from the previous night and his wavy blond hair stuck out around his head. "We made Bourbon Street our bitch."

"You should've told me your plane was delayed, V," Sam said. "Rockwell would've picked you up at the airport. It's not safe to be out by yourself around here."

"I travel alone all the time," I replied, simultaneously warmed and irritated by his overprotectiveness. "Besides, I'm pretty sure I could kick your ass or anyone else who needed it." I stared pointedly at Beckett.

20

"Jesus," Tucker muttered, and inched his chair back.

"Well, we're glad you made it," Dakota said. "We've got a lot planned for today, and it wouldn't be the same without you."

"Is Sydney coming?" Tucker leaned into my side, speaking too low for anyone else to hear, his tone hopeful.

"Later," I replied. "She wanted to take a nap first." Before I could question why he wanted to know, the thread of conversation took an unwelcome turn.

"Beckett had a good time last night. Didn't you, Becks?" Sam's eyes twinkled with mischief as he deftly changed the subject.

"I suppose so," Beckett said. Our gazes collided across the table and bounced apart.

"I stopped by his room this morning. Seems he had some company." In spite of my mental curses, Sam kept on talking. For a reticent man, he certainly had a lot to say this morning.

"What?" Tucker's fork hovered in midair. "You devil. You've been holding out on me."

"No one's holding out," Beckett said. "There's nothing to tell." A silver ring holding a large blue stone adorned his right ring finger. I'd seen it before; it was some kind of basketball championship ring from his college years. He spun it around and around as he spoke.

"Why don't you bring your girl to the wedding tonight?" Dakota suggested.

I pushed a piece of pineapple around the plate with my fork.

"I don't think so," Beckett said, carefully avoiding my eyes. "But thank you for the invitation."

"Beckett doesn't date," Tucker added. "He's a one-and-done man."

"A hazard of my occupation," Beckett said.

I meant to nudge his big foot with my toe beneath the table but kicked Crockett instead.

"Ouch. What was that for?" Crockett scowled across the table at me and reached down to rub his shin.

"Excuse me," I said in my most prim and proper accent. "My apologies."

"Beckett's a divorce attorney," Dakota explained to Crockett.

"It's ruined him for marriage," Sam said. He lifted a tray of beignets and offered it to me. I shook my head.

"I'm not against it, exactly." Beckett took the tray and dropped two of the tasty confections on his plate. "My parents have been married for thirty years, but I believe they're the exception rather than the rule."

"We're going to be married for thirty years." Sam dropped a kiss on Dakota's temple, and she smiled. My stomach turned over, and I had to look away.

"And thirty more after that," Rockwell interjected and lifted his glass into the air in a toast.

"I have no doubt you will," Beckett said, his tone warm. "But I believe you two are also the exception and not the rule. Not everyone is cut out for marriage. Like me, for instance. In my opinion, it's a binding legal contract, a business agreement."

"Wow, that's cold," Crockett said and stuffed an entire beignet into his mouth.

"It's not cold. It's realistic. Statistically speaking, half of all marriages end in divorce," Beckett said.

"And some marriages last a lifetime," Mrs. Atwell said. I hadn't seen her in a decade, but age hadn't dimmed her Nordic beauty. Her blue eyes softened as she watched Dakota caress Sam's cheek. I wanted to shove a finger down my throat but sat on my hands instead.

"Absolutely," Beckett added smoothly. A ray of morning sunlight cast blue highlights on his short black hair. "But if they don't, they always need a good attorney. And that's where I come in." The dimple beside his mouth deepened. Desire skated up the inside of my thighs.

"Have you ever even had a relationship?" Tucker asked.

"Why buy the cow when I can get the milk for free?" Beckett said.

I bristled at his callous remark. His brows drew together as he realized the insult he'd just thrown my way. It was all I could do to resist stretching across the yellow tablecloth and tossing my Mimosa in his lap. He leaned back to regard me with open curiosity, an arm thrown over the back of the empty chair beside him. His square jaw gleamed from a fresh shave. Hidden by my eyelashes, my gaze snagged on the hint of black curling chest hair exposed through the open throat of his white polo shirt. The space between my legs ached from where he'd ridden me. Lordy, he was smoking hot. I had to pinch myself to prove it hadn't been a dream. Then I remembered I was mad at him.

"What about you?" I asked Tucker, eager to turn the attention somewhere else. "What happened to you last night?"

"After Beckett bailed on me, I sat in on a poker game at the casino," he said, leaning his chair back on two legs.

"Alone?" I lifted an eyebrow.

Tucker's cheeks colored, but his smile grew. "I was lucky enough to run into an old friend along the way."

"How'd you do?" Beckett asked.

"With the girl or at the table?" Tucker smirked.

"I never have any luck gambling," Dakota said.

"Unlucky at cards, lucky in love," Rockwell interjected. He patted Mrs. Atwell's hand, and they shared a smile.

"Lost my ass." Tucker lowered his sunglasses and winked at me. I grinned back. Our relationship was much easier than the one I shared with Beckett.

"A fool and his money are soon parted," Sam said.

"Well, you should know all about that," I quipped. Awkward silence descended over the table. Heat flashed into my cheeks. Oh, why had I said that? Damn my mouth. I bit the tip of my tongue.

A muscle in Sam's jaw flexed, and a knot of regret tightened in my belly. I frowned and stared down at my lap. No matter how I felt about Dakota, it was evident Sam adored her. The last thing I wanted was to hurt him. He'd been the only constant in my life. Even during what he and I called the dark ages, when he'd been at war with my father and heartbroken over Dakota's betrayal, he'd been my rock.

"Excuse me. I think I'll visit the ladies room." I pushed back my chair, unable to tolerate another second pretending this event was anything other than a huge sham.

Tension crackled through the room. The walls of my chest ached from the weight of it. Sam and I stood in unison. The legs of our chairs scraped across the hardwood floor. We stared at each other over the elegant china, antique silver, and crystal goblets. Even the birds stopped chirping.

"In the hall. Now." Sam spoke in a low, quiet voice, his words clipped. It was his business voice, the one he used to call order to an unruly boardroom, the one that meant I was about to get a verbal ass-kicking.

My knees wobbled, knowing I'd pushed him too far. The frown on his face reminded me of being eight years old, having trespassed into his bedroom or listened into his phone conversations with a teenaged Dakota. I fought the urge to hang my head and walked into the hallway, chin lifted, lips trembling. He followed on my heels, fingers tight around my elbow, and marched me over the threshold of a nearby sitting room.

"That's it. No more." He took a warrior's stance in front of the fireplace. I stared at my toes and fought back words of hurt and anger. He was all I had left. The only thing worse than his rage was the threat of his emotional pain once Dakota showed her true self and dumped him again. I'd do anything to protect him from that kind of anguish.

"I'm sorry. I just can't keep quiet any longer. You're making a terrible mistake. Don't go through with it. Everyone will understand. You don't have to explain anything. We can just pack up and leave." I conjured my best wheedling tone. "I'll tell Rockwell to get a car for us."

After a painful pause, Sam pointed a finger in my face. "You need to straighten up. Right the fuck now. I'm going to marry Dakota. Tonight. Whether you like it or not."

I batted his hand away, but I still couldn't look him in the eye. "She's making a fool out of you. Again. Everyone knows it. Tucker. Beckett." Once the words started, they gushed out of me. "She hasn't changed. We all see it. Everyone but you. She's going to marry you, pop out a kid or two, then leave and take all your money."

"What money?" Sam chuckled, but his eyes remained humorless. "We both know I'm broke."

"But you won't be for long. You're a genius like that. You'll be back on top in no time." I meant it. My father had filed bankruptcy and still had billions of dollars. Sam was smarter and shrewder than any man I knew, including my dad. "You'll be stuck with her forever. Just wait. She's poison. Can't you see that?" Emboldened by my speech, I ventured further, setting all my misgivings free. "I bet she's still in contact with Dad. You know how he is. Once he gets his claws into someone, he never lets go." Except for me. He let go of me. I squeezed my eyes shut to block out the sight of Sam's anger. I was going to have my say whether he liked it or not.

When I opened my eyes, Sam continued to point a finger at me. "You have no idea about any of this. What she's been through. What our father did to her. The way he manipulated us." The tight lines around his mouth frightened me more than his words. "You have no right to pass judgment."

"I have every right," I snapped. By this time, we stood toe-to-toe, mutual fury unbridled. "You mean everything to me. And I protect what's mine. I won't let her ruin you again."

A little of the heat in Sam's eyes dissipated. He took a step back. The air thinned between us.

Thinking I'd won, I continued, my voice wheedling. "You know I'm right. You know it, Sam. In your heart, you have to admit it's the truth."

He shook his head and ran a hand through his hair. "I get that you're worried. But you need to trust me. Dakota loves me, and I love her." His tone softened. "I'm nothing without her, V. Nothing."

The conviction in his words tilted my world. I'd never heard Sam sound so wrecked with emotion, so convicted, and never over any other woman. Only Dakota. My stomach churned. I was losing him. And to her, of all people. "You'll have nothing if you stay with her. She'll ruin you."

"I already have nothing, and she doesn't care." His shoulders shook with laughter. "Do you really think I'd marry someone I can't trust?" He studied me with somber eyes, eyes that cut through me like a laser beam.

"You did once before."

"You think I'm an idiot?"

"I think you let your dick rule your head where she's concerned." The accusation popped out of my mouth and hung in the air between us. Sam's green gaze flared. I panicked. "I mean—that's not what I meant."

"It's exactly what you meant." He shook his head. "If you felt this way, why'd you even bother coming here?" The way his jaw tensed reminded me of our father when he was angry. Solid as granite and twice as unrelenting. He walked toward the door. When he faced me again, his eyes were icy. "Here's the deal, V. If you're not with me, you're against me. And if you're against me, then I don't want you here. The choice is yours."

His ultimatum struck me with the impact of a fist. I recoiled and placed a hand over my diaphragm, unable to draw breath, fighting back tears. He chose her over me. Just like my father. When Sam opened the door, Beckett stood in the hallway, fist uplifted as if about to knock. He dropped his hand, and his gaze travelled from me to Sam and back again.

"Everything okay in here?" Beckett asked.

"That goes for you, too, Beckett," Sam said. "With me or against me?"

Beckett lifted his hands, showing his palms. "I'm with you, man. Always. All the way. Balls to the wall."

Sam pushed past him and disappeared in the direction of the dining room. Beckett stared at me. From beyond his broad shoulders, I caught the shocked glances of Rockwell, Mrs. Atwell, and Dakota. Tucker's mouth gaped open. He shut it with a snap and dropped his gaze to his empty plate. Crockett smirked. It was going to be a very long day.

Playing witness to my brother's wedding was going to be much more difficult than I anticipated. For some reason, I'd been under the misguided notion that I could hang out with Sam and Dakota while remaining detached from the significance of the event. After our little run-in, I began to think otherwise. Sam was making a mistake of epic proportions. I couldn't stand by and watch him remarry that traitorous bitch. The first time, I'd been too young to understand, but now I comprehended the ramifications all too well.

I splashed my face with water then wandered out a side door and down a narrow gravel path. Gnarled branches dripped with Spanish moss. The humidity bordered on unbearable. Near the stream's edge, a wooden swing swayed in the breeze, suspended from a huge tree by ropes as thick as my wrists. I took a seat and tried to steady my thoughts. At the crunch of footsteps on the gravel, I glanced up to find Beckett rounding the curve of the path.

"Hey." He vibrated to a stop and glanced over his shoulder as if looking for a means of escape. When he caught a glimpse of my face, his expression softened. "What are you doing?"

"Swinging," I replied. "What are you doing?"

"Looking for a place to smoke. The whole grounds are non-smoking." He fished in the pocket of his khaki shorts and came back with a battered box of

Camels and a silver Zippo. He placed the filter between full lips, flicked the lighter, then cupped his hands around the cigarette to shelter it from the breeze.

"I didn't know you smoked."

"Wish I didn't," he said and sighed. "I keep trying to quit."

"Can I have one?"

"No." He regarded me for a second then shook his head and handed his cigarette to me, filter first. "Since when do you smoke?"

"Since now." I took a drag. The nicotine tingled on my lips, and the smoke burned my lungs. I coughed and sputtered until he pounded me on the back.

"Give me that." He snatched the cigarette from my grasp and scowled before lifting it back to his lips. "What's wrong with you?" Twin plumes of smoke drifted from his nostrils and dissipated in the air between us. "Jesus, that's all I need. If Sam found out I turned you into a smoker, he'd really have my ass."

"I think that's the least of your worries, given what you did to me last night." I bit back a smirk at the twin patches of red in his cheeks.

"Don't remind me," he groaned. He flicked ashes onto the gravel with an expert twitch of his thumb.

"Could you be a little less enthusiastic?" I grumbled. "My ego can't take it."

"Sorry. I didn't mean it like that." The smooth baritone of his voice lessened the sting of his words. "I'm sure it was…delightful."

I barked out a laugh. "Delightful? Seriously?" A pair of swans glided past us, buoyed by the current of the stream and disappeared around the bend. "The ballet is delightful. Newborn babies are delightful."

He sighed, leaned his back against a tree, long legs crossed at the ankle, and regarded me. "I really am sorry, V."

"Stop apologizing. You're only making it worse," I admonished.

Beckett finished his cigarette, dropped it to the gravel, and ground it out with the toe of his loafer. I twisted the swing rope tightly and let it spin me in a slow circle. My heels cut a circle into the gravel as the rope unwound.

"What was that back there anyway?" he asked.

"How can you stand by and let him go through with it?" I asked, my anger renewing.

"It's not my business," Beckett said. "Or yours."

"If you were any kind of friend, you'd stop him," I said, my voice climbing in pitch and volume. "You know what she did to him before." The recollection of Dakota's betrayal lit my temper. "She extorted money from my dad. He paid her a million dollars to divorce Sam. What kind of person does that to someone they love?"

"You don't know the whole story," Beckett said, his voice as calm as mine was wild. "Only Sam and Dakota know the entire truth."

"That's bullshit and you know it."

Beckett shook his head while I gathered steam. His laughter scraped across my nerves. "Like anyone could stop Sam from doing what he wants. You of all people should know that. He's going to marry her, and if you're smart, you'll stay out of the way. All we can do is stand by him and be there when—if—he needs us."

"You're not helpful at all." My gaze flicked up to meet his. His eyes were dark with worry. My heart squeezed. Beckett loved Sam almost as much as I did. "You don't approve either?"

He shook his head. "It doesn't matter what I think."

"Coward," I taunted.

Beckett laughed and crossed his arms over his chest. "Not cowardly. Cautious. There's a difference. You should try it sometime." He leaned forward and brushed a wayward strand of hair from my temple. "A little caution might do you some good." The glide of his touch against my skin sent a small shiver down my back in spite of the heat.

"That's not what you said last night. Last night you were all like, *Do it, Venetia. Don't stop, Venetia*," I teased. "Did you know the tips of your ears turn red when you're embarrassed?"

He passed a hand over his eyes. "I blame the alcohol."

"You didn't think it was a mistake last night." I couldn't help prodding his discomfort. "In fact, you were very enthusiastic about the whole ordeal."

"Really?" One of his eyebrows lifted. "So…" His voice trailed off before picking up the thought again. "How was it?"

My gaze snapped up to his. Devilish humor danced in his eyes. Arrogant ass. It was just like a man to worry about his prowess.

"I'm sure it was *delightful,*" I replied. A dimple flashed in his cheek as his face split into a smile. I let him chew on this tidbit for a second before I continued. "And you can stop with the guilt. I might have taken advantage of you in your drunken state."

"I doubt that." His dark brow furrowed into a frown. "I'm the adult here—"

"We're both adults, Beckett." Anger heated my face. He still regarded me as a kid. All the frustration and hurt from the day welled up inside me. A tear threatened to slide down my nose. I blinked it away. *Don't cry. Do. Not. Cry.* The last thing I wanted was to show how deeply his words wounded me.

"Shit." He saw the evidence anyway. "Come here."

"No. I'm okay," I said, but I didn't push his arms away.

"You're not okay. Come here." He nestled my nose into the hollow at the base of his neck. The warmth and strength of his embrace cracked the walls of my defenses, and another tear escaped. "Don't cry, baby girl."

The way he said "baby girl" brought back an abrupt flash of my legs wrapped around his narrow hips, our naked flesh colliding, and his whispered endearments in my ear. *Fuck me harder, baby… Put your leg here, sweetness.* A twinge of lust tightened inside me. I cleared my throat and tried not to inhale the clean scent of his aftershave.

"V. Look at me." The touch of his fingertip to my chin brought my gaze up to his. Dark brown eyes, the color of rich coffee, dipped to my lips. The expanse of his chest pressed against my breasts with each of his breaths, which were coming quicker by the second. I leaned into his embrace.

"Beckett?" I started to whisper his name, but his mouth crushed against my lips. His tongue swept over mine. I moaned, my furious heartbeats spurred on by the tangle of his fingers in my hair. One of his hands edged into my shorts, easing down to claim a handful of my bottom. I felt every inch of his lean body, hard thighs, the button on the fly of his shorts, and the steel behind it.

"What are you doing?" Tucker's voice caused us to bounce apart.

I turned my back, fingers flying over my clothes and through my disordered hair.

"Nothing." Beckett's voice sounded harsh.

The denial stung. Again. Fool me twice, shame on me. I resolved then and there to make sure there wasn't a third time.

"Yeah. I'm pretty sure you were doing something." Tucker smirked.

"Shut up, Tucker." I pushed past him and thundered down the trail without a backward glance. Once I rounded the corner, I found a quiet bench, sat down, and tried to quiet the trembling of my hands.

Chapter 5

Beckett

"DO MY eyes deceive me, or were you just shoving your tongue down young Venetia's throat?" Tucker leaned against a tree and waited for an answer.

I couldn't reply, too rattled by the taste of champagne and orange juice on Venetia's tongue, the sweet smell of her perfume, and the soft slide of her hair through my fingers. God, in that moment, I'd wanted her. No. Not wanted. Desired. The kiss brought back a dozen memories from the night before. Venetia naked. Her honeyed thighs parted while I sank deep inside her. A tangle of bedsheets wrapped around her waist, high breasts peeking over the linen, taunting me to touch, knead, suck.

"I fucked up, Tucker," I said. "Royally."

"You didn't." His eyes lit up with playful excitement.

I scrubbed a hand over my eyes and nodded. "Not a word to anyone about this. Not. One. Word. Understand me?"

Tucker raised his hands, fingers splayed, and shook his head. "No judgment here. But can I just say you're playing with fire, my friend."

Didn't I know it? I had no excuses for my behavior, except... Damn, she tasted good. It had been a few years since the last time I'd seen her, and she'd changed since then, in the best of ways. Her legs seemed longer, her eyes bluer, her breasts bouncier. The minute I'd taken her into my arms, I'd been a goner. All reason had left my head at the same time all the blood had rushed into my cock.

"It's not going to happen again," I said, more to convince myself than Tucker.

"Looks like it was about to," he interjected, "if I hadn't come along, that is." He waggled his eyebrows.

"She was upset. I tried to comfort her."

"With your hands in her pants? Remind me to keep my troubles to myself next time." His laughter scraped over my humiliation, and I winced.

"Things got...out of control." I turned away from him and started down the path. His footsteps crunched on the gravel behind me. Nothing could excuse my behavior. I'd stepped over the line with her for a second time. Damn my traitorous dick, and damn her beautiful big blue eyes.

Once we returned to the house, the group gathered for a game of croquet on one of the smooth plantation lawns. I vowed to keep my distance from Venetia for the rest of the day, but my eyes kept straying back to her. Tanned legs stretched from white denim shorts. The halter top revealed a strip of toned, taut skin above the waistband of her shorts. She'd twisted her blond hair high atop her head in an artful mess. The ends fluttered and danced around her temples when the wind picked up.

Sam, Dakota, and Crockett squared up against Tucker, Venetia, and me. The rest of the group drank lemonade and mint juleps from shaded tables around the perimeter of the playing field.

What should've been a civilized, sedate game quickly devolved into no-holds-barred warfare. Venetia and Sam were ruthlessly competitive. When her ball landed against Dakota's, I braced for the worst. Venetia placed a foot on top of her ball and with a well-placed *thwack* sent Dakota's ball soaring into the distant underbrush.

"Yes. Take that," Venetia lifted her arm and mallet into the air triumphantly. She sashayed in a circle, shaking her round bottom in a victory dance worthy of an NFL quarterback. I choked back a laugh.

From ten paces away, I saw Sam bristle. He pointed a finger at me. "Don't encourage her." To Dakota, he said, "Stay there. I'll get it."

"No. It's fine. I'll get it." Dakota placed a hand on his forearm.

"There might be snakes in there," he replied, and glared at his sister. "Venetia can get it."

"Like hell," Venetia muttered.

"I'll get it," I said, having experienced the wrong side of a Seaforth temper a time or two myself, eager to avoid the drama.

"No one's going to get it," Dakota shouted in a rare show of irritation. "It's my ball." She stomped into the thicket of weeds.

Sam ghosted her footsteps, muttering curses.

"I don't know about you, but that one scares me a little." Tucker nodded at Venetia before driving his ball toward the wicket for a point.

"She's a handful, that's for sure," I replied, letting my gaze drift over her once more. She stood in a beam of sunlight, dappled by the branches overhead. One hand rested on her hip while the other shaded her eyes to observe her opponents. Watching her, I knew exactly why I was so attracted. She was different, more intense, more confident, more beautiful…just *more* than I remembered. A year in Italy with one of Milan's most influential interior designers had served her well. As a Seaforth, she was destined for success. It flowed through her veins and DNA. I had no doubts she'd become as powerful and influential as her father and brother, given enough time.

"I pity the man who tries to tame her," Tucker said.

"I could do it." For some reason, the thought of her with someone else didn't sit well. My fingers curled into fists at the idea of another man, any man, touching her.

Tucker lifted an eyebrow. I coughed and cleared my throat. "Better bring some spurs, cowboy," he said and clapped a hand on my shoulder.

Dakota retrieved her ball and drove it back into play. On my turn, I gave a half-hearted swing. The ball ambled a few feet and came to a stop.

Venetia turned accusing eyes to mine. "Seriously? Is that all you've got?" She frowned. "I expected better from you, Beckett."

"Me, too," Tucker added. He had a mint julep in one hand and twirled his mallet through the air with the other. "You're a professional ball handler. Have some pride, man."

I shrugged. "Was. I *was* a professional basketball player. A million years ago. My specialty is law now. Besides, it's too damn hot." Humidity plastered my shirt to my chest. I plucked at it with two fingers but found little relief from the heat or the tension of the game. "This isn't even a real sport."

"Don't tell me you're afraid of a little friendly competition." Venetia had gotten closer until I could see the smattering of freckles over the bridge of her nose brought out by the sun. Her breath held the faint odor of liquor. With a fingertip, she lowered her sunglasses and peered over the frames at me. Challenge lit her eyes.

"I like competition," I replied, meeting her stare. "Especially when the prize is something I want." What? Wait. Shit. I shouldn't have said that, yet the fire in her eyes made my groin tighten with need and the wish to taunt her more.

"What do you want?" The timbre of her voice lowered, sultry and smooth, so only I could hear. "Care to make a wager?"

"How about another kiss?" My gaze dipped to her mouth.

Her pink tongue smoothed over her lower lip in a decadent slide. Too many mint juleps before lunch had loosened my inhibitions, had my common sense tied up in knots.

"What the hell, Venetia?" Sam's angry voice brought a screeching halt to our wordplay. A half dozen long strides placed him between us. I glanced away, flushed with guilt. He wrapped a hand around her bicep and jerked her to his side. "No drama. You promised."

"The only drama I see is yours." She yanked her arm out of his grip and glared back at him with equal intensity. "It's a game, Sam. Get over it."

"You get over it," he growled.

"Touchy, touchy," Venetia teased. I'd witnessed a hundred similar altercations between them. They were passionate, playful, quick to anger, and quicker to forgive. She loved to irritate him in the way only a little sister can do, and Sam ate it up.

"Give him a break, V," I said. "The man's under a lot of stress." I watched him gather Dakota and retreat in the direction of the house.

Venetia poked me in the chest with the handle of her mallet. "You're so sensitive for a big guy."

"And you're so drunk." I gripped the end of the mallet and gave it a small tug. She stumbled forward and placed a hand on my chest to recover her balance. My heart thudded against her palm. She stared at her hand. A live connection jolted between us. Her gaze lifted to mine, dropped to my mouth, and flickered up again.

"I don't know about you, but I'm done. It's too hot out here." Tucker approached. "Let's go swimming." His gaze bounced between Venetia and me. "You need to put a leash on that anaconda." He pointed his mallet at my crotch.

Venetia's fingers lingered over the swell of my chest. Whatever had sparked between us flickered and died. She backed away, looking everywhere but at me, then turned and disappeared in the opposite direction as Sam. I exhaled in relief, feeling like I'd just passed through the eye of a hurricane.

Chapter 6

Venetia

TO COOL our tempers and sunburned skin, the group headed to the pool following the croquet match. Sydney arrived in time for the fun, wearing a Hawaiian print sarong and matching bikini. She floated on a raft next to me, a mimosa in one hand and her cell phone in the other.

Within seconds of her appearance, Tucker paddled over to greet her, all lazy smiles and quiet stares. "Sydney," he said, drawling out the syllables, making her name sound almost dirty in his Kentucky twang.

"Hey, Tucker," she replied, red lips parted in a brilliant smile of her own.

He rested a hand on the corner of her raft and treaded water next to her. They regarded each other in wordless admiration. The sexual tension between them thickened the air around us until I blinked away, uncomfortable. If I didn't know better, I'd think something was going on. But I did know better. Sydney had a boyfriend, the co-star of her television show, a handsome, charismatic Australian.

"Hey, yourself," Tucker said.

She batted long, black lashes at him. For a second I thought they might kiss or do something equally reckless, but Beckett broke their trance by diving off the board in a perfect arc. His lean form sliced the surface at the opposite end of the pool without a ripple.

I followed the shadow of Beckett's body through the clear depths and felt a small thrill when he passed beneath me, close enough to cause an undercurrent to swirl and eddy around my body, rocking my floating chair. Was there anything this man couldn't do and do well? Handsome, athletic, and smart. The trifecta of male pulchritude. He surfaced a few feet away, shaking his head and flinging water in all directions, dark locks hanging in messy waves over his forehead.

Tucker fist-pumped the air. "Yeah, man. You're the king." Taking Beckett's prowess as a personal challenge, Tucker abandoned Sydney. He splashed to the ladder for a turn, but my attention remained on Beckett.

He was tall enough to stand on the bottom near me, the upper third of his torso above the surface. From behind the safety of my sunglasses, I admired his shape, the perfect slope of his shoulders, the round swell of his biceps, the definition of sinew and muscle roped by thick veins. He had to work out every day to have a body like that, eat right, train hard. I held my breath as he waded toward the side, his gaze flicking over me in the briefest of glances. One look from him sent me back through the years. I was fourteen again, heart hammering in my chest, mouth dry, overwhelmed by his hotness. Droplets of water glistened on the six-pack of his abdomen. Each step revealed another inch of smooth, tanned flesh, a flat belly button, a trail of black hair leading into the waistband of his trunks, the deep cut of muscle on each hip. When he reached the edge of the pool, he hoisted himself to the deck in one effortless motion and sauntered back to the diving board.

"Did you see that?" Sydney whispered. "Holy hell." She grabbed the edge of my float and pulled me closer. "I think my ovaries just exploded."

One of the things I loved best about Sydney was her sense of humor. I laughed, relieved to have a distraction. "You're a goof."

"No. I'm serious. You were with *that* last night, V. My respect for you has reached a whole new level."

"Shhhh." I scowled and cast a covert glance around the area. "In the vault, remember? You need to lock it up tight and never let it out."

"Right." She didn't sound convinced but nodded anyway.

"And stop staring at him. He's going to know I told you."

"Why do you care? If it was me, I'd send out a press release."

While Tucker took his place on the end of the diving board, Beckett stood alongside. Although he was too far away to see his eyes clearly, I felt the weight of his gaze on us. Heat burned in my cheeks, intensified by the afternoon sun. In all the years I'd known him, he'd never shown this much interest in me. I liked his gaze on me. After a lifetime of going unnoticed, I gloried in the attention and the long-overdue boost to my ego.

"Your whole life is public property, Syd. You couldn't keep anything a secret, even if you wanted to."

For a moment, she looked wistful, and my heart squeezed for her. While no one ever noticed me, everyone noticed Sydney. She lived in a fish bowl and had grown accustomed to the total invasion of privacy, the constant swarm of cameras, everyone talking about and watching her.

"What's with you and Tucker, anyway?" I asked.

"Nothing." Her eyes lit with playful fire. "Yet."

"Syd, do I need to remind you that you have a boyfriend? Alex? Remember?"

She dipped a shoulder in a dismissive shrug, smiling again. "We have an agreement. When we're apart, we can see other people."

"Really?" I lifted an eyebrow. "Does Tucker know about Alex?"

"I don't know. Does Sam know you're screwing his best friend?" Her pretty face puckered into a scowl. "Don't be a grandma. I'm just going to play a little with Tuck. No one will ever know." Narrowed eyes bored into me. "Unless you tell."

I groaned. "I wish I'd never said anything."

"You keep my secret, and I'll keep yours." The smile returned to her lips. She splashed me playfully.

"That's blackmail."

"I know." Obvious delight lilted in her voice, and I bit my lower lip to hold back a smile. "Now, get over there right now and stake your claim on Mr. Ovary-Exploder."

For the briefest moment, I contemplated her suggestion. What would it feel like to belong to him? I fantasized about walking up to him, digging my fingers into his thick hair and planting a kiss on his full lips—in broad daylight—in front of everyone. The idea curled my toes. Only his ambivalence stopped me. My gaze wandered back and collided with his. He looked quickly away to chide Tucker.

"This is my specialty dive," Tucker announced. He gave Sydney a wink. Two running steps and one leap sent him high into the air. The tip of the board vibrated from the impact of his feet. He somersaulted, tucking his knees beneath his chin, and landed with a resounding smack a few feet from us. The resultant tidal wave capsized my float. The cocktail in my hand tumbled into the pool.

Sydney shrieked and clutched her raft. "Tucker!" she fumed. "That's not funny. You know I can't swim."

"Don't worry, darling." He stroked through the waves to her side and steadied the raft. "I'll save you."

"Nice," Beckett called after him. "Now, let a real man show you how it's done."

"Jesus. What the hell happened to your back?" Tucker's attention drifted from Sydney to Beckett, who'd turned to mount the diving board.

"What?" Beckett twisted in an attempt to see over his shoulder.

Bright sunshine glinted off his back and highlighted a series of five red scratches from his nape to his waist. Blood rushed into my cheeks. I put a hand to my mouth to hold back a gasp. Sydney laughed so hard I thought she might tumble from her float.

"It looks like a hellcat got hold of you," Tucker chided. "That must've been some good time you had last night."

Beckett avoided my stare. He bounced on the end of the board, testing the spring. "A gentleman never tells."

"That'll be a first." Sam sauntered onto the scene. "Usually you like to regale us with all the sordid details."

I groaned and slid from the chair into the cool depths until the water closed over my head. Beneath the surface, I could hear my heart beat and relished the serenity of the moment. A shaft of sunlight cut through the waves and cast prisms on the concrete floor. I wasn't sure how to deal with Beckett, and I most definitely didn't want to discuss my sex life in front of an audience. Drowning seemed like a viable alternative. A muted splash rescued me. Beckett's form torpedoed through the blue water and glided past me. A sharp pinch stung my bottom. I pushed off the pool floor to resurface, in need of oxygen. Beckett popped up a few feet away, a smirk curving his mouth. For a few blissful seconds, everyone else faded away, and we were alone. I returned his smile and forgot to be afraid.

After Tucker and Beckett completed their diving competition, the atmosphere began to quiet. Crockett stretched out on one of the hammocks beneath the trees. Sydney and Tucker sprawled on a blanket near the garden gate. Rockwell, Mrs. Atwell, Sam, and Dakota sat around a patio table. Their smiles and laughter floated over the mirrored surface of the pool. From my vantage point a few yards away, they looked like a typical family, one to which I didn't belong.

I sat on the edge of the pool and dangled my legs in the water. Mrs. Atwell leaned forward and squeezed Dakota before dropping a kiss on her forehead. An uncomfortable ache filled my ribcage. They seemed happy, contented. I turned my attention to the young man trimming roses in a nearby flowerbed. What was it like to have a mom who gave out hugs and smiles instead of reprimands and admonishments? *Sit up straight, Venetia. Enunciate clearly, Venetia. Not now, Venetia.* The muscles in my forehead tightened. The unpleasant memories were all I had of my mother, yet I clung to them.

43

"If you frown any harder, your face is going to freeze like that." Beckett's deep, smooth voice interrupted my pity party. He sat in the deck chair at my left and stretched his long legs in front of him. Coarse black hair covered the bronzed muscles of his thighs and calves. Mirrored aviators hid his eyes, but I felt them peruse over me.

"Maybe I just have resting bitch face." I lowered my sunglasses from my hair to my nose, abashed to be caught staring at my new in-laws.

"You've got a beautiful face." The praise buoyed my spirits. He smiled, lifting my mood even more when a dimple popped next to his mouth. "There we go. That's better."

"Last night—how did that happen?" I asked, overwhelmed by the need to know. "I mean, what's changed? You barely noticed me before."

His brows dipped lower and furrowed. I wished he'd take off those damn sunglasses so I could see his eyes, because I had no idea how to judge his sincerity. "Oh, believe me, I noticed you before then." The corners of his lips tipped up. "But you were a kid. Off limits. You're still off limits." Even though I couldn't see the direction of his gaze, I felt it slide over my breasts. My nipples tingled behind the small triangles of the bikini top. "As for last night—well—I'm only human."

"I wasn't fishing for a compliment."

"It's not a compliment. It's a fact. And if Sam wasn't your brother, and I wasn't a jerk, you'd have to fight me away with a baseball bat."

Holy hell. This confession muddied the anger I'd been clinging to for self-preservation. I melted a little inside.

"Excuse me," said an unfamiliar voice. "Are you Dakota Atwell?" I looked up into the face of a plantation employee. He held up a small express mail package. "She's got a delivery."

"No. She's over there." I pointed toward Dakota. The young man nodded and made his way across the lawn to my future sister-in-law. She took the package and turned it over a couple of times in her hands, shooting a quizzical look at my brother.

Sam shrugged, a half smile on his lips, but I saw the concern in his eyes. "Don't look at me." He lifted his hands into the air in a gesture of non-compliance.

"Well, don't just sit there. Open it," Crockett prodded.

Dakota tore open the plain brown package to reveal a smaller black velvet box inside. The name Cabot & Cabot, the most prestigious designer of upscale jewelry in the country, was engraved on the top. She opened the lid and gasped. I blinked against the blinding glare of diamonds and sapphires set in platinum.

"Oh my," Mrs. Atwell said and placed a hand over her heart.

"Sam?" Dakota's brow furrowed as she lifted the necklace into the air. Sunlight winked from the gemstones. I'd seen a similar handcrafted piece in Cabot & Cabot's display window and knew it was worth at least ten thousand dollars.

"It's not from me." Sam's eyes narrowed. He withdrew a small card from the box and read it aloud. "All my love and best wishes. You're going to need them. M.S."

"Maxwell Seaforth?" Dakota dropped the necklace into the box like her fingers had been burned. I gaped at her while a hundred contradictory thoughts galloped through my head.

In all of my life, my father had never given me anything. Sure, he'd provided a roof over my head and financed my education, but I'd always felt it was because he had to and not because he wanted to. He'd never bought me a birthday present or a gift for Christmas. Nothing. All I desired was five minutes of his time, his acknowledgment, and to know he cared. He couldn't be bothered to remember his own daughter, but he had time enough to lavish gifts on his daughter-in-law. I dragged my lower lip between my teeth and tried to hold back the hurt.

I fled to a quiet room to change out of my bikini and spent the entire time vacillating between hurt and outrage. After I paced a dozen rounds of the small room, some of the steam began to dissipate from my anger. I sank onto the edge of the bed, exhausted from my fit of temper. Sam still chose Dakota. After the necklace. After everything. After all the lies, deceit, and heartache, he aligned with her. I knew Sam well enough to know once he'd made up his mind, he couldn't be swayed. Beckett was right. I needed to rethink my strategy. Before I could devise a new approach, a knock sounded at the door.

"Come in," I said.

Dakota opened the door. We stared at each other for an uncomfortable beat. The frown must've been evident on my face because she hesitated at the threshold. I gave her an assessing look, wondering what about her had my brother so entranced. Wavy brown hair tumbled over her shoulders. She was shorter than me, a few pounds heavier, with average features. Sam had been chased by supermodels and actresses. Her mom had been our cook, for goodness sake. He could have any woman he wanted, but he wanted her—this normal girl from a working-class family, a fact my parents had never accepted.

"Can I talk to you for a minute?" she asked.

"I guess."

She closed the door behind her and leaned against it. Judging by the furrow between her brows, she'd heard every word of my earlier argument with Sam. I braced for her anger. In fact, I welcomed the chance to unleash my fury on her.

"I love him," she said simply. "I always have. And I get that you're worried about him because you love him too."

"Actions speak louder than words, Dakota." I continued stuffing things into my suitcase. Why had I packed so much for a single day? "You ruined my family."

"I'm truly sorry that I hurt you. I was young and stupid and I did the wrong thing for the right reasons." She sighed and studied the pattern on the rug beneath our feet.

"I don't know about any of that," I said and returned to arranging my clothes. "I only know what I saw." A strange pang of hurt throbbed inside my ribs. "Maybe I should go home."

"No. Please stay for the wedding." She left the door, crossed the room to stand at my side, and placed a hand on my arm to stop my frantic packing. "I know you don't like me. You don't have to. But we need to get along for Sam's sake. He loves you so much and this thing between us is killing him."

I inched away from her hand and sat on the edge of the bed. "You hate me."

"I never hated you." She sat beside me. "I used to babysit for you sometimes when you were little. You were an adorable little girl. I used to brush your hair and put it up in pigtails. Do you remember?"

Until she mentioned it, I'd forgotten. I'd come along well after Vanessa and Sam. An accident, my mother had called me. My care and upbringing had been left to a dozen nannies. None of them had stayed very long. Their faces and names blurred into anonymity. Mrs. Atwell had volunteered her daughter to watch me from time to time. Dakota had been kind and attentive when no one else acknowledged my existence. The memory flashed past, bright and clear, a vivid picture of her crouched on the floor beside me, face alight with laughter, holding a tiny teacup and pretending to sip my latest imaginary concoction.

"I remember." My voice quavered. I couldn't look at her, so I stared out the window at the darkening sky.

She patted my hand and stood to leave. "Please think about staying. I know Sam is angry, but he'll be crushed if you aren't here. You're all the family he's got left. Don't throw that away."

The sadness in her voice added to my distress. I didn't want to forgive her, but it was hard to ignore her sincere concern for my brother.

An angry, confused tear spilled from the corner of one of my eyes. I swiped it away with the back of my hand. "And he's all I've got," I whispered, but when I turned around, Dakota had already gone.

Chapter 7

Beckett

THE DOWNSIDE of my career choice was a jaded outlook toward marriage and relationships. I'd seen the best of them fail and the worst of them implode. Nice people got hurt. Bad people triumphed. Poor people got poorer while the rich got richer. Hearts splintered. As a consequence, I vowed never to fall prey to any woman or the big lie called marriage. No, sir. I intended to spend my life in freedom, drinking to excess whenever I felt the urge, watching TV in my underwear, and never spending two nights in the same woman's arms, as any respectable bachelor should.

With my years of experience came an uncanny ability to predict the length of a marriage. The tiniest shrug of a shoulder or roll of the eyes spoke volumes about a relationship. But as I watched Sam and Dakota exchange vows, I found a lump in my throat and a glimmer of hope. I'd been friends with Sam for the majority of my adult life. We'd struggled together, partied together, succeeded and failed together. I'd witnessed his climb up the ladder of corporate success and his plummet from the pinnacle, only to lift himself up by sheer force of will. Other than myself, no one liked to win more than Sam, yet he was willing to risk it all for this one woman.

For these reasons, I stood beside him on his wedding day, in front of the minister, Dakota at his side. Because that was what best friends did. Through good times and bad, we stuck together. I didn't know if their marriage would last, but I hoped with all my heart it would. They had a dozen things going against their success, but I wouldn't be one of them. Venetia, on the other hand, wore a scowl on her face and her heart on her sleeve. The way she put her feelings out there for everyone to see, regardless of judgment, touched my jaded heart. I admired her bravery, her conviction, and her stubbornness. Over Dakota's shoulder, our gazes collided. A flush of crimson crept up her neck, and she glanced quickly away to focus on the minister.

"I now pronounce you husband and wife." The reverend said the words in a solemn baritone. "Sam, you may kiss your bride."

Sam leaned in to claim his new wife. A lump rose in my throat when he turned to walk her down the aisle, followed by a sharp pang of envy. I'd never known a love like theirs; I denied its existence and swore to never fall prey to its clutches. And yet...what if I was wrong? What if, by denying love, I was robbing myself of something mystical or magical?

I felt the pull of Venetia's gaze and found blue eyes witnessing my internal debate. Her mouth quirked in a smirk. I narrowed my eyes and wiped the emotion from my face. Damn this wedding for making me doubt myself and my beliefs. And damn Venetia for seeing my turmoil. I steeled my jaw and adopted my most intimidating glare. Sam and Dakota joined hands and walked down the aisle. I offered V my arm, and she slipped a hand around my elbow.

"I never took you for a sap," she whispered. "Is a little of the ice thawing around your heart?"

We fell into step behind the happy couple. The sun hovered low on the horizon. Dozens of lanterns hung from the surrounding trees. Twinkle lights illuminated the garden. A bead of sweat trickled down the back of my neck and into my shirt. Thank goodness it was a casual affair. Sam and I wore shorts and short-sleeved dress shirts. Dakota wore a white sundress. I silently thanked her for insisting on the informal attire.

50

"Never. It's too damn hot out here," I growled, embarrassed at being caught. Tears glimmered in Venetia's eyes. If I had to guess, I'd say they weren't the happy kind. In an instant, I forgot my mortification, overcome by the need to soothe her. "What about you? You okay, kiddo?"

She lifted her chin, lips pressed together in a tight line. "Fine," she said, but I knew it was a lie by the quiver in her voice.

"Dakota, you look beautiful." We'd reached the newlyweds by this time. I bent and kissed Dakota on the cheek.

She smiled, a tranquil radiance emanating from aquamarine eyes. Venetia's arm slipped out of mine.

"Thanks, Beckett." Dakota beamed up at Sam.

"Sam, congratulations." I shook his hand.

He clapped a palm to my back and pulled me into a one-shouldered man hug. The rest of the group gathered round. There were more tears, more hugs, and more emotion than I could handle. I backed away, eager for a smoke and a few minutes to come to grips with the evening.

I found a shadowed place beneath an oak tree and lit up. From my hiding place, I watched Sam sweep Dakota into his arms and carry her up the steps to the plantation porch. Their laughter carried across the lawn. Rockwell and Mrs. Atwell held hands as they followed them into the house for cake and refreshments. Sydney, Tucker, and Crockett tripped up the stairs in their wake. Venetia trailed a few paces to the rear, barefoot, sandals dangling from the fingertips of her right hand. I was left behind to take in the starless night sky. Alone. The way I liked it.

Chapter 8

Venetia

A STRING quartet played the soft strains of Debussy on the veranda while Sam and Dakota danced. He held her in his arms tenderly and brushed the hair back from her face. The display renewed my frustration. I couldn't stand by one minute longer and watch his ruin. I'd stayed for the wedding because he needed me and because it was the right thing to do, but now, I saw the truth with sickening finality. My brother had turned onto a new road, one that didn't include me, one of which I didn't approve.

"Come and dance with me." Sydney grabbed my hand and tugged me toward the dance floor.

"It's a slow song, goofy." In spite of my churning insides, I smiled at her silliness.

"It'll be like boarding school." She blinked large, pleading, puppy dog eyes. We'd gone to an all-girls boarding school and, since there were no boys, had been forced to dance together. The memory brought back a flood of good times. I hesitated, unwilling to celebrate such a sorrowful occasion, to pretend I was anything but heartbroken. I wanted to be alone.

A light breeze billowed the sheer curtains on either side of the French doors. Candlelight flickered and cast undulating shadows on the walls. Rockwell pulled Mrs. Atwell into his embrace and twirled her in a circle. It seemed everyone had someone, everyone but me.

"Sydney." Tucker beckoned to my friend with a quirked finger. She lifted her eyebrows, seeking my permission.

I nodded and smiled. "Go on. You know you want to." I gave her hand a squeeze. "Behave." Once her back was turned, I slipped into the dark hall with a champagne flute in one hand and a bottle of Dom Perignon in the other. Random, unpleasant thoughts flitted through my mind. I needed time to process, to wrap my head around the day's events. Why couldn't I just be happy for Sam? Why couldn't I get over the ugly mistrust festering inside me?

At the next turn in the hall, I blundered into the library. The scent of old books mingled with leather from the sofas and the sweetness of magnolias outside the open window. The sheer white curtains floated in the breeze like ethereal ghosts. A faint tinkle of music filtered in from the party, along with the night sounds of crickets and frogs. The figure of a man emerged from the shadows of the room.

"Oh." I stopped short at the unexpected sight of Beckett. His presence caused a frantic beating of my heart.

"I didn't realize you were in here." I placed a hand on my chest to try and regain control of my pulse.

"Hiding out?" His deep voice reverberated in the quiet, evoking an electric hum throughout my body.

"No. Not exactly." I turned to face the window.

"I never took you for a sore loser," he said.

From the corner of my eye, I saw the sharp angle of his jaw. Moonlight and shadow gave him a devilish glow. I paused and filled my glass to the brim with champagne. The bubbles tickled my throat. I downed the first glass and filled it again.

"I didn't realize it was a competition." My fingers tightened around the smooth, cold glass of the champagne bottle, still gripped in my fist.

"You act like it is." He took the glass from my opposite hand and drank a sip.

"Don't be ridiculous," I snapped, but the accuracy of his statement knocked me back a mental pace. Why did I feel so bereft, so betrayed over this wedding? Brothers got married every day. In-laws disliked each other. I lifted the champagne and took a drink straight from the bottle while my mother's ghost chastised my lack of manners.

"Come on. Let's go." Beckett took the flute from my hand and set it on the desk then gestured for the bottle. "I think you've had enough."

I pulled it away, out of his reach. "I can't. Not right now." Tension wrenched the muscles in my forehead. "I won't pretend I approve when I don't. I'm not a hypocrite." My breath came in short, shallow bursts. Unable to look at him, I faced the fireplace and braced a hand on the arm of the love seat next to me, the velvet upholstery plush against my palm.

Beckett's gaze drilled into my back. "No one's asking you to be anyone other than who you are."

"I'm right," I said in a voice too high and too thin to be my own. "You know I am." I felt the heat from his body before I felt the weight of his hands on my shoulders.

He turned me gently until I faced him. "I don't know any such thing, and neither do you."

"But you said—"

"I know what I said." His dark eyes sought mine. I stared into their depths, desperate for reassurance. He traced the line of my cheekbone with his fingertips. "And I was out of line to say it."

"He's going to ruin his life."

"Exactly."

I furrowed my brow, confused by his affirmation. "What's that supposed to mean?"

"That it's his life to ruin. His decision. Not yours. You need to butt out."

An overwhelming urge to flee twitched through my body. I wanted to fling open the window, leap over the sash, and sprint toward the bayou, desperate to lose the gnawing desolation inside me. "If you were me, you wouldn't stand by and let him do this." Even to my ears, I sounded whiny and pathetic. "Am I wrong?"

He studied my face. "Yes."

Heat flashed into my cheeks. His blatant disapproval had me second guessing my outburst to Sam. Had I fucked up with both Beckett and my brother? "What would you do then?"

"I'd suck it up. For Sam's sake. Forget about Dakota. Sam's your brother. He needs you. You need each other." Lines of sympathy softened the sharp angles of his face. "If you don't support him in this, you'll lose him, V. Is that what you want?"

"No." I studied the pink polish on the tips of my toes, the delicate silver straps of my leather sandals, and the cabbage rose pattern of the rug beneath them. I didn't have to think long to recognize he was right, but I was too stubborn to admit it.

A few seconds later, he moved to stand behind me and tugged me against his chest. The heat of his body warmed my backside. One of his hands smoothed over the curve of my ribs, soothing me. Arousal prickled along my skin. The scent of his cologne, spicy and sweet, tickled my nose.

"I didn't think so," he said. The stubble of his chin grazed my temple.

Needing more reassurance, I leaned into him. I couldn't help it, my body pulled to his by a force beyond my control. Taut muscle formed a solid wall against my back. I closed my eyes and savored every inch of him. I drew in a deeper breath. His hand slid around my waist, fingers spread wide over my belly, and pulled me firmly into him. A tight, aching need unfurled between my thighs. I gripped his pant legs and ground my bottom into his pelvis.

Hot, dry lips brushed over the shell of my ear. "What are you doing to me, Venetia?" His voice cracked in a whisper.

I have no idea, I thought, and dropped my head onto his shoulder. His hands skimmed along my ribs to cup my breasts. Large thumbs flicked over my nipples. They tightened into stiff, painful peaks. "Kiss me," I said aloud. "You know you want to." I turned my face to his and pressed our lips together.

Our tongues collided, fingers gripping and bodies melting together. I parted my lips, wanting more, and moaned. His muscles tensed. He pushed away, holding me at an arm's length. Warning sparked in his eyes.

A wave of crushing rejection bowled over me. "What?"

"No." He shook his head and backed up until a yard of distance loomed between us.

"Why not?" Was I so unlovable that no one wanted me? Why did everyone push me away?

"I want you, but this isn't going to happen." He shook his head again, as if clearing away a mental fog. "We can't do this. You need to get it through your head. Zero chance, V."

It was too much, and the thin barrier holding my self-esteem together snapped. "Why? What's wrong with me?" I took a step toward him, and he countered with another step back. "Just tell me. Am I too tall? Too ugly? Too blond for you?"

"You're a beautiful girl, V. It's not that."

"Just tell me then."

His chest lifted and fell with a deep breath. "You really want to know?"

Now I wasn't so sure, but I nodded anyway.

"You're young and spoiled. You bulldoze over everyone, expecting them to cater to your every wish. You say you're an adult but you act like a brat. You need to grow up." Then he did the most humiliating thing I'd ever experienced. He chucked me under the chin like I was a petulant third grader.

A few minutes after midnight, I left the celebration. No one noticed. Sydney and Tucker had disappeared, probably to soothe the itch between them. Beckett, Rockwell, and Crockett lurked in the corner, deep into a heated argument about the latest basketball scandal. Mrs. Atwell had gone to bed early with a headache. Dakota and Sam had gone to their room, eager to be alone and begin their wedding night.

I tapped out a quick text to Sydney.

Me: Heading back to the hotel. Our flight leaves at noon. Don't be late.

Her: I'll be there. Don't wait up.

She didn't explain why, and I tried not to dwell on the reason. It wasn't that I didn't like Tucker, because I did. He was an awesome guy, a gentleman, and a loyal friend to Sam. I feared Sydney would break his heart, as she always did. I also didn't approve of cheating, but who was I to judge? Sydney said what Alex didn't know wouldn't hurt him. In my experience, it had been true. I'd promised to keep her secret, because I had plenty of my own.

Chapter 9

Beckett

AFTER SAM'S wedding, I returned to work in Laurel Falls with unprecedented gusto. I'd only been in New Orleans for a few days, but it took almost a month to catch up and another two weeks to regain my footing. I didn't mind. It kept my thoughts off the fact that I'd screwed my best friend's sister and lost my wingman to the quicksand of marriage. Hard work didn't lessen any of the guilt festering deep inside my gut. I didn't like the way Venetia and I had left things. I didn't like keeping secrets from Sam. And I didn't like the lingering notion that my life had changed without my consent.

Even after a month and a half, I couldn't get Venetia out of my subconscious. At night, I had vivid, erotic dreams of her naked body. In these dreams, we had passionate sex in inappropriate places: on the desk in my office, in a parked car, and the bathroom of a local pub, to name a few. The list continued to grow with every passing night. Each morning I awakened with a painful erection and the need for relief. I blamed these fantasies on a lack of sex. I hadn't been with anyone but V since the wedding. The longest I'd ever gone without was two weeks. If I didn't get laid soon, I was going to combust.

On the next Tuesday afternoon, six weeks after Sam's wedding, I punched the elevator call button and entered the car for the ascent to my office. The Law Offices of Daniels, Quaid, Beckett & Associates occupied the upper floor of a downtown skyscraper in Laurel Falls. There were satellite offices in New York, Los Angeles, and Miami. I preferred to spend my time in the most central location, finding it closest to friends and family. Because my friends were my family, as much or more than my actual blood relatives.

"Good morning, Piers." A sultry female voice interrupted my musings. Margaret Chapman, another junior partner, followed me into my office.

"Margaret, welcome back." We shook hands. "How was Florida?" She'd been working at the Miami office for a couple of months. The glow of tropical sun showed in her smooth, Latino skin.

"Fine. Hot." Her brown eyes drank me in from head to toe before returning to my face. I avoided her gaze. "We have an emergency meeting."

"When?" I frowned, mentally categorizing a list of tasks and goals for the day. Surprises weren't on the schedule.

"Ten minutes. Daniels wants us in the conference room." She rested a hip on the corner of my desk while I rifled through a case file.

"What's this about?" As the most senior partner and founder of the firm, Daniels delighted in testing my mettle with impromptu meetings.

"No clue. He just said it was important and highly confidential." She placed a manicured hand on the center of my desk and leaned in, offering a peek at her cleavage through the open throat of her silk blouse.

"Great." I blinked and focused on the file until she cleared her throat.

"Are we on for Thursday?" she asked. One of her long-fingered hands adjusted the lapel of her navy suit jacket.

"Sure," I replied. "Your place or mine?" Not only was Margaret a respected co-worker, she was also a fantastic lay. I found her intelligent, amusing, and an invaluable asset in the courtroom as well as my bedroom. We fucked every Thursday night, if our respective schedules allowed. The arrangement suited both of us. Work occupied most of our waking hours and left little time for relationships. A quick, no-strings shag helped clear the mind and released the buildup of sexual tension.

"My place. Your place is like a dorm room, and I've got an early deposition the next day," she said.

"That works." I continued to skim the documents in front of me. The success of our hookups depended on a set of strict rules. We alternated the location of our trysts, depending on our schedules, and we never, ever slept over.

"Did you get my notes on the Kennedy divorce?" Margaret picked up the professional thread of conversation without missing a beat.

"Yes, thanks. Good work."

She glanced at her watch. "We'd better head to the conference room."

I followed her out the door. Always a leg man, my gaze dropped to her toned calves as she walked in front of me. They were nice legs, but not mouthwatering like Venetia's. The thought caused me to falter. Another snippet of our tryst haunted me. The soft flesh of her inner thighs against the stubble of my cheek, a breathy sigh of erotic arousal.

"Are you okay?" Margaret stopped at the entrance to the conference room. "Your face is red as a beet."

I cleared my throat. "I'm good. Just a little hot." Hot and bothered, more like. I'd jacked off to those memories of V a dozen times in the past weeks. I gave Margaret a reassuring smile. A night with Mags would quash all those crazy flashbacks.

When I opened the conference room door, however, my temperature raised another degree. Maxwell Seaforth sat at the head of the table like it was his office instead of mine, and here I was debauching his daughter in my mind only a few minutes earlier. The tips of my ears grew hotter.

He stood when I entered and offered his hand. A jewel-encrusted watch face flashed beneath his immaculate shirtsleeve. He was almost as tall as me, dressed in an impeccable navy blue suit. Short salt-and-pepper hair framed an angular face. Except for his age and the coldness in his green eyes, he could've been Sam's twin.

I searched his face for a resemblance to Venetia and found nothing in common. I shrugged off the disparity. Not everyone resembled their parents. I didn't resemble my fair-haired mother at all.

"Piers." Maxwell gripped my hand and released it.

"Mr. Seaforth." I nodded and gave a narrowed sideways glance at Daniels, the sly bastard. He grinned in smug satisfaction. "What brings you here today?"

"I'm getting married."

"Congratulations." We stared at each other while I wondered what he was up to. When a shark swam to your door, you sat up and took notice. You also got out of the water. "So what can we do for you?"

"Straight to business. I like that." He returned to his seat and withdrew a sheaf of documents from his briefcase. "I want you to handle the legal side of the marriage. The negotiation of the premarital agreement is of utmost importance. I want an airtight document. No loopholes. And we'll need to outline the framework for divorce." The blatant coldness of his statement knocked me back into my chair. "I'd like the option to file for divorce at the end of five years on whatever grounds you find to be most advantageous financially."

"Okay." I flipped through the pages of the agreement. His request wasn't unusual, but I'd never heard it stated in such blunt words. "Is your fiancée aware of the five-year term?"

"The future Mrs. Seaforth has no idea," Maxwell said. "I'd like to keep it that way."

Damn, this man was cold. I tapped a finger on the table while I weighed my options. If the decision was mine alone, I'd refuse the case. Unfortunately, Daniels would never allow me to pass on such a profitable opportunity. Maxwell had billions of dollars at his disposal, and his divorce would be quite a feather in our caps. His presence in our office validated my success. With Maxwell on our client roster, the firm would rocket into a new stratosphere, and it would secure a senior partnership for me. I didn't care about the money, but I did care about Sam's feelings. He might view this new alliance with his father as disloyalty.

"I have serious reservations about taking you as a client," I said, choosing to mimic Seaforth's blunt approach. Daniels sputtered on his coffee. Margaret choked back a laugh. "Given my relationship with your son, I don't feel I could give you fair representation. Perhaps Daniels or one of our other associates could better serve you."

"Let me be frank, Piers." He leaned forward and lifted his chin. "I came to you because I only deal with the best, and your reputation is outstanding. How many cases have you lost?"

By the tone of his voice, he already knew the answer. "None," I replied.

"Exactly." A smug smirk quirked the corners of his mouth. "And I know success like yours doesn't happen by accident. Work with me on this. I have contacts. I know people who need a guy like you. I can make you and this firm a household name." He directed this comment to me, but his gaze flickered to Daniels.

A sickening smile spread over Daniels's face. Damn greedy bastard. I liked money as much as the next man, but I had no desire to fuck over my friends in order to get it. "We appreciate your business, Mr. Seaforth." Daniels's eyes gleamed. No doubt he was counting the dollar signs behind the future divorce settlement. It was like money in the bank.

"Great." Seaforth extended a hand to shake, diamond cufflinks winking in the daylight streaming through the windows. "Draw up the papers. We'll meet again next week."

Chapter 10

Venetia

STUPID, STUPID, stupid. The one word kept replaying on a loop through my thoughts as the plane began its descent into the Laurel Falls International Airport. Miniature rows of houses appeared through fluffy cotton ball clouds, and I imagined the people inside looking up at me with tiny accusing faces. *Stupid.* I'd done some asinine things during my life; this one was the granddaddy of all fuck-ups.

"I can hear you mentally chastising yourself all the way over here," Sydney said from the seat next to me. She lifted a penciled eyebrow before handing her empty water bottle to the first-class flight attendant.

After finishing my internship in Italy, I'd spent a month with her in L.A. Six weeks had passed since my hookup with Beckett, but it seemed like a lifetime ago.

"Wouldn't you be?" I shifted in the seat to face her.

She met my gaze with sad but understanding eyes. "Okay. So you had some bad luck." Her hand found mine and squeezed. "Stop beating yourself up about it. It'll all work out."

"I'm glad you think so." I returned my gaze to the window and the approaching ground outside.

"It'll make a fantastic story for your grandchildren."

"Not helping, Syd." The glass of the window felt cool against my forehead until the plane hit a pocket of air and jolted. Sydney sucked in a breath beside me. It was my turn to pat her hand. "Deep breaths." She smiled, but the corners of her lips trembled. "How someone like you can be afraid of flying just stumps me. You're on a plane every other day it seems."

"And every other day, I'm convinced I'm going to die," she said and leaned back into her seat, eyes closed. "Distract me. Tell me what you're going to do about this mess you're in."

What was I going to do? I bit the inside of my cheek. I had no one to blame but myself. Once again, I'd acted on impulse, and once again I was going to pay. Big time. I liked Beckett. Okay, lusted after him. But our brief encounter had been just that. An encounter. Now, our futures were knotted together, possibly forever.

"Can I just pretend it never happened?" It would be so much easier to ignore the situation than face the dire consequences.

"No." Sidney gripped the arm rests, her knuckles white, and opened her eyes. "Things like this can't be ignored." The point of her chin quivered. "This is your wakeup call, sweet pea. You need to get your shit together. You've been in a self-destructive spiral ever since—"

I cut her off with a venomous glance. "Don't."

She drew in a deep breath. "Yes. I will, because I'm your friend and someone needs to say it. You've been hell bent on destroying yourself ever since Sam got back with Dakota and your dad went AWOL."

"He didn't go AWOL. He's just busy." The plane engines whined, and my belly flipped as the jet hit another pocket of air. Sydney gasped. I rubbed her arm and my fingers brushed the edges of two nicotine patches on the underside. "Two, Syd? Really?"

"I'm desperate to quit," she said in an overdramatic whisper. "Alex hates my smoking."

"Alex?" It was the first time she'd mentioned his name in weeks. "What about Tucker?"

"Tucker is sweet." A frown puckered her forehead as she settled deeper into the seat. "I'm not supposed to say anything, but the studio wants us to get married. Me and Alex, I mean. For the next season."

"Sydney Ellen, are you kidding?" I gripped her forearm and gave her a shake. "Do you love him?"

"The ratings will be off the charts," she replied without opening her eyes. "We're going to do a wedding special. The publicity will be insane."

"And you have the nerve to give me crap about my situation?" Misplaced anger burned through my veins and mingled with hurt. "How could you not tell me this?"

"I signed a non-disclosure. I'm not supposed to tell anyone, and now, neither can you." Her voice softened. "You're the only person who knows. Even my parents don't know. I only told you because I trust you and wanted you to know." She gasped as the plane hit a pocket of air.

"You're playing with fire." The thought of the damage to poor Tucker's heart made me queasy.

"This is a brilliant career move for me and Alex. We've been planning it for over a year." She opened her eyes long enough to give me a pointed glare. "Besides, we'll only be married for a few weeks. It's timed to happen right before the release of my movie. Beckett has already drawn up the divorce agreement. It's all settled."

"People in glass houses, Syd." Even though I was irritated, I patted her hand in reassurance.

One of the male flight attendant stopped at my side. "Ladies, seat backs up, please," he said in a firm tone.

"Somewhere deep inside, you want Sam and your father to find out, just to piss them off." Her grip tightened around the armrests.

I wanted to deny her accusation, but she could be right. I wanted Sam to feel the way I felt when I learned about Dakota—betrayed, angry, disillusioned. And my father? Would he even care? Probably not, but if he was even the slightest bit disturbed, I'd be satisfied. How sick was that? I crossed my arms over my chest and trained my attention outside the oval plane window.

"I'm serious, V. You've got to deal with whatever emotional crap is swirling around inside your head and face up to the facts that Sam married Dakota and your dad is a dick." She closed her eyes again and settled back into the seat. "My dad's a dick, but you don't see me going around getting knocked up to spite him."

"I didn't do it on purpose," I snapped. "We used a condom. I'm on the pill. You can't get any safer than that." But it hadn't been enough. Maybe one of the condoms had been defective. I still couldn't wrap my head around the concept. I was pregnant, and Beckett was the father. We were having a baby. Together. The mere thought of motherhood caused my blood pressure to skyrocket. I was too young to be a mom, too irresponsible, too unprepared. This time in my life should be worry-free and filled with adventure, not diapers and domesticity. As if to emphasize the truth, my stomach lurched, and a hot wave of nausea burned my throat. I shut my eyes and drew in a deep breath through my nose.

"What was that?" The landing gear dropped with a *thunk*. Sydney winced.

I took her hand in both of mine and held it tight. "Nothing to be worried about. We're good," I said, forgetting my own discomfort in the need to ease hers.

The wheels of the aircraft touched pavement, bounced, then settled on the ground. We fell silent as the engines whined and the body of the plane shuddered. Sydney's fingernails bit into my palm, her arms rigid.

"It's okay. We've landed. You can open your eyes now," I said.

One eyelid cracked to a slit before a huge smile lit up her china doll features. "Thank goodness."

We disembarked the plane without commentary. A throng of paparazzi swarmed the gate and pushed me aside to get at Sydney. Flashbulbs exploded around us. Sydney lifted a hand to ward them away, annoyance furrowing her forehead. She had to rush to make her connecting flight to Seattle but paused long enough to give me a squeeze. Tears pricked my eyes. She was such a good friend, better than I deserved. I hugged her back.

"Text me when you get to the hotel, okay?" I asked.

"I will." With the strap of her leather bag thrown over her shoulder, she began walking backward. "You're going to be fine, V. I know you will. Now, what's the first thing you're going to do when you get home?"

"Call Beckett," I recited, even though the idea of seeing him again made my hands tremble. Tall, dark, and handsome Beckett. Because of my predicament, my bruised ego would have to take a backseat. I sighed and hoisted my bag higher on my shoulder. Confessing my pregnancy to Beckett ranked right up there with getting a root canal. Unfortunately, it had to be done. As soon as I settled into the limo with my driver, I called Beckett's office and set up an appointment with his assistant to see him the next day.

Chapter 11

Beckett

ONE DAY later, the firm's phone rang off the hook with a sudden influx of high-profile clients. I suspected Maxwell at the root of my newfound popularity. Part of me—the power-hungry, bloodthirsty part—gloated over this windfall. The incoming revenue from these clients would allow me to buy a bigger apartment, a new house for my parents, and maybe something frivolous for myself, like a new car. I'd been driving the same Jeep Wrangler since college. Although it was well maintained, it didn't exactly suit the profile of a man in my line of work. I'd been too busy making a name for myself to worry about unimportant details like cars and decorating my apartment.

Garth, my assistant, hovered at the office door with a dozen messages and an armload of case files. He was in his mid-twenties, tall and slender, dressed in an inexpensive but well-tailored navy suit.

I took off my coat and handed it to him. "Call Sam Seaforth and see if he can do dinner tonight, would you?" I needed to meet with him and let him know about the situation with his father. I didn't want to do anything behind his back.

"Okay. Your two o'clock cancelled. You need to call these people." He shuffled the case files into my outstretched arm when I paused at the door. "These need signed."

"Thanks."

"Oh, and I worked this one in." Garth tapped the top file folder in my hands. "Venetia Seaforth?" Hearing her name sent a strange rush of adrenalin through my veins. "She said it was urgent, and I figured you'd want to see her right away. Since she's a Seaforth," Garth added. "She's been waiting for a while, and I don't think she's very happy about it."

Shit. Venetia? The frenzy of the day had pushed aside my secret obsession, but now it flared again. By this time, most of the hazy details from our night together had returned. The tips of my ears heated at the memory of our sweat-slicked skin, tangled fingers, and moans of pleasure on that hot Louisiana night. I frowned and glanced at my watch. It had been a tedious morning, and I was hoping for a few minutes to clear my head from the oily nastiness of the Reyes's divorce. I wasn't prepared to face Venetia quite yet. She was probably still angry with me. I braced to meet the famous Seaforth temper.

"Just what I need. Another Seaforth," I muttered. "Maybe we should change the name of the firm to Daniels, Quaid, Becket & Seaforth."

"I worked around your schedule to fit her in." Garth's lips thinned into a straight line, as they always did when he took liberties with my routine and expected censure. "I can reschedule if you like."

"No. Not necessary." I entered the office, prepared to meet the willful girl I'd left in Louisiana, but instead found a self-assured woman seated across from my desk. She stood and smoothed the fabric of her straight skirt. The silken length of her hair was pulled back into a low ponytail. The long end of it trailed over one shoulder and across the top of her left breast. When she turned, my heart did a ridiculous dance in my chest.

"V, it's good to see you. You're looking well." It wasn't a lie. I'd never seen her look more stunning. Or maybe I'd never noticed before? Her skin glowed, luminous as a pearl, and I had an uncontrollable urge to stroke her cheek, to see if the translucence was a trick of the light.

"Hello, Beckett." Venetia stretched out an arm to shake my hand at the same time I leaned forward to give her a hug. We bumped shoulders awkwardly. "Thank you for working me in today. You seem really busy."

"No problem." I didn't have the heart to tell her it was Garth and not myself who'd made the concession. "This is a pleasant surprise." Trying to recover my cool, I enveloped her small hand between both of mine. The brush of her fingers over my palm sent shivers of pleasure skittering along my forearm. When I released her hand, she stepped back to put a foot of space between us. Her impersonal smile tamped down my enthusiasm a notch. "I've been meaning to call you," I said. "I've been thinking about you." At night, in the shower, and every single morning.

"Have you?" The way the corners of her mouth turned down suggested she didn't believe me.

I studied her, struck by her sober gravity. How could someone change so much in such a small amount of time? "Yes. Maybe we could do lunch sometime." I gestured for her to sit again and tried not to gawk at the miles of slender leg as she crossed them at the knee. Damn. Had her legs always been that long? I had a quick, inappropriate flash of those fantastic stems wrapped around my waist while I pumped into her. Heat raced up my neck. *Jesus, Beckett. What's wrong with you?* I was acting like a teenager alone with the babysitter for the first time.

"I'll have to check my calendar and get back with you," she said and cleared her throat. When I tore my gaze away from her legs, I found her regarding me with icy blue eyes. The coldness cooled my libidinous thoughts. This Venetia I knew.

"Where are you staying?" I asked and focused on straightening the papers stacked in front of me.

"I rented an apartment until I find something more permanent." As she spoke, she stared at a place beyond my shoulder and toyed with the ends of her ponytail. It bothered me, this loss of eye contact. Without those blazing eyes boring into me, I had no way to judge her intentions. "You'll have to forgive me for rushing this along, but you were late, and I've got a job interview after this."

73

"So what can I do for you? Too many parking tickets?" I teased.

She didn't smile. "No." She smoothed her skirt and eased into the chair. "It's a little more serious than that."

"Okay." I clasped my hands on top the desk, giving her my full attention. "Spill it." I smiled, feeling flattered she sought my help, and curious. Her high spirits and penchant for mischief had gotten her into a few scrapes over the years. Sam had always been quick to rescue her, but given the state of their current relationship, she probably didn't feel comfortable going to him. "I'm happy to help. What's up?"

"I'm pregnant."

Blood drained from the top of my head straight into the tips of my toes. A baby? *My* baby? Panic raced through every fiber of my being. Suddenly, I was fifteen again, hearing my girlfriend confess she was pregnant, looking at the demise of my future. I ran a finger around the inside of my shirt collar, the cloth unbearably confining, and counted the days backward in my head. "Jesus, V. Are you sure?"

For the first time, her tough façade cracked. She drew in a deep breath and clasped her hands in her lap. "I haven't been to the doctor yet, but yes. I'm sure. I took five pregnancy tests from the store. I'm four weeks late. There isn't any other explanation."

My gaze flitted to the bottle of Woodford Reserve at the wet bar on the wall adjacent to my desk. I rose from my chair, poured two fingers into a short glass, gulped them down, and poured two more. "And you're sure it's mine?" The words came out harsher than I intended, but I didn't apologize. This couldn't be true. She had to be mistaken. Surely there had been other guys before or since our hookup. It was a reasonable line of questioning, given the circumstances, and I had every right to rule out other possible candidates.

"Don't you dare," she snapped. Hot blue eyes drilled into mine. "Don't you dare try to make me out as a slut, Beckett. You will not disrespect me."

"And you haven't been with anyone else?" I held firmly to my line of questioning, hoping for a glimmer of reasonable doubt.

Her chin lifted higher. "You're the only person I've been with for months. Do you really think I'd blame someone like you if it wasn't true?"

"Like me? What's that supposed to mean?" My pride bristled. I stood in front of her chair and glared down at her.

"It means you're not the first person I'd choose as the father of my child." She held my gaze firmly. "You're a player. And we both know you're completely against commitment of any kind. I'm not asking you to raise the child or have anything to do with it. I'm here because you're Sam's friend, and I thought you deserved to know."

Her words served as a substantial blow to my ego. I'd always considered myself a reasonable catch. I had a good job. I stayed in shape. I wasn't ugly. To know she considered me less than desirable came as quite a shock. I sank down in the chair beside her and covered my eyes with a trembling hand. "How did this happen? We were careful." I never took chances where my personal safety was concerned. "I used a condom." The facts of the case continued to speed through my brain as I searched for a loophole, some way to prove this was all a mistake. "I thought you were on birth control."

"I am. Or was." Her voice quivered. "But with Sam's wedding and me looking for a job, I've been so busy. I might have missed one." I opened my eyes to find her staring at her feet. "People make mistakes, Beckett."

A wave of guilt slammed over me, and my anger dissipated. It was easy to forget she was only twenty-three. Hell, I'd done some pretty dumb things when I was her age. This was as much my fault as hers—even more mine, because I should have been the responsible one. Since this had happened to me once before, I knew better. I got tested regularly, always used a condom, and never took risks. Never.

I wiped a film of sweat from my upper lip. My life didn't have room for a kid.

I didn't have time to change diapers or babysit. A wave of nervous nausea twitched my gut. "This can't be happening."

"It's happening." She waved a finger between us. "To both of us. You and me."

The solemnity of the situation began to sink into my shell-shocked brain. I was having a baby with Venetia, of all people. I'd never wanted children. Hell, I didn't even want a girlfriend. Now, I had an instant family.

I set the glass of whiskey on the desk and scrubbed my face with both hands. "So what are you going to do? Adoption?" In my mind, it was the only choice. Having been through the anguish of abortion before, I didn't even consider it. "I have contacts. I can put you in touch with some people."

"I don't know. I'm still trying to come to grips with this." She shrank into the depths of the chair, shoulders hunched.

A surge of empathy made me forget all the crap between us. Here I was, thinking about myself, when she was obviously frightened out of her mind. This was no time for selfish thinking. It would benefit both of us to handle the issue as a team instead of adversaries. "It'll be okay." I covered her hand with mine and gave it a reassuring squeeze when I really wanted to run out the door and hide. I pushed aside the panic and took a drink of the Woodford while I waited for her answer. God bless whiskey.

She tugged her lower lip between her teeth and looked away. From the side, her nose had a small tilt at the tip. "I'm not sure what I'm going to do." The swell of her breasts lifted and fell with a heavy breath. "I'm not sure I want to have it."

The Woodford clotted in my throat, and I sputtered. Abortion wasn't an option. At least not for me, not after the hell of the last one. I hadn't considered that she might not want the child, or that—in spite of all my misgivings—I did.

Chapter 12

Venetia

ONCE, WHEN I was six years old, I'd found an injured bird in my mother's garden. With the help of Mrs. Atwell, I'd tried to nurse it back to health. When it died a few days later, I'd been inconsolable, certain it was my fault. The idea of harming something so small, something utterly dependent on me for protection, renewed my panic.

"I'm not sure I can raise a child," I whispered, feeling the sting of tears. For the past week, I'd been wavering between fits of crying and panic. "I don't know how to be a parent."

"Come here." The tension in Beckett's jaw relaxed. He pulled me against his chest and wrapped his arms around my shoulder.

My nose nestled into the crook of his neck. The strength of his embrace flowed through me, and the panic receded. One of his hands stroked soothingly up and down the curve of my spine. "I'm scared, Beckett," I said into his skin and curled my fingers into the lapels of his jacket. His shirt smelled of starch, comforting and familiar.

"Don't be. I'm here. You're not alone in this." His deep voice rumbled in my ear. I let him lead me to the sofa and found myself seated next to him, his arm curled around my shoulders. "We can do this."

"I'll be a terrible mother. You said yourself that I'm immature and impulsive."

My fears tumbled out. "I spent my entire life with nannies and at boarding schools. I don't know how to be a mom."

How could I ever explain my impersonal upbringing? How it felt to wake up in the middle of the night at four years old from a bad dream to be comforted by a stranger? My parents had never taken an active role in my life. My mother had filled her days with charities and fundraisers, too busy to be bothered with a small child. And my father? If it wasn't for the monthly check he deposited into my bank account, I wouldn't know he existed. Even that would stop soon, with the receipt of my trust fund. Sam had been more of a father to me than Maxwell. I didn't want that for my child.

"Nonsense." Beckett tucked a loose strand of hair behind my ear and smiled, a little weakly. He must be as panicked as I was. "It's a natural instinct. You'll be fine."

"You really think so?" Only a man could say something so naïve. I searched his face and found nothing but sincerity in his eyes. I wished for one drop of his confidence in my abilities.

"Absolutely." His gaze dipped to my lips. The cadence of my pulse bobbled. He looked strong, unperturbed in his smart black suit and red power tie. It was easy for me to believe I was safe with his maleness filling the room.

He leaned forward and brushed his lips over mine in the sweetest of kisses. The taste of Woodford sizzled on my lips. The impromptu show of affection caught me off guard. I wavered between wanting more and needing distance. Why did this guy tie me up in knots? Even now, after weeks apart, my body melted into his. I placed both palms flat against his hard chest to create a barrier between us. The situation called for a clear head, impossible to have when he was touching me.

"Sorry." Beckett tensed and pulled back. "I shouldn't have."

"It's a little late for that." I smiled up at him, nervous again. Had the kiss held desire, or was it only my schoolgirl fantasies at work?

"Yeah. I guess it is."

A strand of hair drifted down over his forehead. I pushed it back from his eyes. My fingers lingered a little too long on his face. Heat rushed into my cheeks. This wasn't going to do at all. I let my hand drop into my lap.

"You don't have to decide anything right away," he said. "About the baby, I mean. There's plenty of time for decisions."

"Right." Listening to his deep, smooth voice, I could almost believe it was true.

"Make an appointment with the doctor." One corner of his mouth curled up into a shy smile. Now that the shock had worn off, he seemed to be coming to grips with the idea. "I'll go with you."

"You don't have to," I said, although the idea of facing the doctor made my stomach flip-flop.

He put a finger to my lips. "Not an option." On impulse, I playfully bit the tip of his finger, desperate to lighten the mood. The warm brown hue of his irises darkened to black. "Careful there. I might bite back."

The urge to flirt with him came as naturally as breathing. My face heated with embarrassment. This wasn't a date. We weren't a couple. He'd made it clear—first in New Orleans then a few minutes ago when he'd apologized for the kiss. I didn't want to humiliate myself by chasing after a man who wasn't interested and emotionally unavailable. The sooner I reconciled myself to the fact, the better.

I straightened my posture, drew on every bit of composure I possessed, and stood. He stood alongside me, unfolding his long limbs with athletic grace. "I'll call your assistant with the date and time. Garth, right?" I plastered a polite smile on my face, the best I could manage under the circumstances.

"Yes. Give me your number," he said, and drew his phone from the inside pocket of his suit jacket. I rattled off the digits. He bit his lower lip in concentration while he programmed them into his phone. The gesture reminded me of how soft and full that lip felt pressed against mine.

Stop it, stop it, stop it. Getting over this obsession might take a bit more effort

79

than I first realized. A few seconds later, my phone buzzed inside my purse and stole away my attention.

"There. Now you've got my personal cell number. Text or call me any time." He stared down at me from his lofty height. "I mean it. Any time. Night or day. Got it?"

I hesitated by the door, uncertain if I should shake his hand or give him a hug. We were saved by Garth's voice on the intercom.

Beckett picked up the received, frowned, and glanced at his watch. He covered the receiver with his palm to speak with me. "We'll catch up later, okay?"

I nodded and slipped out the door. Once inside the elevator, my knees began to weaken. I sagged against the wall in a combination of relief and shock. Earlier in the day, I thought telling Beckett would be the worst of my problems, but now it only seemed to be the beginning.

Chapter 13

Beckett

VENETIA LEFT, and Garth came in the door two seconds later. "Here are the documents you requested, and your next appointment is here." He took one look at my wan face and bit his lower lip. "Are you okay?"

"Fine," I growled. "Just give me a minute."

I stalked into the adjoining bathroom and splashed cold water on my face. Holy hell. A tremble ran through my hands as I dried my face and smoothed back my hair. I studied myself in the mirror. I looked like the same schmuck whose face greeted me every morning, but the change was there. In the space of thirty minutes, I'd gone from bachelor playboy to a father. *A father.* I just couldn't wrap my mind around the idea. A baby changed everything. How could I make senior partner with a kid on my knee? My panic renewed. This wasn't the plan. My life had been carefully mapped out since college, and a baby was nowhere in it.

"Mr. Beckett?" Garth knocked on the door.

"I said in a minute." Jesus. Couldn't a guy get five minutes alone in the john? It wasn't Garth's fault, but my emotions were raw and unfettered, and he was conveniently in the way. I straightened the collar of my shirt and took a second look at my pale face. A blown-out knee hadn't been in the plan either. One ill-timed rebound during NCAA finals had ended a promising future in the NBA, but I had survived, adapted, *thrived*. So what if my plan had been trashed this morning?

The word "defeat" had no place in my vocabulary.

When I came out of the bathroom, I put on my game face and got down to business. Years of discipline on the basketball court and in the courtroom had taught me to work under pressure and put my personal issues aside. Business was business.

I went into meeting after meeting, fueled by the desperation to forget—if even for a few hours—that my life had been shattered. I threw all my efforts into ending another marriage, but this time it felt different. These people were parents, families. Children would be hurt. Fathers would be ripped away from their sons and daughters. Mothers would be forced to give joint custody to men who'd cheated and lied to them. I thought about my real father, not the man who'd adopted me and gave me his name, but the one who'd abandoned my mother when she was pregnant. It left me sick to my stomach.

By the end of the day, a few points became clear. I didn't want to be the kind of dad who lived at the office, missed baseball games for conference calls, and put his job above his family. I'd make a new plan, one that allowed for birthday parties and ballet lessons and bedtime stories. Anything worth doing was worth doing well. If I had to be a father, I'd be the best one possible.

I made it through the meetings, but dinner with Sam had my palms sweating and my heart racing. I was used to keeping other people's secrets. Some were small, like the woman who smoked cigarettes in the bathroom to hide the habit from her husband. Others were enormous. A mistress in New York City. A vacation home in Aspen under an assumed name. Fifty million dollars sheltered in offshore accounts. The estranged spouse had no idea, and as the claimant's litigator, it was my job to protect those assets from greedy hands. I could dismiss those secrets as a necessary evil to win a case. But Sam? How in the hell was I going to avoid telling my best friend that I'd knocked up his little sister? If he found out before I told him, he'd go ballistic, and I couldn't blame him. I'd violated his trust; our friendship might never recover.

"Beckett." Sam's voice cut into my musings. We were seated at a private table in Sam's favorite restaurant. I'd been so deep into my own head I'd forgotten he was there. "What the hell is wrong with you tonight?"

I rubbed the back of my neck and tried to snap out of it. "Nothing. Long day." His curious gaze regarded me. Oh, God. Could he see the guilt on my face? Perspiration beaded on my forehead. "Where's Dakota this evening?"

"Out shopping with some of her girlfriends," he said. A furrow deepened between his brows. "We're having a bit of a rough patch."

"Really? Why's that?" In my experience, Sam and Dakota were always at odds over something. The friction between them sparked their relationship. Dakota was the only person besides Venetia who had the balls to stand up to him, and Sam loved to challenge his wife at every turn.

"I think it's time to start a family. She wants to wait."

I'd been about to take a sip of my wine but halted the glass in midair. "Excuse me?"

Smiles for Samuel Seaforth were few and far between, but he smiled now, broad and proud. "You heard me."

"That's huge." I shoved back in my chair and clapped a hand on his shoulder. "Are you sure? Kids are a big deal." My pulse stuttered. I drew in a deep breath and tried to remain calm.

"I'm sure. What's to think about? We're married. In love. Kids are the obvious next step."

"To another generation of Seaforths." I raised my glass in a toast. Sam reciprocated. My hand trembled a little. We drank and set our glasses back on the table. This was the perfect opportunity to confess, to come clean, to take whatever punishment he had in mind. We could commiserate, celebrate, or whatever the hell it was I felt. My emotions seemed to change on a whim. But I couldn't make myself do it. The words hovered on the tip of my tongue. I bit them back. I'd promised Venetia I wouldn't say anything until she'd made her decision, and I couldn't break my promise to her.

"Dakota—she's not happy about it," he said after a long silence, voice low and confiding. "She says the timing's off. I say, why wait? Neither of us is getting any younger." For the first time since I'd met Sam, he looked uncertain.

"Please tell me you didn't make disparaging remarks about her age." I held back a chuckle, knowing he wouldn't appreciate it.

He scratched his jaw. "I might have mentioned it. Now she's not speaking to me."

"Not good, my friend." I concentrated on the color and clarity of the wine while Sam shoved back in his chair. "Do I need to draw up the divorce papers?"

"Hell no. I'm in this for the long haul. Tactical error on my part, but she'll come around." An arrogant smirk replaced his scowl. "The best part about fighting is the makeup sex. Phenomenal."

"Yeah, well, I wouldn't know about that." I'd never been in a relationship long enough to have a fight. I had to admit, it sounded intriguing. With Venetia's hot temper, we were bound to have a disagreement over raising a child together, and the idea of fucking it out sent a bolt of white-hot lust straight into my crotch. I lifted my gaze from the wine to find Sam's eyes narrowed on mine.

"Your ears are turning red," he stated. "Are you looking at the hostess? She's been eye-fucking you since the first course."

"No."

As if sensing our conversation, the hostess shot a seductive smile in my direction. Honestly, I hadn't even noticed her until then. Short skirt, nice rack, pretty face. Definitely my type but not on my radar this evening. The only woman on my mind was Venetia, a naked, moaning Venetia.

I cleared my throat. If Sam knew I was mentally shagging his sister, he'd choke on his appetizer. I wiped my mouth with the napkin and struggled to deflect the conversation. "You'd be a good dad," I told him. "No question about it." The words of confidence were as much for my sake as his. I emptied the last of the wine bottle into my glass and signaled the waiter for another.

"You think?" He shook his head. "My dad hasn't been the best example of a loving parent. Hell, Vanessa got married and moved to a different continent just to get away from him. I don't think he's talked to her or Venetia in years. And you know what he's done to me."

"Well, thank God you're not your dad. And Dakota will rock as a mom. That kid's going to be the luckiest child in the world." And what about my child? What kind of father would I be? The kind who shagged strange girls in elevators. The kind who had one-night stands with flight attendants. Venetia's words returned. *You're not the first person I'd choose as a father.*

For the second time that day, I felt the burn of shame. I couldn't fault her observation. Without a doubt, Sam would harbor the same prejudice. He'd hate the idea of a guy like me raising his nephew, and the knowledge caused a bitter taste in my mouth. My unborn child linked the three of us as a family, a bond more important than friendship. I couldn't change my past, but I could change their minds. I *would* change their minds. Our future depended on it.

A team of waiters arrived at the table bearing platters of poached salmon and filet mignon. We fell silent while they cleared away our salads, served the main course, and refilled our wine glasses.

For the past ten years, I'd been secure in my bachelorhood, accompanied by Tucker and Sam. Secrets aside, I was overcome with the unpleasant premonition that the introduction of children into our sacred circle of men was about to change our relationship forever. No more late-night drinking sessions. No more impromptu vacations in Cabo. Our weekends would be filled with diapers and bottles. A renewed surge of panic shook my confidence. I didn't want that kind of life. Not yet. Maybe not ever.

"Something wrong with the steak?" Sam asked. "You look like you just ate something bad."

"No. It's fine." I set my fork down. "Talked to Tucker lately?" I picked up a new topic, eager to veer away from the unpleasantness of my predicament.

"Yesterday. He's in Seattle working on a new video game concept. Some big-time producer wants to pair Tuck's newest video game with a movie. He'll be back by the end of the week, he said."

"Damn. That boy is on fire," I said, unable to hold back the admiration in my voice.

"And Venetia? Heard from her?"

At Sam's question, my guts clenched. A wave of heat rushed up my chest and into my neck. "Uh, yes. Why?" I threw my napkin on the table and pushed the plate away. My heart pounded against my ribs. *Steady, Beckett.* "I met with her yesterday."

"She called you?" Sam lifted an eyebrow. "For what?"

"Yes." I scrambled for an excuse. "She needed some legal advice on a few things. Nothing important. She said she has an apartment here and some job interviews. She didn't tell you?"

"We aren't exactly talking." Sam signaled to the waiter, requesting he take away our plates, and wiped his mouth with the linen napkin before his reply. "How is she?"

"She's fine. She seemed...sad." I followed the guidelines of a successful cross-examination. Stick to the truth and omit the details. Deflect and redirect. "Maybe you should give her a call. I'm sure she misses you."

"Why? She made her feelings clear when she left the wedding." The line of his jaw hardened. "She needs to apologize first." The Seaforth wall of stubbornness slammed down between us.

I cleared my throat and choked on the omissions. Needing to redeem myself, I raised a palm in the air. "Okay, okay. Not my business." I decided to lessen a little of the betrayal by breaching my professional code of ethics. "Look, I need to make a confession."

"Do tell?" Sam's eyes flashed with mischief. "Have you knocked up one of your interns?" I paled. "Shagged the dog walker?" If he only knew how close to the truth he was.

"Nothing like that. It's about Maxwell."

"What about him?" He waved away the dessert cart with an irritated twitch of his fingers.

"He's asked my firm to represent him—me in particular." I waited for a reaction but got none. Sam's face smoothed into a blank.

"What he does is none of my concern." He looked away and straightened the knot of his tie with a twitch.

"I just wanted you to know. He insisted I handle a few personal issues for him. Daniels and the other partners, they've got me backed into a corner. But if it's a problem for you, I'll drop him." I waited while Sam stared across the restaurant.

When he looked back, his gaze burned into me. "It's not a problem. Unless you intend to go over to the dark side with him." He quirked an eyebrow.

"Hell, I'd just as soon throw him over a cliff, but the law seems to frown on that kind of behavior."

"I trust you, Becks," Sam said. Guilt rampaged inside me. I didn't deserve his confidence. "Besides, it's good to have tabs on him. Might come in handy. Keep your friends close and your enemies closer, right?" He studied me with cool green eyes. "You realize that he doesn't do anything without an agenda. If you're on his radar, he's got something in store for you. Be careful."

We paid the bill and made our way out of the restaurant. Sam's warning about his father echoed my own thoughts. Any contact with Maxwell required careful and cautious planning. I vowed to take his advice to heart.

The head valet radioed to the parking garage for our cars. We stood in silence. I hesitated to open my mouth, afraid I'd break my promise to Venetia. My entire body tensed with the effort. Sam seemed lost in his own thoughts, giving me a temporary reprieve. When my Jeep arrived at the curb, the valet tossed the keys over the hood, and I snatched them from the air.

Sam's Porsche arrived next. He rounded the front of the car but paused before opening the door. "You're still driving that thing?" he teased.

"There's nothing wrong with my ride." To underscore my comment, the engine faltered and choked. A puff of blue smoke billowed from the exhaust. The valet coughed and waved a hand in front of his face.

"You can afford better." One corner of Sam's mouth curled up in a puckish smirk. "You deserve better. You work hard. You should play harder."

"I'll keep that in mind," I said, and opened the car door. "Tell you what. I'll get a new car when you stop being such a stubborn ass."

"Ha. Point taken." He lifted a hand in concession.

"See you next week. Tell Dakota I said hello."

"Will do. And keep an eye on V for me, will you?" His eyes met mine, dark with the concern he was unable to voice. "Let me know if she needs anything."

"You got it." I nodded. His trust increased my guilt. I spun the championship ring around my finger, hating myself for risking our friendship.

He drove away into the night, leaving me alone to deal with all the lies. I turned my Wrangler in the opposite direction, heading for my downtown apartment to contemplate his warning and to bask in the quiet solitude of my bachelor life.

Chapter 14

Venetia

AFTER MEETING with Beckett, I went to a job interview for an entry-level interior design position. Finding a job created a pleasant—albeit nerve-wracking—distraction from the problems of Beckett and the baby. I didn't need a job. Money had never been an issue for me. My billionaire father dropped a fat deposit into my bank account once a month, and I would receive a ton of money from him whenever he passed. When my mother died, she'd left a trust fund that I'd received on my twenty-third birthday. This substantial sum, with careful planning, provided enough income for the rest of my life. Although I never needed to work, I wanted more—a career, a success story all my own, to make a name for myself beyond Seaforth.

Garrison-Tafflinger was a topnotch architectural firm, rapidly expanding and known for its cutting-edge style. I sat in the lobby, briefcase at my side, and pondered the odds of getting this position. After completing an internship with a prestigious designer, I'd been on dozens of interviews across the country. None of them had resulted in an offer. With dual degrees in architecture and interior design, I was over-qualified. The recent decline in the real estate market made skills like mine unpopular. In spite of my education, I'd yet to manage a second interview anywhere. Now that I was pregnant, no one would want to hire me, no matter how impressive my resume. I decided to keep that tidbit for myself. After all, I might not even have the child. In which case, no one ever needed to know.

When the receptionist finally called my name, I straightened my skirt to hide the tremor of my hands and followed her down a corridor of closed office doors to an expansive conference room. A lone woman gave me the once over as I sat in the chair opposite hers.

"You've got exceptional grades and impressive references," the interviewer said after a lengthy barrage of questions. "But I have to wonder, why aren't you working for your father or your brother?" She steepled her fingers in front of her.

I drew in a deep breath, formulating the answer before I spoke. Being Malcolm Seaforth's daughter and Sam's sister didn't help my cause. Although I'd never mentioned their names, they'd played a key part in losing out on previous opportunities. After the last few interviews, I'd downplayed my familial ties. This time I vowed to avoid excuses. I squared my shoulders and looked her in the eyes.

"I want to make it on my own," I said following a lengthy pause. "It's important that I build a reputation independent from my family." And it was. Until I'd said the words aloud, I had no idea how vital this concept had become for me. Sam had made it on his own. Ten years from now, I wanted to look back on my life and know I'd made a success of myself without the benefit of their help.

She smiled and nodded. "I can respect that. But, frankly, I have concerns that you'll leave us after a few years to join with them. There are rumors that your brother is circling the wagons for a comeback, that he's got a new company in the works. I can't have you leaving us, taking away our clients, and divulging secrets to align with your family."

Her words unleashed my insecurities. I rallied a mask of self-assurance and dropped my smile. I spoke the next words with clipped accuracy. "We both know there are no guarantees in life, Ms. Levine. I don't have a crystal ball, and I can't see into the future. What I can tell you is that I have no desire to work for either one of my relatives at this time. I'm interested in learning from the best, and I'd consider a position in your company to be a feather in my cap." Her eyes widened, and she leaned back in her chair. I stood, intending to leave on a positive note. "Unless you have more questions, I'll be on my way. But let me leave you with this thought. I'm an asset for any company I choose to work for. You'd be lucky to have a Seaforth on your staff. My name alone promises dedication and excellence. I can assure you, I'm well worth the money."

"It's been a pleasure, Ms. Seaforth. Someone will give you a call within the week," she said. We shook hands. I left the interview with a sinking feeling and my confidence rattled.

Following the fiasco of my interview, I returned to my new apartment. Prior to this, I hadn't really had a place to call home. The majority of my life had been spent in boarding schools then college. My parents' house felt more like a hotel than a house. After my mother had died, I avoided going there. Instead, I bounced around the country, staying with friends or hanging out with Sydney in Los Angeles. Now that I was finished with school and the internship, I looked forward to having a place of my own, somewhere I could put down roots and make a life.

On the advice of Sydney's real estate agent, I'd rented a furnished three-bedroom penthouse on the edge of downtown. The doorman tipped his hat as I entered the building. Upstairs, unpacked boxes cluttered the foyer and held the few personal items I'd brought with me. I rummaged through a few boxes then sank onto the sofa in the living room to catch my breath. I seemed to tire more easily these days. Before Sam's wedding, I'd been barreling through life at breakneck speed, trying to forget all the mistakes I continued to make. Too much downtime led to too much introspection, and I didn't like the turn my future had taken. If I stayed in place for too long, the self-doubt and remorse crept in.

With a hot cup of tea in hand, I took five minutes to regroup. From the twentieth floor, the arched windows offered a view of the setting sun. Swaths of crimson, lavender, and gold streaked across the sky. In the distance, the twin skyscrapers of Seaforth Towers loomed above all the other buildings. They served as an ominous reminder of my father, his power, and the emotional distance between us. Was he there now, working on a new master plan to conquer the world, counting his billions of dollars? Every minute, every move in his life was plotted with careful deliberation. How disappointed would he be to learn his daughter was such an abject failure in her life? He'd never been the understanding type. Maxwell Seaforth didn't make mistakes. Neither did Sam. It was expected, mandatory.

"Can I get you anything before I go?" The housekeeper stopped on her way out the door. Her unfamiliar, yet kind face, offered little comfort.

"No, but thank you for asking. Have a good evening." I watched her leave. The door shut behind her with the finality of a prison gate.

My mind continued to race. Beckett had taken the news reasonably well, considering. He must be in shock. Maybe I'd been wrong to tell him. Maybe I should've taken care of it—I still couldn't bring myself to call it a baby—on my own. I rubbed a hand over the flatness of my belly. The image of an infant with black curls and long, dark lashes flashed through my imagination. Would it be dark like Beckett, or blond like me? Protectiveness swelled inside me, and I locked the fingers of both hands over my stomach. It needed me. *Someone* needed me. This baby would be mine. It would belong to me, and I would belong to it.

I glanced at the clock. Midnight. Sleep pulled my eyelids shut, but they fluttered open when I realized Sydney hadn't texted since I'd left her at the airport yesterday. It seemed a lifetime ago. I found her name in my speed dial and called, knowing she kept late hours.

"Hey, V." A yawn came through the speaker. I pictured her lounging on the hotel bed, phone in one hand, diet soda in the other.

"You were supposed to text me last night when you got in. I worry about you, you know?"

"Sorry. I'm so tired. I can't think. I had to go straight into a radio interview when I left the airport. Then there were costume fittings and meetings with the producers." The tension in her voice carried through the phone. "I only got about three hours of sleep last night."

"Don't let them work you to death," I warned. "Take care of yourself."

"Oh, I'm good. You know me. I thrive on this shit. What about you?" she asked.

I heard a deep, familiar male voice in the background and sat up a little straighter. "Who is that? Is that Alex? I thought he was in New Zealand." It didn't sound like her boyfriend. "Don't tell me it's Tucker."

"Nobody. Don't worry about it," she said, a hint of mischief in her tone. "Did you call Beckett? How'd it go?"

"I think he's in shock." Shoot, who was I kidding? I was *still* traumatized. "He's going to the doctor with me." The pressure inside my head increased, and I rubbed the space between my eyebrows to ease it. "He was pretty cool about it, considering."

"Beckett's a good guy. He'll take care of you," she said, and I knew it was true. Beckett's confidence had lessened the churning worry in my gut, but only a little. "Did you decide what you're going to do?"

"No, but he wants me to keep it." How could I explain the complicated emotions I felt around him and the baby when I didn't understand them myself? "He was very adamant about it." I feared he might try to pressure me into the wrong decision.

"Just remember, I'm here for you either way," Sydney said. She must have covered the phone with her hand because I heard muffled murmurs.

"Syd? What's going on?"

"It was room service." She cleared her throat. "Sorry."

"I've been thinking about what you said, about getting my shit together, and I —" My voice cracked. Tears stung my eyes. "You're right. I'm doing the wrong things for all the wrong reasons."

"Maybe you should go talk to someone about it. Someone impartial."

"Like a therapist?"

"Sure. I've been seeing Dr. Bob for a couple of years. It helps me stay grounded and deal with work. All this fame can make a person crazy."

"Seriously? I had no idea." One of my boarding school teachers had suggested a counselor when I was younger, but my mother had been adamant in her denial. Therapy was for the weak or the crazy, two things a Seaforth could never be.

"I can give you his number. Maybe he can recommend someone for you."

"Okay. I'll think about it." I bit my lower lip and sniffed to curb a sob. An outlet for all the pent-up frustrations might be nice. On the other hand, confessing my shortcomings to a complete stranger seemed out of the question. "Thank you for putting up with me. I don't know what I'd do without you."

"Aw, don't cry, pussycat." Sydney's voice softened. "You're my hero. You dive headlong into life, and I admire you for it."

"I'm an idiot." A solitary tear rolled down my nose. I swiped it away with the back of my hand.

"Yes, you are. But I love you anyway." The warmth in her words shored up the cracks in my confidence. "You need to think things through a little more. These are big decisions. Give them some time."

"I know. You're right. I will." I drew in a shaky breath and straightened my shoulders. "This is a bump in the road, right? I need to shake it off and move forward."

"Yes! That's my girl." I imagined Sydney's fist pump into the air. "You're a Seaforth, and Seaforths kick ass."

"They do." The tightness in my chest loosened. "I won't let this get me down."

"Now get your shit together and fix this." The edge to her voice strengthened my courage. "It's never too late to start over."

"I will. I will."

"And promise me you won't do anything else stupid while I'm gone. I'll be back in a month. Do you think you can stay out of trouble until then?"

"Probably not." I covered my mouth to stifle another yawn.

"Well, at least wait until I get back." She sighed into the phone, and I heard the man's murmur in the background again, deep, intimate, and tinged with a southern drawl. "I've got to go. I'm going to fall asleep on you."

"Okay. Sleep tight." A smile twisted my lips. "Tell Tucker I said hello."

Over the next week, I went to two more interviews. Neither appointment lasted longer than fifteen minutes, a bad sign. After the last one, I returned home, dejected but not defeated, and stuck a frozen dinner into the microwave. Every time I received a rejection, it only intensified my determination to succeed. I still hadn't heard back from Garrison-Tafflinger and chalked up the experience as another failure. Tomorrow, I'd try harder. Eventually, someone had to give me a chance.

The timer on the microwave dinged. I opened the door to withdraw a steaming tray of rubbery lasagna and sniffed the contents. I'd never learned to cook. For the duration of my childhood, I'd been waited on by servants, my meals prepared by trained chefs like Dakota's mother, and later, when I'd gone to college, I'd dined out every night. The need to cook had never seemed necessary or important. Now, staring at my pre-made pasta, I vowed to make cooking a priority, maybe take a class or two.

I transferred the meal to a china platter, poured a glass of red wine then remembered the baby and poured it into the sink. I took a seat at the dining room table. Alone. I missed my friends. I missed Sam. What was he doing? Was he happy? I'd pushed him away to punish him when all I'd done was punish myself. I wasn't ready to call him. Not yet. Not until I'd reached a decision about the baby. Not until I got my life together. I set my fork alongside the plate, appetite gone. Before I could spiral too far into self-pity, the phone rang in the kitchen. I went to it. My pulse leaped at the sight of Beckett's name.

"Hello?" I said.

"Hey." The deep timber of his voice shimmered over me. Excitement stirred butterflies in my stomach. I never expected him to reach out to me after the awkwardness of our previous meeting. "What are you doing?"

"Um, nothing." I dropped the lasagna into the trash can and leaned against the kitchen countertop. "What's up?"

"Well, I was just thinking." He paused. A mental image of his tanned fingers curled around his phone and his full lips close to the speaker sent prickles of gooseflesh along my arms. "If you're not doing anything, and I'm not doing anything..." My heart tripped, absurdly excited to hear his next words. "Maybe we should do nothing together."

"I don't know. What did you have in mind?" An insane smile curved my lips. He'd been thinking about me. It was silly, but the notion made my hands tremble.

"Come over," he said. "And I'll cook for you."

Butterflies fluttered in my belly as I sat on a barstool in Beckett's kitchen. The studio apartment had good bones with soaring ceilings, exposed brick, and a view of the city park, On the downside, the bare walls lacked personality. There were no family pictures, no knick-knacks. It seemed a lonely place, and my heart twisted for his solitude. I understood loneliness. Maybe we had more in common than I thought.

In my head, I painted the walls a buttery yellow and chose eclectic metal sculptures to complement the bare pipes stretched overhead. He had only a few pieces of furniture. A sofa and chair clustered around an enormous TV to create a living area. Beyond, a mattress and box springs sat on the floor to form the bedroom. I tried not to think about Beckett asleep on his bed, naked to the waist, wearing only a pair of boxers...

"V? Are you okay with garlic in the sauce?" By the slant of his brows, he'd asked more than once.

"Yes, sure." I swallowed and watched as he expertly smashed a clove of garlic beneath the flat side of his knife blade. He moved easily about the galley kitchen, opening cabinets, rummaging through drawers. Country music played from an invisible sound system, the soft notes a pleasant background to the sizzle of butter and herbs in a saucepan on the stove. When he turned his back to retrieve the chicken from the refrigerator, I stole a chance to admire the width of his shoulders beneath a soft pinstriped shirt and the hard curve of his ass inside over-washed blue jeans. He hadn't bothered to gel his hair, and the inky black locks curled softly above his ears.

"Why so quiet?" He flicked a drop of water into a skillet and watched it sputter before placing the chicken breasts onto the oiled surface.

"I was mentally decorating your apartment." It was a half-truth. I'd been dressing his living area before mentally undressing his body, but he didn't need to know that. "How long have you lived here?"

He glanced up from the chicken and pursed his lips. "A year. Maybe two."

"Seriously? Beckett, that's terrible. You don't have one picture on the walls." I wrinkled my nose. "It smells like bachelorhood in here."

"I work all the time. I haven't had time." His easy shrug and boyish grin sent a tingle of sexual awareness along the inside of my thighs. "Besides, I'm not into it. Give me a comfortable couch and a flat screen TV, and I'm good to go."

His dark eyes connected with mine across the kitchen island and reminded me of feelings I didn't want to have, shouldn't have. He'd hurt my pride in New Orleans, and I couldn't quite forgive him. Not yet. Not until I knew the fortress around my fragile inner self had been shored up. We could be friends to raise this baby, nothing more.

To break the line of electricity sizzling between us, I stood and walked to the window. The weight of his gaze followed me across the room. A black, starless sky stretched over the city beyond the glass. The yellow globes of streetlights lined the sidewalks of Everest Avenue. A few leaves, liberated by the cool day, danced along the pavement and skittered between the parked cars lining the avenue.

"Nice view," I said, glancing back at him over my shoulder. A chill travelled the length of my body, and I wrapped my arms around my waist.

"Cold?" Beckett lifted a remote control and with the press of a button, flames flickered around the gas logs in the fireplace next to me. The concern in his voice warmed me more than the heat of the flames.

"I'm not used to this weather," I admitted. "I've always spent the fall and winter in warmer climates."

"Why not this year?" He poured two glasses of wine and carried them to me with long, graceful strides. I could watch him move for hours, admiring his easy athletic grace. "You could live anywhere in the world. Why Laurel Falls?"

"I need to settle in somewhere. Even before I found out about the—about it." I still couldn't bring myself to say the word "baby", so I shrugged. "Sam is here, and Sydney has family here too." He offered the wine to me. I frowned at it, knowing I shouldn't drink alcohol.

"It's sparkling grape juice," he said.

The thoughtful gesture chipped a crack in the shield around my heart. I took the goblet from him. His fingertips grazed mine, and I struggled to keep my features neutral at the sizzle along my nerve endings.

While the chicken cooked, he sat on the arm of the sofa, attention trained on my face. The tails of his pinstriped shirt were untucked, the sleeves rolled up over muscular forearms dusted with black hair. He was big, male, and smelled clean like soap and aftershave. It unnerved me to be so close.

I took a step back and nearly tripped over something on the floor. Stacks of plain brown boxes lined the wall near my feet. "What are these?" I nudged one with my toe.

His eyes followed mine, lingering on the stretch of my calf before dropping to the hardwood floor. "Care packages for the homeless." His gaze returned to meet mine.

I kneeled and lifted the lid on the first box. It was neatly packed with bandages, deodorant, protein bars, hand warmers, and other miscellaneous toiletries. "You make these?"

"Sure. I carry them to work and give them out to the displaced people on the streets." The timer on the stove buzzed, and he rose to his feet. "It's starting to get cold out. They'll need all the help they can get."

A curious mix of tenderness and warmth washed over me at his unexpected generosity toward strangers. I'd seen the disproportionate number of homeless along the streets, camped in doorways, and huddled on park benches. I passed by them, averting my eyes. My mother had been a huge proponent of charities, but never advocated direct contact with the less fortunate. I'd paid little attention to her causes, too absorbed in the petty dramas of my life to care. Shame left me cold once again.

Beckett returned to the stove. "I'm sure you're involved in some charities, right?"

"No. I don't know. I mean, I'm not sure." I couldn't tear my gaze from those boxes. They taunted me from the floor. "My accountant handles all those things." A team of accountants, actually. Set up by my mother to handle the trust fund, later managed by Sam. "I'll ask Sam." If we ever spoke to each other again, that is.

"Have you talked to him yet?" With practiced ease, he shook the skillet then flipped the chicken over. The pan sizzled. The sound called me to the kitchen, where I stood next to the breakfast bar and admired the sight of a man cooking for me.

"No." With every passing day, the rift between us grew wider and hurt a bit more. I was too stubborn to consider I might be wrong, and Sam was too stubborn to concede. As far as I was concerned, we were at a stalemate.

"I had dinner with him last week. He asked me to keep an eye on you." Beckett shot a sideways glance in my direction.

"Did he?" Hearing this meant more to me than I cared to admit. An ache surrounded my heart. Maybe Sam was coming around. Maybe I wouldn't have to apologize. I fiddled with the edge of a dishtowel.

"Sure." He drained the pasta through a strainer, tossed it with olive oil, and plated it on thick paper plates. "One of you needs to make the first move, you know."

"I know." Capitulating had never been easy for me, even when I was wrong. I still held to the belief that Sam had made a mistake by remarrying Dakota, and until I knew otherwise, I had no intention of apologizing. "But it's not going to be me."

"Dinner's ready." The aromas of sage, garlic, and chicken drifted across the room and rekindled my appetite. He nodded to the small folding table and chairs set for two. "I hope you don't mind. I haven't gotten around to purchasing a real table." He'd thrown a bed sheet over the surface and placed a pair of candles in the center. The twin flames danced as he dimmed the overhead light. If I didn't know better, I'd think he was coming on to me. I snickered at the implausibility of the idea.

"What?" He settled the plates onto the table and raised an eyebrow.

"Nothing." I drew in a deep breath. The food smelled delicious. My stomach growled. I couldn't help but be impressed with the pile of angel hair pasta and perfectly prepared chicken, garnished with sprigs of rosemary.

"Are you appalled by my meager offering?" A mischievous glimmer sparkled in his black eyes. "Horrified? Have you ever eaten on a paper plate before?"

"Give me some credit," I retorted. "This is very thoughtful." Was I so vain?

Did he think I was a snob? My shoulders drooped a little. Who was I kidding? I *was* a snob—of the worst kind. Servants, tutors, chauffeurs—I'd taken for granted all the niceties and never considered how hard my life could be without them. "I hate to admit it, but when you called I was heating up a microwave dinner. I don't even know how to boil water."

His laughter brought out his dimples again. "Oh, come on."

"No, really. It's embarrassing." I paused to take a bite of the chicken and moaned at the play of spices across my tongue. "This so good. I'm impressed. If I could cook half this well, I'd weigh a thousand pounds."

"What if I made you a deal?" He sat across from me, his long legs bumping mine beneath the table. "Sorry," he said and eased his knees alongside my thighs in the cramped space. An absurd thrill raced up the lower half of my body. Maybe it was wrong, but I couldn't wait for it to happen again.

"What kind of deal?" I asked.

Before answering, he took a bite and chewed it thoughtfully, teasing me with his silence. His eyes twinkled with challenge, and there was nothing I loved more than a good challenge. "How about if I teach you to cook a few basic meals and you help me decorate this place?"

Chapter 15

Beckett

LOOKING AROUND my apartment, I saw it through Venetia's eyes, and I wasn't impressed. The bulk of my days were spent at the office, my free time in the gym or out with clients. I'd been so bent on making junior partner, senior partner, and making money, that I'd never taken the time to fully move into my apartment. It was merely a place to rest my head at night or screw the occasional girl when time permitted.

"I don't need much," I said. "A nice TV, a comfortable couch, and a good bottle of wine. Do you mind if I have a glass?" I lifted the pinot noir to show her the label before filling my glass. "Or would that be rude?" It was full-bodied but light and paired well with the chicken.

She took the glass from my hands. Our fingertips brushed. She held the goblet to the light, swirled the liquid around the sides, then lifted it to her nose for a delicate sniff. "Nice," she said. "You'll have to tell me how it tastes." Her smile instigated a rush of warmth straight into my dick. Wow. Pouty lips parted to show even, white teeth. I hadn't seen that smile in a long time, and I was instantly addicted. It became my personal agenda to wring more smiles from her pretty mouth before the end of the evening.

We chatted about sports over the meal. She was an avid Bulls fan and followed basketball. Her knowledge of statistics and the players astounded me. Before long,

I became lost in the flutter of her eyelashes, the curve of her hair around her shoulders, and the tantalizing peek of full breasts every time she leaned forward.

"I've got court side seats for next week's game. You should go with me." I heard my voice offer up the precious tickets before my brain had time to stop the madness. Had I lost my mind? Those tickets had cost a pretty penny, and I'd had to call in a few favors to get them. I'd planned on taking a client, but she seemed like a much better alternative. "It would get your mind off things."

Up to this point, we'd managed to avoid the topic of the baby. The minute I alluded to the situation, her eyes filled with sadness.

"Oh, no. I couldn't." She pushed her chair back from the table. "But thank you." The wall of formality lifted between us again. I became desperate to tear it down, to see the sparkle return to her eyes, and the smile to her lips. "Maybe another time."

"Sure." Disappointment crushed hopes I hadn't known existed until that very second. "It's doesn't have to be a date." She glanced down at her lap, a small furrow between her brows. I caught her hand in mine.

"Do you want it to be a date?" She lifted clear blue eyes to mine.

"I don't know." I looked away. Relationships and commitment had never been my style. I didn't want to hurt her feelings with the truth, but I didn't want to lead her on either. It was better for both of us if we were up front about our expectations. "No. Not really."

"Okay. Good." The relief in her expression kicked my ego in the nuts. "I think we should both be free to see other people."

"Good? What's that supposed to mean? Are you seeing someone?" For the first time, it occurred to me that she might have a man in her life, someone other than me. I stood up straight and squared my shoulders. I didn't like the idea of some stranger kissing her or raising my kid, but I wasn't sure what to do about it.

"No," she said with a slight shake of her head. "But I might want to."

Ouch. The more I thought about it, the less I liked the idea. However, it seemed unfair to tether her social life when I had no intention of curbing my own. I forced out a breath to dispel my anxiety. "We'll work it out."

"This is going to be so complicated." Her lower lip trembled, and she glanced up at me with worried eyes. "If I have this baby, it's going to change both our lives forever."

"But it doesn't have to be a bad thing." A small white lie, a half-truth at best. I came around the table and drew her to her feet. With my right hand, I swept the hair away from her face and tucked it behind her ear. "One of these days, we'll both laugh about this."

"Somehow, I don't think I'll ever laugh about it." She sighed and shook her head.

"You will if I have anything to say about it." I hooked a finger beneath her chin and lifted her face up to mine, needing to comfort her.

Her gaze dipped to my mouth before locking with my eyes. The way she looked at me, like I was half god and half superhero, erupted a primitive need to claim her and fueled my ever-starving ego. It sent a surge of testosterone rocketing through my veins, headier than the sweetest wine.

It would be so easy, so very easy to kiss her. One tilt of the head, a shift of our bodies, and our lips could meet. I imagined the brush of her mouth against mine, the succulent fullness of her lower lip when I dragged it between my teeth. Would she taste like grapes? Behind the fly of my jeans, my cock pulsed. I brought both hands to the side of her face and cupped the fragile bones gently. I wanted this kiss. I needed it in the worst way, if only to prove my imagination outdid the reality and put an end to my suffering. I closed my eyes and leaned in. One kiss, and I could end this ridiculous fantasy.

"I should go," she said. Her breathing quickened.

"Right." I dropped my hands and stepped away. An uncomfortable silence thickened the air.

"Or maybe we could watch some TV?" She turned huge, hopeful eyes up to mine. My mouth went dry, and every question about what we were doing disappeared from my head.

"Great idea." I took her hand and pulled her toward the sofa. We could do this, be friends. We were already friends. I felt a responsibility to Sam, Tucker, and now Venetia. Their wellbeing mattered to me, more than I cared to admit. And now, Venetia needed me. As angry as I was at our foolish mistake, I couldn't blame her. It was as much my fault as hers.

"Have you thought any more about what you want to do?" The question scared me, but I had to ask. If she chose to terminate the pregnancy, we were going to have a fight on her hands. I didn't want a child, but I'd been down this road once before, long ago, and I knew the pain of regret over such a permanent decision.

"I'm still not sure, but I'm leaning toward having it," she said after a lengthy pause.

"Just consider it. Please." A loose strand of hair fluttered over her eye. I swept a finger over her temple, tucking the strand behind her ear. "It's all I ask."

"I can't think about anything else," she admitted. "I feel like my life is in limbo until I decide how to handle this."

The profound sadness in her voice tugged at my heart. If only I could take away some of her indecision, help her realize this wasn't the end of the world. It had happened to me before, and I had lived through it. I wanted to tell her about my experience, but I couldn't summon the words or the trust to confide in her. No one knew about my teenaged mistake, and I intended to keep it that way.

For the rest of the night, she sat on the sofa next to me, one leg tucked beneath her, a pillow on her lap. Halfway through the movie, her eyes closed and her head fell onto my shoulder. The weight of her, trusting and innocent in sleep, stirred my protective animal instincts. Instead of waking her, I picked her up and carried her to my bed. Venetia never flinched, and I couldn't blame her. She had to be exhausted. I tucked her beneath the covers and brushed the hair from her forehead before grabbing a blanket and heading to the couch for the night.

Chapter 16

Venetia

I AWOKE in an unfamiliar bed to the smell of coffee and toast. Once I'd rubbed the sleep from my eyes, I took a glance around and remembered the comfort of sitting next to Beckett on the sofa, his thigh pressed to mine, the accidental brush of his bare foot to my toes, and the way my body reacted with tingles of sexual attraction deep inside my core. The glow of sunrise lingered in the apartment, along with the scents of aftershave and shower gel.

"Morning, sleepyhead," Beckett called from the kitchen.

I ran a hand through the mess of my hair then followed his voice. He stood behind the counter, the picture of success in a charcoal suit, white dress shirt, and ice-blue striped tie. I made a mental note to thank his tailor. Each of his suits had been cut to accentuate the inverted triangle of his broad shoulders. I swallowed and blinked away before he caught me watching him. "What time is it?" Judging by the heaviness in my limbs and the fog in my brain, I'd been asleep for a very long time.

"Six," he said.

"I can't believe I dozed off. I'm sorry." I caught a glimpse of my tumultuous appearance in the polished stainless steel refrigerator and cringed. There was nothing sexy about rumpled bed hair or smudged mascara. As irrational as it sounded, I wanted him to want me even if neither of us could act upon it.

"It's okay." His lopsided grin eased my embarrassment. I exhaled the breath I'd been holding when he turned to rinse his coffee cup in the sink. The sight of his rock-hard ass beneath the wool blend of his trousers reminded me of our history, and I curled my fingers to stifle the urge to touch him. "I've got to get to work or I'd have breakfast with you. Stay. Help yourself to the fridge or the shower. Whatever you need." His dark gaze travelled the length of my body, and a shiver of lust stiffened my nipples. In spite of our declaration to keep our relationship platonic, the sexual chemistry between us was off the charts. "Or I can drop you at home? It's on my way."

"I live down the street, Beckett," I said. "I can walk." A flash of heat brought a clammy sweat to my brow. I frowned and dragged a hand over my forehead.

"Are you sure?" His concern brought a blush to my cheeks. "It's cold outside."

"I'm sure. I could use the exercise." A strange bitterness lingered on my tongue. "Can I borrow a shirt?"

"Absolutely." An uncomfortable silence cooled the air between us. He cleared his throat and backed toward the front door.

I ducked my head, unsure what to say or do next. "Okay. Thanks."

The unease must've been obvious in my voice, because Beckett pulled me into his chest, tucking my chin into the hollow of his sternum. The scent of starch and laundry soap mingled with the spiciness of his cologne. I melted into the warmth of his body and closed my eyes.

"You're a strong woman, V." His deep voice reverberated through his chest and into my ear. "Everything will work out."

"I'm glad you think so," I mumbled. My hands, unable to resist the temptation, slid up his chest and curled into the fabric of his shirt. An unpleasant rumble wracked my belly. Bile rose in my throat. I clapped a hand over my mouth.

"What?" Beckett asked, eyes round.

I pushed him away and galloped toward the bathroom but only made it as far as the kitchen sink. The few remaining contents of last night's dinner raced up my throat. Strong, masculine fingers gathered my hair at the nape of my neck and held it out of the way as I hurled into the garbage disposal. Within seconds, the nausea subsided.

Beckett released my hair and smoothed a soothing palm down my back. "Are you okay?" he asked, his deep voice filled with shock.

I turned on the water and flipped the disposal switch to destroy the evidence. I brushed the back of my hand over my mouth. He handed me a paper napkin then turned to fill a glass of water from the refrigerator tap. "Yes, I'm fine," I said, but my hands shook as I took the water from him. I drank two sips. The liquid hit the bottom of my stomach and bounced back up, splattering the floor and Beckett's shoes. Oh. My. God. I covered my face with both hands, horrified beyond speech, too humiliated to look at him. "Oh, Beckett, your shoes."

"Fuck the shoes." Before I could open my mouth, he scooped me into his arms and deposited me on the sofa. Worried brown eyes locked with mine as he kneeled beside me. All the color had drained from his face. He lifted his phone to his ear. "I'm calling the doctor."

"Beckett, no." I sat up and put a hand on his forearm. "It's just morning sickness. I'm starting to feel better already." He lowered the phone but didn't seem convinced. "I think I need something to eat. Do you have any crackers?"

He rushed to the kitchen and returned with a box of saltines. While I nibbled the corner of a square, he watched me like I was a bomb about to explode. God, he was so sexy. In his turmoil, he'd loosened the knot of his tie and unbuttoned the collar of his shirt. A few rough hairs peeked through the opening at his throat. Even when he was worried, he exuded a primal vibe that curled my toes.

"I'm calling in." He reached for the phone in his pocket. "When's your appointment with the doctor?"

"Next week." The crackers began to absorb the acid in my stomach. My head stopped spinning. I breathed a sigh of relief. "You don't need to stay here with me. I'm fine. Really." To prove it, I stood up and smiled. "See? All better. I'm sure you have important things to attend to this morning."

"No." His dark gaze took in every detail of my face. One of his arms slipped around my waist and tugged me into his chest. "I'll stay," he murmured. His hand stroked my hair as he spoke. "Nothing is more important than you. If you need me, I want to be here for you. For the baby."

No one had ever said anything like that to me before. Words like those made me forget to keep an emotional distance between us. Words like those made my hands slip inside his suit jacket and slide up the groove of his muscular back. I rested my cheek against his chest and savored the steady, solid thump of his heart. "Thank you. For caring. It means a lot to me."

"It means a lot to me, too." His lips brushed the crown of my head and left me wondering where we stood with each other. Were we friends? Was it even possible after the night we'd shared, with a baby on the way? I had no idea how to categorize the unusual position we were now in. "Beckett." I pulled back to look at him. "Is this weird?"

"Not to me." The irises of his eyes warmed into a rich dark chocolate, almost black, then he frowned and dropped his hands to his sides. "Is it weird for you?"

"A little," I admitted. So many questions flew through my head. There were things I needed to know, boundaries to set, before I could feel at ease with him. "I'm not sure how to act." I waved a finger between us. "Are we friends? Not friends?" A groove deepened between his eyebrows. "I mean, I didn't ask if you're involved with someone. Are you? Seeing someone, that is?"

"We'll always be friends, V. No matter what," he said, but didn't answer my question about the women in his life. The warmth in his eyes chilled. He backed away and put a hand on the door, and left me to improvise the answer. "I guess we need to iron out some details, don't we?" I nodded, and he bent to pick up his briefcase. "Let's talk tonight. No, wait. I've got some things to take care of this evening. Let me look at my calendar, and I'll call you later. Promise me you'll call the doctor if you get sick again."

"I promise." I nodded and watched him walk out the door then I ran over to the window. Beckett exited the building onto the sidewalk, his steps confident and sure like he owned the street. At the curb, he lifted a hand to hail a taxi. An elderly woman hovered at his elbow, waiting for a ride of her own. He turned to smile at her, spoke a few words, then helped her into his cab and waved down another one for himself. The gesture was so sweet, so selfless, that I felt a surge of pride and something more, something that made my chest ache. Maybe he was a playboy, and maybe he wasn't the ideal candidate for a father, but he was a good person, and that was enough for me.

Chapter 17

Beckett

BECAUSE I got a late start this morning, I was off kilter for the rest of the day. Between depositions and research, I tapped out a quick text to Venetia. When noon rolled around, I still hadn't heard from her. Was she okay? She'd seemed fine by the time I left her, but worry consumed me. What if it wasn't simple morning sickness? What if she had some kind of serious medical complication? She might be lying unconscious on the floor of my kitchen. I had no experience with the symptoms of pregnancy. I had three younger brothers, all of them unmarried, and no close female relatives except my mother.

"I'm sorry, Mr. Beckett. No messages from Ms. Seaforth," Garth said when I stopped by his desk.

"Tell Margaret I'll be a few minutes late for the next meeting," I told him and drew out my phone to call Venetia. I stepped into an alcove next to the conference room, away from the buzz of voices and the ring of telephones, and cupped a hand around the phone.

She answered on the second ring, her voice harried. "Hello?"

"V? Thank God." I melted against the wall at my back. "Are you okay?"

"I'm fine." Car horns beeped in the background, and I heard the whoosh of traffic.

"I've been texting you all morning." I thrust a hand through my hair and fought to keep my voice level. "Why didn't you text me back?"

"I told you I had an interview," she replied, frustration evident by her clipped speech.

"You couldn't find two seconds to text me back?" My voice rose and several of the paralegals peered at me over their cubicle walls.

"I've got a life, Beckett," she said, her voice sharp. "I have two job interviews today."

"Right. Sorry." I paced the length of the alcove, all three steps of it, and turned to do it again. "I was worried."

Her voice softened, and the sweet tone of it made my head spin. "I'm fine. Fit as a fiddle."

"Great." Until that moment, I had no idea how heavy my concern had weighed on my mind. I didn't want to care so deeply, but I couldn't help it. I'd promised Sam to keep an eye on her. I might have let him down by impregnating her, but hell if I'd disappoint him again.

I met Margaret in the conference room. She closed the door behind us. I went straight to the conference table, where she'd laid out the last will and testament for Maxwell. It was a full ream of paper. I picked it up and riffled through it one last time.

A man of Maxwell's stature and wealth required careful planning and detail for his estate. There were corporations, subsidiaries, and land holdings to take into account, as well as each of his three children, and now a wife and her children. Margaret and the assistants had spent hours combing through the technicalities.

"This can't be right. Venetia's not in here anywhere. Or did I miss it?" I frowned.

"I'm not sure." She peered over my shoulder, skimming through the pages after me. "Are we missing a page?"

"Not that I can see." I scratched my head.

"I saw her picture on the internet yesterday with that reality star. What's her name?" Margaret asked.

"Sydney."

"Right. That's the one." A few beats of silence passed before she said, "Venetia's pretty."

"Yes. Very," I replied, still studying the document.

"You're friends with her?"

"Yes." I gritted my teeth, ill at ease with this line of questioning, afraid I might spill my guts to the first willing listener. Until I had Venetia's blessing, I had to keep our little problem under wraps.

"She seems young. How old is she, anyway?" she asked. Even with my back to her, I felt the burn of her gaze.

"Um, twenty-three, I think." I scanned through the pages of the will, slower this time, looking for anything out of place.

"She's just a girl," Margaret said. "I thought she'd be older."

"Well, she's not," I said. For some reason, I felt the need to defend Venetia, but bit my tongue. The more I said about her, the more apt I was to incriminate myself. I tapped a finger on the page, drawing the conversation back to business. "This. This is different, isn't it? Did someone authorize changes to the beneficiaries?"

Margaret approached and peered over my shoulder. "Oh, that. Yes. He called in those changes yesterday. I thought you knew about it."

"No." The terms of the will left the bulk of his estate to Sam and a nominal sum to Vanessa, but there was no mention of Venetia anywhere. I read through the details once more, unable to believe my eyes. The pages hissed as I thumbed through them.

Maxwell was a coldhearted bastard, but this went beyond comprehension, even for him. How could a father turn his back on his flesh and blood? I knew the answer. My own father—the real one, not the man who'd raised me—had done the same thing. I'd never met him. The only thing he'd ever given me was his hair and eye color and funding for an education, but none of the things that mattered. Not his name, nor his love, nor his presence in my life.

"Sam and Vanessa are the beneficiaries. Rayna receives the property and money detailed in the prenup. They won't have any kids. That's also been agreed upon in the prenup." Margaret crossed her arms over her chest and lifted an eyebrow. "I didn't even know he had a third daughter until you mentioned Venetia the other day."

"That's weird. Why would he leave her out?" I pushed a hand through my hair. Did Venetia know about this?

"All I can say is she must have done something to piss him off. When I asked him about the beneficiaries, he said all of his heirs were accounted for."

"I'm not signing off on this. Not until I talk to him," I said. "Everything else is good. Make a note for Garth to get hold of him, would you?"

"Nope. No mistake," Maxwell Seaforth said an hour later. "As I said before, all my heirs are accounted for."

I didn't like the unemotional tone of his voice or the way he didn't seem to care about leaving his youngest daughter in the cold. "You've got billions of dollars, yet you can't spare a few million for one of your kids?"

"It's not your place to question my motives," Seaforth said, and he was right. I needed to get a rein on my personal feelings. By the absence of background noise, he must've been inside the quiet opulence of his limo, shuffling between meetings. "Really, Piers. You surprise me. Maybe you don't have the stomach for this."

"I'm looking after your interests, Maxwell. If you don't mention her in the will, she could contest. A nominal sum will show intent, prove you didn't overlook her." The instant the words came out of my mouth, I felt the sharp sting of betrayal. As Maxwell's attorney, my first obligation was to him, but another part of me wanted to take care of Venetia and now our child. Shit. Things were starting to get complicated.

"Hmm, good point," he said. I heard the rustle of clothing, murmured voices, and a few seconds of traffic noise followed by footsteps echoing on a hard surface. "Truth is, she's not mine. Her mother had an affair. I agreed to raise Venetia with my name for reasons you don't need to know, and to see her to the age of twenty-three when she'd receive the final installment of her trust fund."

This red-hot piece of news knocked me back in the chair. Not his daughter? Maxwell spoke with same casual unconcern as a man discussing basketball scores while I reeled from the shock.

"Now that her mother's gone, I don't see any reason to continue the charade. She's got a trust and the money from her mother's estate. She'll be fine."

"Does Venetia know this?" I asked when I could formulate a sentence.

"No," Maxwell replied. "And you aren't going to tell her, either."

"Of course not." I twisted in my chair, trying to ease the tension in my back.

"Now that you mention it, I want you to draw up an NDA for her. Once she knows, I can't have her going around, spouting off about it." He barked out a few terse orders to someone next to him before returning his attention to our conversation. "Make sure it's airtight. And do it yourself. I don't want anyone outside of you to know about this."

Client confidentiality prohibited me from discussing any of Maxwell's legal doings outside the firm, but this felt wrong. I dropped my head into my upturned palm, feeling old and weary. I'd already violated that sanction by confiding my legal relationship with Maxwell to Sam, and I didn't intend to commit another breach of ethics by telling Venetia. I pushed the unease aside by telling myself it wasn't my business, but guilt kept me awake for hours that night.

Chapter 18

Venetia

ABOVE THE morning stillness of Laurel Lake, the sun peeked over the tops of the trees. Streaks of pink, orange, and yellow reflected off the surface of the water. I covered my mouth with a hand to stifle a yawn. The last time I'd been up at this hour was to catch a morning flight to Jamaica.

"This had better be good, Beckett. If you dragged me out of bed on a Saturday for nothing, I'm going to be pissed." In retrospect, I had no idea why I'd agreed to a hike around the lake at what seemed like the middle of the night. On second thought, the sight of Beckett's bitable ass in a pair of ripped and faded jeans on the trail in front of me might have been worth the lost sleep.

He cast a glance over his shoulder, brown eyes black in the shadow of his baseball cap. "Stop complaining. You're going to love it." He extended a hand, and I took it. Warm, strong fingers closed around mine and helped me scramble over a rock. The feel of his calloused fingertips on the back of my hand sent a delicious shiver of gooseflesh up my arm. As soon as we cleared the obstacle, he released my hand. I missed the feel of him at once.

"How much farther?" We'd been walking over an hour on an incline, working deeper into the surrounding hillside, and my legs ached. The lake below us shimmered and danced as the wind skittered across it.

"Almost there." The anticipation in his voice brought a smile to my lips. I liked this side of Beckett; playful, relaxed, and carefree.

We rounded a bend in the dirt path. The terrain grew uneven as we ascended. Fearful of tripping, I focused on the ground until Beckett stopped, and I bumped into his back. One of his arms curled around my waist and pulled me to the trail in front of him. My eyes widened at the amazing tableau stretched in front of us.

"Oh." It was the only word I could manage, and not nearly worthy of the sight. Across a narrow ravine, a waterfall plummeted over the precipice and crashed into the creek dozens of feet below. Rays of the sunrise streaked across the chasm, lighting the water in ribbons of scarlet and gold. Around us, the forest came to life. Birds twittered, their voices rising in joyous song. The wind rustled through autumn leaves at the height of their fall glory. "Beckett, it's amazing."

"I thought you'd like this." His arm tightened around my waist. I let my head fall back against his chest. When he spoke, his words buzzed in my ear, his breath warm against the sensitive shell. "I come here a lot when I need to think or get away from the damn city."

We stood in silence, listening to the birds chirp and the splashing water. The rise and fall of his chest against my back caused a pleasant tingle between my legs. I pressed into him. His warmth seeped through our clothes and chased away the early morning chill.

"Being here, it makes me realize how out of touch I am with reality." I turned in his arms and placed both palms on the broad swell of his chest. He licked his lower lip, the motion drawing my gaze to his mouth. "It reminds me that I'm just a tiny part of a bigger universe."

"I was hoping you'd see it that way." His hands rested on the swell of my bottom. Butterflies pinged the walls of my belly. "Whenever I have problems or I'm under a lot of pressure, this place helps me get my head straight."

I couldn't imagine Beckett ever being anything less than perfectly in control. Even now, surrounded by wilderness, he dominated the outdoors, all bronzed skin, taut muscle, and primal male. Standing so close together gave me an appreciation for how virile he was. I curled my fingers into his chest and felt the flex of his pectorals. Oh, my. And then I had a second, less comforting realization, that I'd been feeling him up for longer than appropriate. I tried to push away, but his hands pressed harder against my bottom until I could feel the rigid outline of his cock behind the denim of his jeans. A delicious shiver rippled down my back. Oh, God. It felt too good, too right, to be in his arms. I wanted more, needed more, but this wasn't the agreement. He was bending the rules, and I was too weak to protest.

"Are you ready for some breakfast?" He dropped his hands and stepped back, crushing me with disappointment, adding to my confusion. For a few brief seconds, I'd thought he was going to kiss me. I'd *wanted* him to kiss me. Friendship be damned. He might think I was a kid, a nuisance, a problem to be solved, but for one tiny instant, I'd recognized the flicker of heat in his dark, dark eyes, and I'd liked it.

"Don't tell me you have food in there?" I nodded to the backpack he'd dropped at his feet.

"Sure. You're going to need energy for the walk back." The zipper growled as he opened the top and began pulling out items—two plastic-wrapped bagels, cream cheese, and a Thermos.

"If you have hot chocolate, I'm going to kiss you." The declaration slipped out before I realized the implication. I bit my lower lip, hoping he hadn't noticed, but one of his eyebrows lifted, his gaze shimmering with mischief.

"Well, then." He withdrew two coffee mugs and set them on a stump. "You'd better pucker up."

I felt the blush travel up my neck and settle into my cheeks. His laughter didn't help my embarrassment. Why did he unsettle me so? I'd never been anything less than confident around other guys, but Beckett put me off balance. Maybe because I'd worshipped him as a kid, and getting to know him as an adult conjured up all those childish notions, refueled my fantasies.

Once he'd filled our cups from the Thermos, he handed one to me and perched on the stump. He patted the top of his thigh. "Have a seat."

I looked around, hesitant, but finding nowhere else to sit, settled gingerly on his knee. "Are you sure I'm not too heavy?"

"Are you kidding? You're light as a feather." With a grin, he turned his baseball cap around to put the brim at the back. Now I had full access to his long-lashed eyes and the black flecks in his coffee-colored irises. We stared at each other. His gaze dipped to my mouth. We blinked away in unison.

For the next half hour, we savored the quiet solitude. Beckett ate his bagel in three large bites, while I nibbled around the edges of mine. I'd learned if I ate early in the morning and slowly, I could avoid morning sickness. When we were finished, I made a move to stand, but he held me in place with a hand on my knee. My heart skipped a beat at the familiar touch to my bare leg, the callouses on his fingertips scratching my skin in the most delicious way.

"Can we talk?" he asked in a voice rich with intimacy. He shifted my weight, angling my torso to face him.

"Sure." More heart palpitations. Sitting so close, I felt the heat of his body and the swell of his chest with each breath. And his smell? I detected hints of aftershave and shampoo, the scent so enticing I had to resist the urge to buy my nose in his neck.

"About the baby."

I tensed, bracing for a lecture, and dropped my gaze to the grass beneath my boots.

"No, V. Look at me." He put a finger beneath my chin and tilted my face to his. "I need you to hear this."

A nervous tremor shook my hands. I clasped them together in my lap and tried to concentrate on breathing. "All right."

He studied my face as if trying to formulate the proper sequence of words. When he finally spoke, the amount of unchecked emotion in his deep voice sent a shiver up my spine.

"My girlfriend got pregnant when we were both fifteen." I opened my mouth to express surprise, but Beckett shook his head. "Let me get this out then you can ask questions."

"Okay," I whispered.

"We were too young to raise a kid. We both knew it. Our parents knew it. After a lot of talk, her family decided she should have an abortion."

I stroked a hand over Beckett's stubbled cheek. "I'm sorry. It must've been hard, being so young."

"It seemed like the best thing for both of us." His jaw clenched beneath my hand. "At first, it didn't bother me. Even though I was a kid, there was already talk about college ball for me, maybe a professional career after that. We went to a very strict school. We would've both been expelled if anyone had found out."

I didn't know what to say, so I sat mute on his lap and watched the expressions flit across his face. He didn't bother to hide the regret or the glimmer of tears that came along with it. So much raw vulnerability in such a masculine man shook me to the core. I wrapped my arms around his neck and pulled him into a tight hug.

"It must've been frightening to be so young." I murmured into his hair.

His hands stole up my back and held me close. "It was. I could've lost my entire basketball career over one careless experience." He shifted, burying his nose in the crook of my neck. "But she was the one who suffered. She had a breakdown our junior year, spent a few months in an institution. Before she got pregnant, she used to be a really fun girl, but after that she changed. She was serious and quiet, very withdrawn. I don't want to see that happen to you."

His confession brought the prick of tears to my eyes. It was so sweet—his concern—and it chipped a hole in my defenses. "Do you know what happened to her?" My heart cried out for the memories of a young love ending in heartbreak and tragedy.

"No. We never talked about it and went through the rest of high school like strangers." He sat up, his chin scraping across my jaw with the change in position.

125

"Oh, Beckett." My fingers found his hair and brushed through the short, silky strands, wanting to soothe his obvious pain. "I can't imagine how that felt."

"It changed me—us." He turned his face to mine. "Maybe it wasn't the best decision for her, but I think it was the best decision for me at the time. I can't go around second-guessing something I can't change. I haven't thought about it in years, but I have to tell you, now I wonder if it was a mistake. I think about how old our kid would be, how different my life would've been with a child in it. I don't want you to ever feel that kind of regret."

I pressed my lips together and tried to process this peek into Beckett's private life. For the first time, I realized I didn't know anything about him beyond his friendship with Sam, and it seemed a real tragedy. The more I learned of him, the more I admired his principles. All my life, I'd seen him as a two-dimensional god, far removed by the pedestal I'd placed him on, but he was really just a guy with flaws and insecurities like all the rest of us mortals. Like me.

Chapter 19

Beckett

ASIDE FROM my parents, no one knew about the girl I'd gotten pregnant until I told Venetia. My parents had been eager to forget the situation. As a boy of fifteen, I'd been happy to comply, but I'd never forget the disappointment in their eyes every time they'd looked at me that year, or the shame of betraying their trust. With Venetia, things were different. I was a man now, with the means and ability to care for a child, and I intended to act like one.

Venetia shifted on my lap. She wore one of my baseball caps with her ponytail pulled through the back, cargo shorts, and hiking boots. As she moved, the long strands of silk brushed the hand I held on her back. I don't know how I'd convinced her to accompany me on one of my early morning hikes, but now it seemed like one of the best ideas I'd ever had. This was my private place, a place to contemplate and decompress from the mounting pressures of work, but it seemed right to have her here.

"I can see why you want me to have it." Her gaze drifted to my mouth then flitted away. "Thank you for telling me. I understand better how you must feel."

"I'll always be honest with you, V. You can count on it." But was I lying to her by keeping Maxwell's secret? I pushed the topic out of my head. After all, he was my client, and I was sworn to uphold his secrets by the law.

Our eyes met, and I couldn't deny the irresistible pull of my lips to hers. The soft, moist feel of her flesh caused an eruption of need deep in my groin. I didn't push for more. I just wanted to taste her, to enjoy the relief of sharing a secret hidden away for so long. To my surprise, she opened her mouth and her tongue swept over mine. I groaned, overcome by her sweetness and the feeling of a pretty girl on my lap. Her hands fisted in the front of my hoodie.

We were already in a fragile place. I didn't want to upset the balance of a perfect morning, but damn if I could resist. Her breasts flattened against my chest. My hands gripped her bottom and pushed her down hard on my growing cock.

"Wait." The instant she resisted, I loosened my grip. We moved apart, open-mouthed and panting. A pretty pink blush tinted her lips from our frantic kiss and the scrape of my stubble. "I thought we weren't going to do this." The raw edge of her voice buzzed in my ear, heating my blood. "I don't want you to be sorry."

"I'm not going to be sorry," I said.

"Kisses like that make me forget we're just friends." Her gaze locked on my lips in a way that made my mouth dry. "You said this wouldn't happen again."

"Don't friends kiss?" I was playing with dynamite, but to hell with caution.

"What about Sam?" She kept staring at my lips until I could only think about how they might feel wrapped around my cock. "What about your 'bro code?'"

"I have nothing but the deepest respect for Sam. He and Tuck are the best friends a guy could have." I cupped her chin and redirected her gaze to meet mine. "But right now, I'd ditch them both for another kiss like that."

"Well," she said and smiled before she kissed me again.

Deep kisses. Slow kisses. Wet kisses. The kind of kisses a guy dreamed about getting and receiving. I devoured her mouth. She kissed me back like she was starving for me. We kissed until my lips chafed and my balls ached.

I wrapped her ponytail around my wrist. She turned to straddle my lap. If we kept this up, I was going to fuck her on the ground, hard and embarrassingly fast.

"Venetia." Her name ripped from my throat. I cupped one of her breasts in my hand, admiring the weight and fullness of it, the way it fit my palm perfectly, upturned and perky.

She dipped a hand between us and gripped my cock through my jeans. I groaned and pressed into her palm. A shudder of need rippled down my abdomen and straight into my groin. She rolled her hips, lighting explosions of desire inside me. "Come on, Beckett. Where are all those smooth moves I've heard about?" Her lips brushed against my open mouth as she spoke. I felt her smile.

"I've got moves," I said. The hiss of my zipper released the pressure behind my fly as her hand slipped into my jeans to stroke me.

"Show me." Long fingers wrapped around my cock and pulled up from the base to the end.

"Ah, God," I muttered. Who was I kidding? I wanted her, wanted to do wicked, dirty things to her. I thrust into her hand, enjoying the glide of her soft palm against my hardness, horny beyond reason. She stood and pushed her shorts over her hips while I dug a condom out of my wallet. I unrolled it over my dick and held it by the base. I hissed as she lowered herself onto me. She was tight and wet and slippery. I tried to hold back, but when she lifted and slammed down, I lost all control.

With one arm around her back and the other on her hip, I held on to her while she rode me, fast and furious. Short whimpers of pleasure ripped from her throat. Frustrated by the need to drive into her, I laid her on the grass next to the stump. I hammered her soft flesh, sinking balls deep, and kept going. Her legs tightened around my hips.

"Faster, Piers," she whispered.

The sound of my first name on her lips spurred my efforts. At this point, I'd do anything to please her, to get her off. I doubled my speed, ramming against her until my knees ached from the hard ground. She tilted her head back, eyes closed,

129

lacy lashes fanned over her cheeks. The morning sun bathed her skin in gold light. Fuck me if she wasn't the prettiest thing I'd ever seen. I dipped my head to tongue one of her nipples through her shirt. She groaned, deep in her throat.

"You feel so good," she said, her breath tickling my ear.

The pressure of her fingernails cut through my hoodie and into my back. The pain gave clarity to my thoughts, sharpened the sensations of the friction and heat between her legs. I tried to absorb the moment, savor the taste of salt on her skin, the scent of her body spray, and the slick wet heat of her gripping my cock.

"Don't let go," she begged.

"I won't. I've got you." The vulnerability in her plea drove a crack into the shell around my heart. I forgot about my own aching need and focused on hers. She responded to every brush of my fingers, every kiss of my lips, with a new sound. The power went straight to my head then to my dick. I murmured into her hair, praising her, letting her know how much I appreciated her, and took pride in her gasping cries. "So good. So sweet. Just like that, baby."

A rush of fire shot through my veins. Venetia tensed and stilled beneath me. I came with a jerk, relief flooding through my legs and into my toes. Her pussy clenched and spasmed around my erection, wringing electrified jolts of ecstasy from me. Air burned in my lungs as I gasped for breath.

I buried my face in the curve of her shoulder and tried to regain my composure. What the fuck had just happened? The power of the experience obliterated the memories of every girl I'd ever been with. There was only her. Beneath me, her body trembled from head to toe.

I pulled back to look at her, alarmed. "Are you all right? Did I hurt you?" I searched her face, relaxing a bit at the flush in her cheeks and the brightness of her eyes. I brushed aside the tangled mess of her ponytail then plucked a blade of grass from her shoulder. To my smug satisfaction, she looked well and thoroughly fucked.

"I'm good." Dimples I hadn't seen in quite some time deepened in her cheeks as she said, "You can hurt me like that anytime."

Chapter 20

Venetia

BECKETT INSISTED on accompanying me to the doctor's office for my first visit, even though I'd told him it was unnecessary. Neither of us addressed the sex by the waterfall, agreeing by unspoken consent to ignore the chemistry between us. Lately, it had been all I could think about. The touch of his fingers, the abrading stubble of his five-o'clock shadow, the way he'd grunted and groaned as he'd hammered into me. Sex like that could turn a girl's head, but I vowed to put my lust for him aside for the sake of our baby.

As I sat in the waiting room, I still couldn't believe this was happening. He sat in one of the hard plastic chairs at my side, large, square-jawed, and overtly male amid the expectant mothers. He paid no attention to their admiring sideways glances, but I heard their hums and whispers. I stared back at them, a prickle of possessiveness lifting the fine hairs along the back of my neck.

Beckett glanced up, catching my gaze. "You okay?" he asked in his rich voice. The sound of it hummed through me. My nipples, which seemed to have a will of their own these days, tightened. Brown eyes studied me.

"Yes," I said, giving him a shaky smile.

He winked at me then returned his attention to whatever he'd been typing into his phone.

While I tried to quell the butterflies in my stomach, he scrolled through texts and emails on his phone, briefcase at his side, absorbed in his work. How could he be so calm? It took all of my self-control to keep from breaking into hysterics. By contrast, he looked like he'd done this a thousand times before. He must have rearranged quite a bit of his schedule to be here, and it warmed me to know our child was a priority for him.

I bit the inside of my cheek and tried to breathe through my panic. This was just a preliminary visit. I already knew I was pregnant. Getting the results of the test was a mere formality. It wasn't going to change the fact. Then I saw it, the telltale sign of his anxiety. Using his thumb, he spun the silver championship ring around and around his tanned finger, over and over. I put my hand on his, calming his fingers, and gave a small squeeze. He smiled and squeezed back. The flash of white teeth did a thousand crazy things to my insides.

"Thank you for being here," I whispered.

"Wouldn't miss it," he replied, and I knew without question he meant it.

The woman next to me smiled kindly. She balanced a toddler on her lap, mindful of the huge swell of her pregnant belly. A second child, a curly-haired girl, sat at her feet and hummed a happy tune while coloring in a book. The mother caught my gaze. "Is this your first?"

It took a few seconds before I realized she was talking to me. Strangers never spoke to me. "Um, yes," I replied, hesitant to share the details. "Is it obvious?"

"You have that deer-in-the-headlights look," she said. "So does your man." She nodded at Beckett, who was engrossed in his phone.

"It was a bit of a surprise." Even though I rarely shared the private details of my life with anyone, this tidbit popped out of my mouth. The need to tell someone overwhelmed my common sense, and the confession rushed out before I could stop it.

"Mine too." She pulled the toddler's fingers from his mouth. He squirmed on her legs until she handed him a colorful rubber dog. "At least this one was."

"I'm a little scared," I confided.

"No need to worry. This is my fourth," she said, resting a gentle hand on her stomach. The little boy blinked at me with round, innocent eyes and made an ineffectual grab for my pearl necklace. His mother thwarted the attempt with a practiced hand. "And every one of them has been a blessing."

Four children? She couldn't have been more than twenty-seven or twenty-eight. Her hair was pulled into a messy twist and secured with a plastic butterfly clip. Shadows of fatigue darkened her eyes, but her smile held warmth and happiness. The little boy gurgled and kicked his feet.

"How do you manage?" I asked. "Isn't it a lot?"

"It is, but you do it anyway." She captured the boy's feet with her hands to still them. "They're totally worth it."

"He's adorable," I said, admiring his chubby cheeks and pink lips. Children had never held much interest for me before this, but I felt a profound tug deep inside. I smiled and the boy clapped his hands gleefully.

"Thank you. He's a hellion is what he is," she said with a shake of her head before dropping a kiss on his forehead. "Takes after his daddy."

"Daddy," the little boy mimicked.

She nodded toward Beckett. "I'm sure your baby is going to be beautiful. With that one as the father, there's no way it could be anything else."

Beckett shifted in his chair, too large to be comfortable and decidedly out of his element. Sensing our scrutiny, he looked up from the phone and frowned. "What?"

"Nothing." I smiled and shook my head. The woman was right. Beckett's broad shoulders, sinful good looks, and natural athletic ability guaranteed our child would be blessed. A bit of my anxiety disappeared. How lucky was I? I'd hit the alpha male genetic jackpot.

"Venetia Seaforth." The nurse called my name.

I stood, expecting to undergo the exam on my own, but Beckett rose to his feet and followed me. "You don't have to—" I began, but Beckett waved my hand away.

"No, I don't, but I'm going in." He sounded as if preparing for battle.

"You can get dressed now," the doctor said and patted my hand before leaving the room. Beckett turned his back while I slipped into my dress. Aside from being pale, he seemed to take the news in stride. It was real to me now. So freaking real. According to the doctor, I was due sometime in late April.

"I want to have this baby," Beckett and I said in unison. We stared at each other.

"Are you sure?" I asked. "I'm not talking about adoption. Because you don't have to be a part of it if you don't want. I can do this on my own." I wasn't at all sure I could, but it was important that I gave Beckett the option to choose his level of involvement. "You need to be certain."

"I'm sure." His jaw flexed, a familiar gesture of stubbornness.

"It's a huge commitment." A tingle of awareness prickled over my skin as he took a step closer and stared down at me. "We can't do this halfway."

"When have I ever done anything halfway?" he asked; a touch of cockiness twinkled in his gaze. All-star basketball champion, Ivy League law graduate, and successful attorney. Everything he did, he did with dedication and gusto. "You and I are going to be kick-ass parents."

"I'm sure you will be, but I'm not so sure about myself." Making the decision did nothing to calm my insecurities. I still had a mountain of issues to work through.

"I hope it's a little girl," he said. "With pretty blond curls and big blue eyes, like yours." His words filled my insides with warmth. I smiled up at him. At my side, his hand found mine and squeezed.

Chapter 21

Beckett

A LITTLE past eight the next evening, I picked up my phone and hovered a thumb over Venetia's name in my contact list. I thought about the miracle of our baby with a mixture of panic and awe. We were doing this. I was going to be a dad. No matter how many times I rolled the title over my tongue, I couldn't say it out loud. The man who'd raised me, the one I called Dad, was one of the kindest men I'd ever met. He'd nursed my skinned knees, taught me how to shoot a basketball, and loved me like I was his own flesh and blood. Until now, I'd never fully understood the magnitude of the gift he'd given me or the sacrifice it must have been to raise another man's child. If I could be half as wonderful to my kid, everything would turn out okay. I had to believe it.

By contrast, Venetia had little to work with in the way of role models. Maxwell's arrogance still rankled, the way he referred to her as if she was no one of importance, more nuisance than blessing. The burden of his secret burned in my chest.

I needed to see her. Dozens of excuses rolled through my thoughts. We needed to discuss custody arrangements and child support, names and religious views. I opened a new text message.

Me: Hungry?

Venetia: Always. You?

Me: Let me take you to dinner. My treat.

Venetia: Is this a date?

The same dilemma had nagged my thoughts for the past twenty-four hours. What, exactly, were we going to be to each other? We'd been through too much in the past few weeks. I already felt an unfamiliar ache in my chest every time I thought about her and the baby—which was constantly. Labeling our relationship as "just friends" seemed to belittle the strong bond growing between us. Then again, she'd been adamant about setting boundaries.

Me: Not a date. Dinner.

Fifteen minutes passed and no answer. Had I offended her? Maybe she wanted a relationship. I had to admit I was beginning to warm to the concept. A few weeks ago, the thought of more had sent a shudder of pure bachelor fear down my back. Today, it seemed more palatable. I liked spending time with Venetia. She was funny, mischievous, and reminded me there was more to life than work. Raising a child would require us to spend a lot of time together. We might as well get started right away.

I studied the piles of legal briefs on my desk, the list of unopened emails in my inbox, and the number of appointments on my calendar for the next day. The responsible thing to do was to stay at the office, eat Chinese takeout from the restaurant down the street, and power through the night. The longer my text remained unanswered, the more desperate I became for her reply. When she still hadn't answered after twenty minutes, I fired off another message.

Me: I've had a hell of a day. I could use a friend. Maybe you could, too?

With Tucker out of town, I had no one to talk to but Sam, and I'd promised Venetia to keep the baby under wraps until she was ready to tell everyone. The secret swelled inside me until I felt like bursting. I needed to talk to someone about the situation. Who better than her?

Venetia: I'm at the building next door. Give me twenty. I'll pick you up.

Me: Meet you in the lobby.

After I splashed cold water on my face, shaved, and changed shirts, I boarded the elevator and rode down to the lobby. Venetia waited near the exit. She turned when the elevator door opened. The sight of her smile caused excitement to replace the unease in my gut. I forgot the mountain of work waiting upstairs and realized with a jolt how much I missed her during our short time apart. Maybe this baby was our wakeup call. A child might be the anchor we both needed to finally put down some roots.

"Hey." I gripped her elbow and leaned in to kiss her cheek. The soft brush of her skin against my lips left me hungry for more than food. "I'm glad you could get away. I couldn't stand the idea of eating alone again tonight."

"Me either," she replied. Her hand brushed over my sleeve. "Thanks for asking."

"No problem." I opened the door. A pleasant tingle electrified my chest when her shoulder grazed my shirt. "I feel like we should celebrate. And we can get a few business details out of the way while we're at it."

She nodded and passed by on a subtle cloud of expensive perfume, trailed by undertones of her shampoo. I resisted the urge to bury my nose in her glossy hair and followed her to the curb. Crisp fall air swirled around us. I drew in a deep lungful to cleanse away the hypnotic pull of her scent. Walnut and elm leaves in colors of gold and orange skittered and skipped along the sidewalk at our feet, escapees from the small park across the street. She stood a few inches in front of me, balanced on a set of the highest heels I'd ever seen. The heat of her body warmed my chest as I closed the gap between us.

"I'm driving," she announced.

"Are you sure?" I asked. My chin hovered over her shoulder and next to her ear.

She tossed a saucy glance back at me. "Absolutely." Our lips were close. Her gaze flicked to my mouth, hints of blue irises barely visible through the lacy fans of her lashes. I could kiss her so easily. Just a shift of weight to the balls of my

139

feet, and our mouths would meet. I leaned in until her back rested against my front. We were in the dying light of day on a busy street, but I didn't give a damn. I needed to claim those full, sexy lips for my own. Before I could act, the purr and whine of a twin turbocharged engine interrupted.

I cleared my throat, straightened my tie, and tugged down the sleeves of my dress shirt. Few things excited me anymore except pretty women, front-row seats at an NBA game, or a well-crafted automobile. This, however, wasn't just a car. This was a Bentley Continental GT Speed, the car I'd been lusting over for the past six months, a perfect mix of luxury and performance. Tinted windows, black paint so deep it looked bottomless, and chrome wheels sparkled from the pavement. I hoped to buy one for myself someday, maybe with the proceeds from the Seaforth case.

"This is your car? You've got to be kidding." I let out a low whistle as the driver's door opened and the valet exited.

"Yes, it's mine, and no, I'm not kidding," she said with a wide smile.

"Jesus, V," I muttered. "I'm in love."

She took the key fob from the valet and crossed to the driver's side while I stared—make that panted—on the sidewalk. The sight of a gorgeous blonde next to the car of my dreams sent testosterone rushing through my veins.

"Put your tongue back into your mouth. It's obscene," she said. The easy way she teased me only exacerbated the testosterone speeding through my body.

"Can I drive?" I tried to tamp down the enthusiasm in my voice.

"No." She gestured toward the passenger door then slid into the car.

"You could have pretended to think it over before you answered." I opened the door on my side and drew in a deep breath, filling my lungs with the sweet combination of sumptuous leather interior and new car scents.

"Maybe I'll let you drive later if you behave," Venetia replied. She cast a coy sideways glance in my direction. The sultry spark in her eyes excited me more than the car. "Buckle up and prepare to be dazzled."

I'd barely secured the seatbelt when she tromped the accelerator to the floor and swerved into traffic. The shock of her impromptu launch from the curb sucked all coherent thought from my head. I gripped the dash with one hand, the armrest with the other, to keep my balance as she slalomed between cars.

"Have you decided on a color scheme yet?" She slammed a foot on the brake to avoid ramming the rear bumper of the van in front of us then accelerated to race through the yellow light at the next intersection.

"W-what?" I stammered.

"For your apartment?" Tires squealed. The driver of the Volvo beside us raised a middle finger when Venetia cut him off. She continued at breakneck speed, oblivious, her frown directed at me. "You said you'd think about it. I can't get started if I don't have a palette to work with."

"Uh, no."

The Camry in front of us flashed brake lights. I stomped a foot into the floorboard, willing Venetia to stop before we rammed into it.

She jerked the steering wheel to the left, missing the car by a hair's breadth, and glanced into the rearview mirror to check her makeup. My heart hammered against my ribs. "It's not that difficult, Beckett. What's your favorite color?" Her gaze flitted to meet mine.

"I don't care." I stiffened my legs and braced for impact.

"Are you okay?"

"You can do whatever you want."

"Okay." She blazed a brilliant smile in my direction, but I was too intent on praying for my life to admire it for long. "I've got a few ideas then."

Thank God, we'd reached our destination. I blew out a sigh of relief when she slid the gearshift into park and the car stilled. I wiped a bead of sweat from my temple. Venetia turned to me, blue eyes wide, head tilted to one side. I stared back at her. Something rumbled in my chest, a small bubble that pinged inside my chest before lifting to my throat. The left corner of my mouth twitched upward. A chuckle shook my shoulders. I tried to choke it back until she smiled, her expression brimming with mischief. We broke into full-fledged laughter.

"You tried to kill me," I said, brushing tears from my cheeks.

"Don't be a baby," she replied before biting her lower lip in a gesture so appealing I had to curl my fingers to keep from touching her. She gave my shoulder a playful shove.

"I almost had a baby, and believe me, that's a big deal for a guy," I chastised. "You're the worst driver I've ever seen."

I chose a trendy place on the top floor of the Milton Bank Building. The firm had a standing reservation for entertaining clients, so we were able to walk in. Every head in the room turned to look at Venetia. She seemed completely unaware of their attention. I couldn't fault their stares. Maybe it was the pregnancy glow or her growing confidence. Whatever it was, she was becoming irresistible to me. Smug male pride swelled my chest. I put my hand on the small of her back to direct her toward our table and to let the men know she was with me, only me, and they'd better stand the fuck back. I did it out of a sense of protectiveness and because she was carrying my child, not because I was totally, completely head-over-heels crazy about her.

A sea of stars scattered across an ocean of inky blue sky outside the floor-to-ceiling windows. Candlelight flickered over our secluded corner table. While she made a trip to the ladies room, I worried over the details. Was the location too intimate? Maybe I should have requested a table in the center of the dining room, where the low hum of conversation floated on air scented with herbs and filet mignon.

Since meeting the Seaforth clan, I'd done my best to emulate their high standards. They demanded excellence and suffered nothing less. Venetia had been born into a layer of society I could never understand. She'd just returned from a year abroad, for goodness sake. Before then, she'd attended Swiss boarding school, summered in Cannes, and spent weekends with the richest of the rich. I, on the other hand, had spent my summers baling hay, wrangling livestock, and wearing thrift store bargains. We were worlds apart in every way.

Then again, she wasn't a Seaforth by blood, which raised an entirely new set of problems. How could I sit across the table from her, knowing this secret, and not say a word? She was the mother of my child. Our lives would be forever entwined. I owed her my honesty as well as my loyalty.

The next time I looked up, she was there, heading toward me. Our eyes met and locked over the heads of fellow attorneys, government officials, and the city's most popular celebrities. The way she moved across the room, a vision of flowing blond hair and graceful limbs, stole my composure. A tight skirt showed off the long stretch of her legs. I stood, straightened my tie, and pulled out her chair to seat her.

"This is nice." She glanced around the restaurant, offering a prime view of her delicate profile.

"They just remodeled a few months ago," I replied.

"They seem to know you here." Her gaze swept over the trio of waiters hovering around the perimeter of our table, and the crystal stemware in front of her. "Are you a regular? Is this where you bring your girls?"

"Something like that." Lame, lame, lame. I was usually much more debonair around women. You wouldn't know it from the way my words knotted on my tongue. I'd never cared what other women thought of me, but Venetia's opinion mattered. I wanted her respect as well as her admiration.

"Oh, come on. You can tell me." She peered at me over the rim of her water glass. "Sam said you had a girl for every night of the week."

Most of my nights were spent at the office, working late, or out with the guys.

143

The occasional weekend shag and Thursdays with Margaret served to satisfy my physical needs. I realized with a jolt that the occasional hookup had turned into a rarity. In fact, I hadn't even looked at another woman since Venetia.

"Honesty, remember?" She tossed my words back at me.

"Okay. If you really want to know." She nodded, so I continued, even though the topic made me uneasy. "I do have a regular. Her name is Margaret. We hook up now and then."

"This Margaret. Is she pretty?" Her fingers curled around the water glass and usurped my attention. For a second all I could think about was how they might feel wrapped around my cock. Her lips pressed against the gleaming crystal. The smooth column of her throat moved as she swallowed.

"Yes."

"And you like her?"

"I respect her as a colleague," I replied. "But it's not a thing." Venetia narrowed her eyes before returning her attention to her plate. "What about you? I know you said there wasn't anyone, but I find it hard to believe you don't have a guy somewhere."

"Before Sam's wedding, I was dating Etienne Guillaume," she said without looking up.

"The race car driver?" I knew of the guy. Arrogant, handsome, and an international playboy. He'd dominated the Indy car circuit for the last few years and splashed the media with his womanizing antics. "He's a douche."

"Beckett, you don't even know him."

"I don't need to. I know his type." It wasn't a complete lie. I was his type. I ran a finger along the collar of my shirt to loosen it before I choked.

"Are you jealous?" A tiny smile twitched the corner of her mouth.

"Of course not."

"Then why are you gritting your teeth?" One of her sleek eyebrows arched. "You don't approve?"

We fell silent when our waiter returned to run down a quick list of specials. My mind wandered. I didn't want to be that guy anymore—a boozing, womanizing playboy, an Etienne Guillaume. I scrubbed a mental hand over my face to wipe away the dust of my hedonistic past.

"Okay. Maybe I'm a little jealous." I picked up the thread of conversation where we'd left off. "I just don't want a guy like that around my child."

"*Our* child," she corrected me, the smile gone from her lips.

"Sorry. *Our* child." The water did nothing to quench my thirst. I set the glass aside, wishing for something stronger.

"Do I need to get your approval on everyone I date? Should I have them fill out some kind of application? Set up an interview?" The words were spoken facetiously, but I gave them serious consideration.

"Are you going to date? In your condition?" Beneath the table, my fingers curled into tight fists.

Venetia's features sobered. A tide of crimson swept up her neck and evolved into twin red patches on her high cheekbones. "Are you saying no one will want to go out with me?"

"No. Of course I'm not saying that. I'm—I'm—" I floundered for the proper words to state my case. In my career as an attorney, I'd made closing arguments in the Supreme Court and never blinked, but Venetia robbed me of my extensive vocabulary. Never mind that I was in the wrong or that I was treading on dangerous territory.

Her nostrils flared. "So, it's okay for you to date around, but I need to sit at home and knit baby clothes? No, thank you, Piers Beckett." She ripped the napkin from her lap, tossed it onto her plate, and braced both hands on the table, preparing to storm out of the restaurant.

No, no. no. Stupid fucker. I shook my head and covered one of her hands with mine. What was wrong with me? "That's not what I meant."

"It's exactly what you meant."

145

We glared at each other. Frustration sparked my temper.

Her chin quivered when she spoke through gritted teeth. "I never took you for a misogynist."

I growled then drew in a steadying breath. "I merely meant that you're in a delicate state." Her eyes narrowed. *Wrong tactic, Beckett.* I tried again. "A pregnant woman is a sacred thing." The furrow between her brows relaxed. Now I was on the right track. I plunged ahead. "You have to be careful, now more than ever. We both do. We have more than ourselves to think about. We really need to think about who we expose our child to."

The tension in her shoulders disappeared. She leaned back in her chair, and her breasts—mouthwatering beneath her blouse—lifted and fell with a heavy breath. Had they gotten bigger? "Okay. I get that. So, you want me to introduce you to my dates?"

"Yes. I think you should. And I should do the same."

"Okay. I want to meet your Margaret then."

Hell fucking no. I leaned back in my chair. "There's no need. Margaret will never be around our kid."

"Maybe my guy won't be around our kid, either. Maybe I'll just have him around for sex."

I choked on the bite of bread in my mouth. Venetia chuckled and bit her lip. Once my gaze tore away from the fullness of her mouth, I saw the teasing glint in her eyes.

"I'm sorry." She smiled. "You left yourself open for that one. I couldn't resist."

"You need a good spanking." I shook my head and smiled back.

"Okay." Her answer sent my cock on high alert. I had a mental image of her turned upside down on my lap, round bottom pink beneath my palm. She glanced from side to side as if about to divulge a secret. "I haven't been able to think about anything but sex lately," she whispered. "I think it's a pregnancy thing."

All the blood left my head in a dizzying rush and flooded into my dick. I shifted in the chair to adjust the pressure behind my fly. Holy hell. Did she really just say that? Was she serious? My appetite for food disappeared, and all I could think about were the creamy tops of her breasts peeking through the opening of her shirt.

I coughed and changed the subject because I was completely down with the idea. If we continued along this line of conversation, I'd be forced to drag her into the ladies room and fuck her against the wall. I was pretty sure by doing this, I'd violate our friendship treaty. "So, you had an interview this afternoon? Tell me about it."

One of our wait staff stepped forward to refill her water glass then melted into the shadows behind us. I sat back in my chair and waited, hoping she relaxed enough to confide in me, because I wanted her trust.

"I'm having trouble finding a job." She took a sip of water then set the glass next to her plate and traced the rim of the crystal with a manicured fingertip. Her opposite hand rested on the table, fingers long and delicate. I covered it with my own. "I've been on six interviews, and none of them went very well. They all think I'm a female version of my father, or that I'll leave to work with Sam." The candlelight flickered over her hair as she shook her head. "And I can't blame them." Her face fell, disappointment clear in the set of her features. "I didn't think it would be this difficult."

"And I didn't help matters by knocking you up, did I?" She pulled her hand away and hid it beneath the table, but her eyes didn't leave my face. I felt the tug of attraction rekindle deep in my groin.

"No, you didn't." Her honesty intrigued me almost as much as the fullness of her bottom lip.

"Why are you even bothering with a job?" I asked with sincere curiosity. "You could start your own design firm. You don't need to begin at the bottom."

"You sound like Sam." A small, impatient snort accompanied the flash of anger in her eyes. "It's not like I can snap my fingers and open a business. I need to build a client base. I want to develop respect and earn a reputation as a serious designer. It's important to me. But I'm sure you wouldn't understand. Everything you touch turns to gold."

Nothing was further from the truth. I could've followed in the footsteps of my adoptive father, taken over his hardware store in our small town, but it had never been my dream. Although he was proud and supportive of my career choice, his disappointment showed in his eyes and tone whenever he spoke about the store. Unless my youngest brother decided to step up when he graduated from college, the store would close or be sold when my dad retired, ending a legacy of three generations.

"I get it, V." By the roll of her eyes, she didn't believe me. "You're absolutely right." My chest warmed with admiration for her tenacity. She'd matured a lot since New Orleans, and I felt guilty for underestimating her. "I respect what you're doing, and I have no doubt you'll do your family proud. You've already made me proud."

Her gaze connected with mine. The blue of her eyes softened. Venetia had a mountain of preconceptions to overcome. Her father was one of the most powerful men in the country, her brother a close second. The name Seaforth graced hospitals and schools and banks across the country. She couldn't cross the street without facing evidence of her family's success. I couldn't imagine the kind of pressure that came along with a legacy like hers.

"Thank you." The muscles in her graceful neck tensed and relaxed as she swallowed. "I don't think anyone has ever said that to me before."

One corner of her mouth twitched then both corners lifted. Her eyes brightened. My pulse skipped a beat. I had missed the tiny dimples on either side of her lips. They flashed and danced as her smile intensified. I had the weirdest need to lean over and kiss one of those sweet indentations.

"That's a shame," I said instead, "because you're a force to be reckoned with, and I'm sorry if I made you feel any other way."

Her gaze flitted to my mouth. She licked her lips before disconnecting and focusing on her plate. "So what did you do today?" she asked while rearranging the napkin on her lap. "Working on anything interesting?"

And just like that, the tone of our dinner changed. Her shoulders relaxed, and the lines of suspicion around her eyes vanished. I found her witty and charming and easy to talk to. I told her, in the most general terms, about the divorces I had working. She listened, chiming in with an occasional observation here and there. The way she focused on my words, nodding and sometimes laughing, sent me into an utter tailspin. I began to seek out those smiles, my ego fueled by her attention.

"I really enjoyed tonight," she said at the end of the meal. Her hand slid across the table toward the bill. "Let me take care of this."

"I'll get it." I nudged the leather holder out of her reach and shook my head. "I invited you."

"Beckett." Her features darkened into a scowl. The mercurial changes in her mood fascinated me. I could hardly wait for the next one.

"A gentleman always buys." Once the waiter returned with my card, I signed the credit slip and gave her a wink.

"Okay." Those delicious dimples peeked out again. "Next time I get to pick the place."

"Deal." The idea of seeing her again sent a surge of adrenalin through my veins. "But I'm driving."

"Chicken," she replied.

We laughed and stood from our chairs. I placed my hand on the small of her back to guide her toward the door. It felt right to touch her there, like I'd done it a thousand times before, like it belonged nowhere else.

"Have you ever been to—" Her words and feet halted. She stared at something or someone at a nearby table. My gaze followed hers across the room and landed on the curious stare of Maxwell Seaforth.

Chapter 22

Venetia

MAXWELL LOUNGED at a private corner table across from a smooth-haired brunette. The lean of his torso and the tilt of her head suggested intimacy. My stomach lurched at seeing my father with a woman who wasn't my mother. He'd been a known philanderer during their marriage, but it still bothered me. I don't know why. Mother had been gone for many years. It was only natural for him to move on.

"Do you want to go over?" Beckett's breath puffed against my ear.

I shook my head, unable to move or speak. "No." The denial came out breathy and short. "I mean, yes." Before I could contemplate the consequences of my actions, I forced my feet to carry me toward the couple. The moisture disappeared in my mouth. It had been so long since I'd seen my dad. The lines around his mouth had deepened. All the blond in his hair had been replaced with salt and pepper. He looked the same yet different than I remembered.

Maxwell looked up and met my gaze without a hint of warmth. Only when I stood directly in front of him did he acknowledge me. "Hello," he said. He stared at me like I was an interloper instead of his flesh and blood. After an interminable second, he stood and offered his hand to shake.

"Hi." I swallowed down the knot in my throat. What kind of father shook hands with a daughter he hadn't seen in five years? I kept my hands at my sides, fingers clenching.

"Good evening, Piers." Maxwell turned away from me without acknowledging my snub and shook hands with Beckett. "Nice to see you again."

"Maxwell," Beckett replied. Did I imagine a flatness to his tone? My father returned to his seat. Beckett's hand rested on my hip, calm and reassuring. I straightened, buoyed by his strength, grateful for his presence. Without saying a word, I knew he had my back.

"This is Rayna Whitman, my fiancée." Maxwell gestured toward his companion.

Fiancée? Shouldn't this be something I knew about? I placed a hand on my diaphragm and tried to remember to breathe. Hurt barreled over me. I didn't know why the lack of communication came as a surprise. For most of my life, I'd been nothing more than an inconvenience to him, an obligation, a nuisance to be tolerated. In desperation, I tried to shore up my defenses before he could hurt me again.

Sensing my discomfort, Beckett moved closer until I felt the solid steel of his chest against my shoulder.

"Rayna, this is Piers Beckett, Sam's friend. And Venetia." He said my name, almost as an afterthought, as if he'd forgotten I was there. Not *my daughter, Venetia.* Just *Venetia.*

"Nice to meet you." I forced a polite smile to hide the hurt.

"Hi. It's a pleasure," Rayna said without a smile.

"I had no idea you were getting married," I said, surprised by the calmness of my voice. Meanwhile, my insides churned. "Congratulations."

"Thank you," Rayna replied. Her catty gaze flitted over my hair and outfit, and I was grateful I'd chosen the figure-flattering dress.

"My wedding invitation must have gotten lost in the mail." My mouth circumvented my brain and took control of the conversation. "Or did you lose my address again? Really, Daddy, you should be more careful."

Beckett's chest shook against me as he choked back a laugh.

"We're having a private civil ceremony," Maxwell replied, unaffected. His gaze locked on mine, green eyes swirling with thoughts I didn't want to unravel. His lips twitched as if amused. That one small gesture turned my malaise to anger. My body trembled with the force of it.

"Sam and Dakota are married now," I said, pleased to see the smile slide from his face at the mention of my brother. "They seem really happy. I'm sure they'll be popping out babies any time now." Of course, I had no idea about the state of their marriage, but it was nice to see his nostrils flare and the color climb up his throat. The briefest flicker of anger turned his green eyes to fire.

"Rayna and I were in the middle of a business discussion," he said after an uncomfortable beat. "What can I do for you? Is there a problem with your trust?"

The question slapped me across the face. All he cared about was money and business. I took a step back, treading on Beckett's foot. His grip tightened on my waist. He drew me against his stomach and held me there, steadying my body as well as my thoughts.

"I don't need anything. I just wanted to say hello." When I glanced up at Beckett, he was watching me from beneath thick, dark lashes. "After all, it's been years."

"We're running a bit late," Beckett interjected, his eyes locking with mine in understanding. "We'd better go." His gaze flicked to Maxwell, reflecting my father's coldness. "Have a nice evening."

"Beckett." My father nodded, dismissing us. "Goodbye, Venetia."

Beckett took my hand in his and pulled me toward the door. I followed without a backward glance to my father. Neither of us spoke. At the curb, the valet handed him the keys to my car. I hesitated. Up until the time we saw my father, I'd had an excellent time. For a brief time, I'd considered putting the moves on him, maneuvering another visit to his apartment or mine. Now, I just wanted to crawl into a dark corner and recover from the shock of the encounter.

"Are you okay?" Beckett held my hand, his grasp warm and steady.

"No. Yes. I don't think so." Feeling the sting of tears behind my eyes, I glanced at the valet.

Beckett's fingers tightened around mine. "Get in. I'll drive." The undertone of his voice scratched over me. "You're pale as a ghost. And the way you drive, you'll probably have a wreck and kill us both." By the scowl on his face, he wasn't going to accept anything but compliance. The valet opened the car door, and Beckett handed me inside.

Once he'd slipped into the driver's seat, he pulled the car smoothly from the curb and merged into traffic. Thoughts of my father, Rayna, Sam, and our complicated relationships raced through my head. I bit into my lower lip, so lost in my own head that I forgot Beckett was there until he spoke.

"It's bullshit," he said, his voice low and raw. His long fingers tightened around the steering wheel until his knuckles turned white.

"What?" I glanced over at him. The passing shadows of street signs and buildings flashed over the planes and angles of his face.

"The way he treats you. It's not right, Venetia." He thumped a hand on the steering wheel. "Motherfucker."

The anger on my behalf, made my heart squeeze. I put a hand on his knee, needing to comfort him. "It's no big deal. I don't know why I expected anything different. Once a dick, always a dick."

Beckett chuckled, and the sound soothed my frazzled nerves. "True." He shot a sideways glance at me before returning his attention to the street. "I take it you haven't talked to him in a while?"

"One time since my eighteenth birthday. He deposits a check into my account each month, but he doesn't talk to me." I realized my hand was still on his knee, and I withdrew it into my lap. "He had me sign some documents regarding my mother's trust and a few other issues. Everything else was handled by his people." Streetlights and store fronts and cars flashed by us in a blur. "The last time I saw him, he gave me this big, long lecture about the importance of being independent and finding my own path in life. Basically, he told me to fuck off."

"Maybe you're better off without him in your life," Beckett said. The tone of his voice caused me to turn and study his profile. The sharp angles of his nose and forehead stood out in relief against the night sky. "You're in good shape financially, right? And you've got a top-notch team of advisors?"

"Yes, Sam made sure of it." Sam had stepped in when I'd received my trust to make sure I'd be in good hands. He'd always been there when I needed him. Now, I realized it was to protect me from my father, and because he cared when no one else did.

Chapter 23

Beckett

THE HAUNTED look in her eyes made my chest ache. Even though she managed a smile, I knew she hurt inside, and it made me admire her all the more. I wanted to take away her self-doubt and erase the damage done by her cold-hearted father, but I wasn't sure where to begin or if she'd even let me.

When we reached her building, I walked her to the door of her apartment. She unlocked the door and went inside. I followed her, wordless, and lingered in the foyer while she turned on the lights.

"Do you want something to drink?" Her brow furrowed in thought. "I've got water, iced tea, wine."

"No." We stared at each other. I needed to leave, but my feet wouldn't take me to the door, not until I knew she'd be fine. A strand of hair fluttered over one of her blue eyes. On instinct, I tucked it behind her ear. "Are you going to be alright?"

"Sure. Why wouldn't I be?" She busied her hands by rearranging a bowl of polished marbles on the foyer table.

"Come here." I stilled her fingers, took her fragile hand in mine, and pulled her to me.

"I'm fine. Really." Despite her protest, she didn't shift away. With a deep sigh, she rested her forehead on my shoulder. I moved to hold her closer. Her breasts pressed against my chest, soft against my hardness.

"You know," I murmured into her hair, "my dad's a dick, too."

"Really?" Her breath puffed against my neck. "Sam always said he liked your dad."

"Not the guy who raised me, my real father." I lifted a hand and buried my fingers in the silky strands of her hair. I couldn't tell her Maxwell wasn't her father, but I could ease a little of her insecurities about him with my own story. "I'm a bastard."

"I had no idea." She pulled back, eyes wide in disbelief.

"He wasn't married to my mom. She got pregnant when they were in college, but he didn't stick around. He said he wanted more out of life, that he had ambitions. A wife and kid would just drag him down." I'd held the secret all my life, but it slipped out easily. She was the first person I'd wanted to tell, the only one I felt might understand. "I've never met him, and I have no desire to."

"But you know who he is?" Her lips brushed over my collarbone when she spoke. My skin prickled with awareness.

"Yes, and so do you." I drew in a shaky breath. "Supreme Court Justice Emerson Conrad. He paid for my college, but he's never initiated any contact with me. As far as I'm concerned, he's not my dad." My dad was the man who'd welcomed me into his home, taken me fishing every Saturday morning, and taught me how to knot a necktie.

The parallels between my conception and that of our child glared back at me. I didn't want to be Emerson Conrad, but maybe I had no choice. Maybe serial philandering was a genetic curse. The absurdity of an idea like that made me laugh. Behavior was learned. I didn't have to repeat the sins of my biological father. I could be a better man. I *had* to be a better man for my child. For Venetia.

Her hands crept up the front of my shirt and around my neck. I smoothed a palm down the groove of her spine. With every breath, her ribs pressed into mine. The warm, flesh-and-blood feel of her renewed the sexual fantasies I'd been fighting. I wanted her, needed her, in a way I'd never experienced. This wasn't about fucking—this was about getting closer to someone I cared about, someone who shared my dirty secrets.

I dragged my lips along the curve of her neck and planted a kiss below her ear. The beat of her heart thudded against my chest. My pulse raced to sync with hers. On an earthy groan, she turned her head, mouth open, and closed her eyes. I fisted a hand in the hair at her nape, angled her face to mine, and claimed those pouty lips for my own. To hell with the bro code, to hell with friendship, and to hell with my fears. None of it mattered. She was having a baby. *My* baby. *Mine.*

Chapter 24

Venetia

PREGNANCY ENHANCED my senses. Food—when I could keep it down—tasted better. My nose detected the slightest odor, like the hotdog vendor down the street or the laundry soap in Beckett's shirt. The fabric of my bra teased my sensitive nipples into tight peaks. The mere thought of sex caused my thighs to squeeze together. And believe me, I thought about sex a lot.

An evening spent in close proximity with Beckett didn't help matters. Why did he have to be so damn sexy? Humidity from rain earlier in the day curled the hair above his ears. He'd been clean-shaven when I'd picked him up at his office, but hours later, dark stubble peppered his cheeks. On the drive home, he'd ditched his jacket and tie, opening the throat of his shirt to reveal a sliver of tanned sternum dusted with black hair.

When his fingers sought purchase in my hair and jerked my mouth to his, I was a goner, my willpower nonexistent. Somewhere, along the path from the foyer to the bedroom, my blouse disappeared. I drew in a deep breath as he laid me on the bed, willing my thoughts to still, to enjoy the moment and not read anything into what we were about to do. The air filled with Beckett's scent, his spicy-sweet cologne, his fresh shower soap, and the musk of his skin. Smooth cool sheets rustled beneath me. Everything seemed more vibrant, more intense.

"Are you sure?" he asked.

"I'm sure. You?" I didn't wait for his answer. My fingers made quick work of the buttons on his shirt. I laid open the front and held my breath at the sight of his abdomen and the dark trail of hair leading into the waistband of his trousers.

"We haven't talked about where we're going, what we're doing, about this…" As he spoke, I pulled off his shirt and stared, mesmerized by his rippling eight-pack and the indentation of muscle on his hips.

"Later." I didn't care where we were going as long as it ended with his cock inside me. The greedy fingers of desire ripped away my composure. I could see the long, thick outline of his erection behind his zipper. He closed his eyes and dragged a palm along its length before lowering the zip. "I need sex."

After all, this was Beckett, a known player. Only a fool would give her heart to a guy like him. I might be impulsive and headstrong, but I wasn't stupid enough to mistake lust for love.

He rocked back on his knees and dragged his pants down over his hips. His erection fell forward, the long shaft nestled in a thicket of trimmed black curls. The smooth tip of his cock bobbed over my tummy. The muscles below my waist clenched in anticipation. While he fished a condom out of his wallet, I shimmied out of my panties and tossed them to the floor, eager to get on with it. When he'd sheathed himself, I curled a hand around his neck and pulled him onto me, opening my legs and inviting him inside.

One of his large hands slipped between us. The tip of his middle finger teased my clit and dipped lower to my entrance. I was wet and ready and had been for most of the night. He dragged the wetness along my seam, preparing me, then plunged his finger inside to the knuckle. The walls of my channel instinctively clenched around him. We groaned in unison.

"Inside me, Beckett. Now." I wriggled beneath him, impatient and wanton.

"What about foreplay?" His deep, ragged voice held a note of amusement. The lights were still on in the room. He stared down at me, all broad shoulders, round muscles, and sharp angles. His finger curled, hitting the sweet spot deep inside me. A smirk lifted the corner of his mouth as I gasped.

"Later," I managed to grit out. If only he knew how badly I needed the release, he wouldn't tease me. I jerked my hips. In another few seconds, I was going to beg him for it, and I hated to beg.

"Careful what you wish for." Before the words were out, he thrust into me, balls deep, and pushed hard into the notch of my thighs. I closed my eyes, and a violent shudder rippled up my body. When I opened my eyes, he was staring down, eyes black as midnight and nostrils flared. "Jesus, V. It's like that, is it?"

Sweet relief washed through my veins, like warm bathwater, replaced by burning desire when he started to move. Slowly, he pulled all the way out, holding the condom in place by a finger against my gripping muscles, then pushed in again. Wetness coated my thighs. He slipped in and out easily, building speed and intensity, each thrust deeper and harder than the first until our flesh met with resounding slaps.

"So fucking wet. So tight," he rasped, his voice more textured than I'd ever heard it. I liked the way he talked dirty, ordered me around, moved my body where he liked it, the way he liked it. "Put your legs on my shoulders. Squeeze me harder."

The headboard banged against the wall. I didn't worry about the dents in the drywall or the damage to the custom wallpaper. All I cared about was following his instructions. The bed squeaked. Our bodies slammed together. The tendons in Beckett's neck stood out. I dug my fingers into the tense muscles of his back and held on for dear life.

"Is this how you like it?" From between my open thighs, he gazed down at me with burning black eyes. "Hard? Deep? Do you want more?"

"Yes." God, yes. I wanted more. I wanted it all, everything he had. "More."

He redoubled his efforts. Beads of sweat glistened on his temples. I threw my head back onto the bare mattress. The pillows had fallen to the floor long ago. He shifted over me, drawing one of my legs to his side, opening me further, and braced a hand on the wall above the headboard. "How's that? Are you going to come for me, V?"

A warning rippled through my muscles. "Yes. Yes. Like that. Just like that."

An overload of sensations filled my head; Beckett's grunts and groans, my whimpers and cries, the scents of sex and sweat, the feel of heat and dampness. Our bodies rocked together, separated, and rejoined in perfect synchronicity. Another ripple, this one strong and undeniable, jolted along my lower half. I reveled in the power of his body, the way he claimed me, and the obedience of my body to his commands.

I climaxed in a flash of lights and colors behind my eyelids. Beckett jerked against my pelvis, ramming into me with such force that the top of my head banged the headboard. His graveled groans extended my pleasure into the longest orgasm I'd ever had. The length of his cock twitched inside me.

"God damn," he muttered after a lengthy pause. With gentle pressure, he lowered my leg from his shoulder. "That was fucking unbelievable."

"I know." At least I wasn't the only one awed by our chemistry. "No wonder I'm pregnant."

I was too weak, too sated to do anything but lie there. With a leisurely moan, he pushed back on his knees. His pants puddled around his ankles. My skirt gathered around my waist. I watched as he pulled off the condom then kicked off his pants. I closed my eyes. Gentle hands tugged my skirt down my legs. The mattress shifted, and I heard his footsteps travel to the bathroom, the sounds of running water, splashing, and his returning footsteps. Then the warmth of a damp washcloth between my legs as he cleaned me up. The intimacy of his touch, the gentleness of his hands, totally undid my composure. I threw a forearm over my eyes to hide my face and the threat of tears.

Was this what pregnancy did to me? Made me an emotional mess? Horny one minute, tearful the next? I drew in a shuddering breath and braced for the next wave of hormones. The bed shifted as Beckett stretched out on the mattress beside me.

"What's going on in there?" The tip of his finger traced the slope of my nose and tapped my forehead.

"Give me a minute," I said, still struggling for composure. After a few seconds, I became aware of his gaze sliding up and down my bare body. When I opened my eyes, I found him leaning on an elbow, head propped in his hand, staring at my belly. The tan, lean length of his body contrasted with my pale, soft curves. I wasn't overly modest, but I placed a hand on the tiny fullness below my navel, instinctively protecting it. His big hand slid beneath mine, warm and rough, but tender in its touch. An uninvited swell of emotion filled my chest. I pushed aside the feelings, blaming the hormones again.

"This," his voice rumbled, rife with undertones of possession. "This is mine. I did this."

"Well, not by yourself. I had a little something to do with it." I couldn't keep the smile from my voice. Sometimes he was so freaking alpha, so completely male.

He threaded his fingers through mine, palm resting against our small baby bump. "Yeah, but it was my super sperm that knocked you up." His smug arrogance caused a laugh to escape before I could stop it. "Don't laugh. You know it's true."

"You're a specimen. That's for sure." I couldn't help noticing he was hard again. His cock nudged my leg. "You're ready to go again?"

"I have a high sex drive," he said. "Especially when you're around."

Awareness prickled along my skin. He leaned forward and nipped one of my breasts, tugging the nipple between his teeth, and let it go. Dampness pooled between my thighs as my body prepared for more sex.

This time, he was slow and leisurely in his lovemaking. He entwined his fingers with mine and stretched my arms over my head, undulating his hips in a gentle rocking motion. He took his time, stroking all my sensitive places, kissing my belly, licking my neck. I'd never had a man pay so much attention to my pleasure. It was as if he took pride in wringing every bit of response from my body. Afterward, he tucked me into the curve of his torso, one arm slung around my waist, his chest to my back, and we slept that way until morning.

Chapter 25

Beckett

WHEN WE parted the next morning, we agreed to keep things casual. I understood casual. It meant no strings, no expectations, no commitments, everything I believed in. Except maybe I didn't want that anymore.

Those feelings scared me. Hell, I didn't even know how to begin a relationship. What if we started dating and she changed her mind, broke up with me? I'd never been dumped, not since eighth grade, and I didn't care to risk my feelings again.

It wrecked me, that night with Venetia. We weren't a couple, but holding her in my arms, feeling the swell of the baby I'd put inside her, it changed my attitude toward monogamy. I couldn't stop thinking about her, about the soft heat of her pussy or the way she'd clawed my back with her fingernails as I'd fucked her. I spent most of the next week thinking about excuses to see her again, but I didn't call her and she didn't call me.

During one of my deep contemplations, Margaret sauntered into my office. Everyone else had gone home hours ago. The hallways were dark and silent. She went straight for the liquor cabinet and poured a glass of sherry.

"Can I just say, the Zabbos are something else? I've spent the entire day slogging through internet pictures of them both. Mr. Zabbos is screwing the nanny and his wife's assistant. Mrs. Zabbos is having an affair with the gardener." She lifted the sherry decanter into the air. "You want one?"

"No, I'm good." I shoved a hand through my hair and rubbed the back of my neck to ease a few of the kinks. The long hours and late nights were beginning to take a toll.

"Here. Let me." She moved around the desk to stand behind my chair and kneaded the knots at my nape with warm, strong fingers. I groaned and closed my eyes. "Better?" she whispered into my ear.

"Definitely."

"Want to have sex? It might help." Her hands left my neck and smoothed down my arms. "It's Thursday, you know." She sat on the edge of the desk beside me and ran her stockinged foot up the inside of my calf.

"You always know what I need." I cupped her chin in my hand, gave her a lingering kiss, and waited for the ensuing lust. Nothing. No tightening of the groin, no hardening of the cock. The only thing I felt was crushing guilt. I pulled back and studied her oval face, admiring the clean lines of her bone structure. She was in her late twenties and fit, dressed in an expensive linen suit and skirt. Most men found her attractive—hell, I found her attractive—but when I closed my eyes, it was Venetia's face in front of me, not hers.

"Come here." I fisted a hand in her long brown hair and jerked her mouth to mine. This time, I put everything I had into ravaging her mouth. It was a weak attempt to exorcise Venetia from my thoughts. I tried to make excuses for my behavior. We weren't in a relationship. By mutual agreement, we were both free to pursue other partners. Margaret's hands found my shirt and made quick work of the buttons. An animal noise tore from her throat. I eased her down onto the desk. Nothing like an impromptu fuck in the workspace to clear a man's head. My dick didn't agree. For the first time in my life, it failed to raise its head and acknowledge the woman beneath me.

"I've been waiting on this for weeks," Margaret panted into my mouth.

I hadn't been with anyone but Venetia since Sam's wedding. Maybe that was the problem. I needed to sink into another woman, and fast. After all, one woman

168

was as good as another, wasn't she?

Jesus. I ran a hand through my hair. What kind of man thought that way? Not the kind of man I wanted to be. I grabbed Margaret's hands in mine and clutched them together between us. This wasn't fair to V or to Margaret. I respected them too much to use them like that.

"What's wrong?" She peered up at me, hair in wild disarray from my hands, and lips swollen from my brutal kiss. "Piers?"

"Goddammit." I let go of her hands and walked to the window. "Get dressed, Maggie."

"Want to talk about it?" When I turned to face her, she'd righted her clothing. Her gaze searched my face. "Is there someone else? It's okay if there is. I'll understand."

That was the awesome thing about Margaret. She understood a great deal more than she let on. "No." I scrubbed a hand over my mouth to wipe away our kiss. "Well, yes. Sort of. There is. I'm sorry."

"We've never been exclusive." Although her expression remained stoic, disappointment flared in her eyes. Another wave of guilt cramped my guts.

"It's nothing. Really." I wasn't sure who I meant to convince—her or myself. By Venetia's decree, we were free to see other people. I just never thought I'd be the one who didn't like the idea. "I met someone."

Her mouth tightened before she donned a brave smile. "And, this girl, you can't stop thinking about her?"

"Yeah. I don't get it." We stared at each other for an instant before Margaret shook her head.

"Of course you don't. You're a man."

"And here's the kicker." I paused for dramatic effect. "I knocked her up, and I don't think she wants to be together."

Margaret's jaw dropped. "Shut up. You've got to be kidding me."

"Do I look like I'm kidding?" I gave her my best serious face.

169

"Oh my God. There really is such a thing as karma." A riotous guffaw burst from her lips. She bent over and clutched her stomach with both hands.

"What's that supposed to mean?" Her amusement sent a rush of heat into my face. "Why are you laughing? This is serious shit, Mags."

"It means the city's biggest playboy has been played." With a genuine smile, she ran a hand through the tangles of her hair then patted my leg. "Oh, don't look so freaked out. You're going to be a fantastic dad." A furrow dented her smooth brow. "Beckett?" She set a hand on my forearm, and I flinched. "Just because this girl is pregnant doesn't mean you have to be with her, you know?"

"I know." No one knew that better than me, but I had a strange sense of accountability toward Venetia. She wasn't just anyone. Now more than ever, she needed someone in her corner, someone to take care of her, to look out for her. And that someone was going to be me.

Chapter 26

Venetia

BECKETT AND I settled into an easy friendship. In the interest of our relationship, we decided to put sex aside for a time and work on getting to know each other. We met for lunch when his schedule allowed, and I spent my spare time shopping for his apartment. I looked forward to seeing him and told myself it was important for the baby, but I knew it was more than that. Beckett made me feel important, like I mattered. After a lifetime of being ignored, the attention was addicting. I was powerless to resist him, but I worked to keep a barrier between us, a small wall of indifference to protect my heart. I couldn't afford to fall in love with him, when my self-esteem was already so fragile.

Three weeks after my night with Beckett, Sydney showed up at my doorstep. Tears streaked her cheeks. She pushed past me and into the living room before collapsing face first on the sofa. I sat down beside her and smoothed a hand over her hair. We hadn't spoken in a couple of weeks, which wasn't all that unusual. She was busy with filming. I'd been overwhelmed with Beckett, the baby, and looking for a job.

"What's going on, Syd?" I asked when her tears had stopped long enough to fit in a question.

"I'm so confused," she said, her words muffled by the pillow beneath her. "I think I'm in love with Tucker."

"Oh, really?" No surprises there. I tucked a strand of her hair behind her ear. "What's the problem? Tucker's a great guy."

"I know," she wailed. "That *is* the problem. He's a great guy." The sofa shifted as she sat up, clutching the pillow to her middle. "We've been seeing each other for a while now, sneaking around."

"I still don't see the problem." I smiled indulgently. Sydney loved drama almost as much as she loved falling in love.

"The studio is putting on the pressure. They want Alex and me to get married soon. They're really pushing us." She buried her face in her hands. "What am I going to tell Tucker? I don't know what to do, V."

"Don't marry Alex." The answer seemed obvious to me, but maybe not to Sydney. Like me, she'd been raised to value career over family. Her father had been married at least six times, maybe more. I'd lost count over the years.

"And give up a priceless opportunity?" The absurd notion slowed her sobs. She reared back and eyed me like I had three noses. "Are you nuts?"

"Well, no." I bit my lower lip and thought about the reasons behind my answer. "If I had a guy who loved me, and I loved him back, there's nothing I wouldn't do to be with him." Until I said the words aloud, I had no idea how true this was. Now that I was pregnant with Beckett's baby, the possibility of love seemed out of the question.

A suspicious gleam twinkled in Sydney's long-lashed eyes. "Who are you, and what have you done with my friend?"

"Stop it. I'm right, and you know it." I gave her a playful shove.

As quickly as her tears started, they stopped and her smile brightened. She reached for my hands and lifted my arms to the sides. "You're looking good. Definitely have a glow about you." One eyebrow arched. "So how's Beckett?"

"Fine." My lips pressed into a tight line. I didn't want to talk about him with her or anyone else for that matter. Once, we'd dished every detail about the guys we dated, but now my relationship with Beckett seemed too personal, too sacred.

He was a secret to be savored.

"Is everything fine with the baby? And Beckett?"

"Yes." I couldn't hold back the smile, remembering the way Beckett had caressed my belly. "We're working it out."

"Good, I'm glad." She stared at me, shrewd eyes assessing the story behind my words. Her lips parted to say more, but her phone jangled with an incoming call. She lifted a finger. "Hang on. We'll continue this in a second." The tone of her voice softened and blurred as she walked into the powder room. "Hey, Tucker."

An hour and a half later, she was back, all sunny smiles and sparkling eyes. I was in one of my two spare bedrooms, measuring out the space. Once the baby came, it would need a room, and I couldn't decide which one to convert into a nursery.

"Change your clothes," she demanded. "We're going out."

"Um, no." I bit my lower lip. A night in the bars no longer appealed. The quiet solitude of my apartment seemed preferable to a rowdy bunch of college guys searching for a one-night stand. I also had an insatiable need to clean and organize my living spaces.

"Yes." She landed a playful swat on my bottom. I frowned at her. "You don't have any food in this mausoleum, and I'm starving."

"A mausoleum is a burial tomb," I replied, taking offense.

"Well, then quit acting like you're dead. Just because you have a baby in there doesn't mean your life is over."

"I can't drink alcohol, you know."

We stared at each, at an impasse. Back in college, we'd gone out every night, come hell or high water. It seemed like a very long time ago.

"Oh, come on," she said. "We have a ton of catching up to do." Her glossy lower lip protruded in a perfect pout. "Besides, I have a surprise for you."

"Really?" Sydney always knew how to manipulate me into giving her what she wanted. "What is it?"

"I'm not telling. You'll have to wait and find out."

Loud music pumped from a jukebox near our table at a pub down the street from my apartment. Sydney fidgeted in her seat. A group of guys gawked at her from a nearby booth. They'd clearly recognized her and, after collecting their courage, approached for autographs. I scrolled through emails on my phone while she chattered with them. Once the crowd cleared, I yawned and gave her a rueful smile.

"Are you ready to go?" I asked.

"Not yet, party pooper. Tucker's on his way. Don't you want to see him?"

"Sure." I hadn't seen Tucker since the wedding. It would be nice to catch up. I settled back into the seat and ordered another glass of water. "But then I'm out." Past experience told me how the night would go. Tucker would appear, Sydney would be all smiles and flirtations, they'd disappear together, and I'd be left to catch a cab home alone.

"Don't forget your surprise," she said. "And here it is." I followed her gaze to the door, where Etienne Guillaume was crossing the threshold. I hadn't seen him in almost six months, but he looked as good as ever. His eyes searched the room until they found mine, and a smile curved his sensual mouth. "I found him at the airport this morning," Sydney confessed. "Aren't you glad to see him?"

I smoothed a hand over my belly, hidden beneath a flowing tunic top. I still looked trim, even though none of my jeans fit anymore. Instead, I'd worn stretch leggings with riding boots. My breasts, rounder and fuller than ever, surged upward. I tugged the neckline to provide a little more modesty.

"What's the matter? You don't look happy." Sydney's brow furrowed.

"*Cherie.*" By this time, Etienne had reached our table. "*Comment ca va?*"

"Etienne. Hello," I said.

Once upon a time, he'd made my pulse skyrocket, but tonight I just felt numb and I couldn't explain why. He looked every inch the European race car driver, out of place among the basketball jersey-wearing guys in the pub. A blue scarf looped around his neck and skinny jeans hugged a body taut with muscle. I stood to give him a hug. He placed a quick kiss on each of my cheeks.

"You are looking well," he said in his thick French accent. He shook back the wavy brown hair from his blue eyes and let his gaze drift from my head to my toes.

"You, too," I replied.

Over his shoulder, I spied Tucker entering the pub with Beckett close on his heels. My heart banged against my ribs, and a rush of heat raced into my face. Not because of Etienne's expensive cologne or his handsome face, but because of the guy who made my thighs tremble and my breath catch in my throat. Because of Beckett.

"How's it going?" Beckett walked straight up to Etienne and stuck out his hand. His black gaze glittered, brimming with danger. He was a foot taller than Etienne and twice as broad. "Piers Beckett."

My knees dissolved. I sank back into the booth, afraid I'd fall if I didn't sit. Etienne shook Beckett's hand, introduced himself then slid in beside me. Tucker and Sydney sat across from us. Beckett pulled up a chair on the end, turned it backward, and straddled the seat. He was wearing worn blue jeans and a navy Henley, long sleeves pushed up to his elbows, revealing the thick veins along his muscular forearms. By contrast, Etienne looked slender and small, and I couldn't remember why I'd ever found him irresistible.

After a round of pleasantries, Sydney and Tucker fell into deep conversation, punctuated by long kisses. Their defection left me alone to deal with Beckett and Etienne. The two men studied each other. Beckett twirled his championship ring around his finger. Testosterone emanated from the men beside me and thickened the air.

"Tell me about you." Etienne stretched an arm along the seat behind me and turned, cutting Beckett out of the conversation. Etienne traced my lower lip with his thumb, a gesture I'd once found panty-melting. "What have you been doing all these long months?"

"Nothing. Looking for a job." I could feel Beckett's eyes boring into me. From my peripheral, I saw a muscle jump below his cheekbone. "Moving into my new apartment."

"Ah, you have a new home? Perhaps you can show me later?" Etienne was smooth and exotic next to Beckett's raw American masculinity.

"What are you doing in the city?" I finally managed to ask.

"Promotional tour for one of my sponsors," he replied. If he was nervous about the Neanderthal glaring over the table, he didn't show it. I, on the other hand, had sweaty palms. Beckett's stoicism screamed at me. "When Sydney told me you were here, I begged her to set up a surprise. You are pleased, no?"

"Yes." *No.* I smiled and nodded politely, even though I wanted to push him aside, straddle Beckett's lap and run my fingers through his hair. I ventured a glance in his direction. The darkness in his eyes made my knees weak. "How've you been, Beckett? Is the new chair working okay in your living room?"

"It's good," he said in a voice gritty with tension. "You should come by and see it."

"I'm decorating Beckett's apartment," I explained to Etienne.

"Ah, I see." Etienne nodded. I knew he didn't care one way or the other about me and Beckett. Etienne had multiple girls in every city. He probably had one waiting at his hotel room this very minute. But Beckett? I got the feeling he was smoldering inside. I didn't know if I should be angry or flattered by his possessiveness. He didn't want a relationship, but he certainly acted like he did.

"I thought maybe you could take me shopping this weekend," Beckett said. Compared to Etienne's smooth tenor voice, Beckett's deep bass rumbled and bounced inside me, stirring up feelings and thoughts I didn't want to have.

"Maybe. I'll have to get back with you." I stood. Beckett stood with me, like the gentleman he was. Etienne relaxed deeper into his seat. Those gestures, no matter how miniscule, differentiated Beckett from every other guy I'd dated. "Excuse me. I need to visit the ladies room." It seemed I had to pee every ten minutes. Drinking four glasses of water in the space of an hour hadn't helped either. I gave both men a smile. Let them figure out their territorial differences.

When I came out of the restroom, I found Tucker leaning against the wall, waiting for me. A rush of fondness made me smile. He smiled back and brushed his surfer boy hair away from his face.

"V, you got a second?" He raised a hopeful eyebrow. "Sydney's signing autographs again. You know how that is." He rolled his eyes. "I wanted to ask your opinion about something, while she's busy."

"Okay. Sure." The shine in his eyes caused an unpleasant premonition to cloud my mood. He was such a good person. As much as I loved Sydney, I loved Tucker too. Whatever they were doing, it was going to end badly for Tucker.

He pulled a tiny velvet box from the front pocket of his jeans and revealed a diamond engagement ring inside. "What do you think?"

"It's beautiful, Tuck." A thin silver band sparkled with baguettes and perfectly framed a huge, round diamond. I traced the edge of the center stone with a fingertip.

"Do you think she'll like it?" The hope and enthusiasm in his voice brought a lump to my throat. He was going to propose to Sydney. She was going to marry someone else. I swallowed hard. "It's perfect for her."

"You can't say anything. I'm going to surprise her with it. I just wanted your opinion on the ring. I don't want to give her something she's going to hate." He snapped the box shut and shoved it back into his pocket. "You have to swear."

"Alright. I won't say anything." I resisted the urge to touch his arm and avoided his gaze, certain he'd see the concern in my eyes. He and Sydney had both sworn me to silence. I couldn't confide in one person without betraying the other.

My neck and shoulders ached with the weight of their secrets. One or both of them was going to be devastated. I had enough secrets of my own without the added responsibility of theirs. I had never been a romantic, but my chest hurt thinking about their predicament. In the past, I never believed in happy endings. Tonight, I wanted to believe in them with all my heart—if not for myself, for them.

Chapter 27

Beckett

WHEN TUCKER invited me to tag along for a beer with Sydney, I only accepted because I hadn't been away from the office all week, and I needed a break. Work had been crazy busy, and I'd only gotten a few hours of sleep each night. Hell, I hadn't even paused long enough to text Venetia. Now, I regretted the oversight. Damn, she looked good. As soon as I saw her, I wanted to march up to her, fist my hand in her hair, and plant a hot, wet kiss on her mouth.

Her cool reception dampened my enthusiasm, as did Guillaume's unexpected appearance. At the sight of him, my senses went on high alert. Were they together? A hot rush of jealousy scalded my veins. I disliked the way his eyes slid over her, like he owned her, like he knew her secrets. Jealousy gave way to panic. What if they were on a date? My guts atrophied at the thought of her—my girl—in his arms. *My* girl. Mine. The single word repeated in mind. Mine. Mine. *Mine.*

"How long are you in town for?" I asked Guillaume. I studied him, wondering what she saw in him, comparing his foreign flavor to my American flair. Next to him, I felt big, clumsy, and awkward.

"Two days. No more." One shoulder lifted and dropped in a casual French shrug.

"I thought you'd be bigger," I said. Although he was muscular, he couldn't have been more than five-eight or five nine compared to my six-foot seven.

"Size is relative," he replied, meeting my gaze evenly. "I've gotten no complaints."

I had to give it to him. He didn't back down from my glare. I hadn't been in a fight since high school, but I had the irrational urge to drag this guy to the parking lot and drag his pretty face over the pavement. His sense of calm pissed me off even more. The way he sat there, casual and cool, the intimate tone of his voice when he spoke to Venetia, raking her with his eyes, incited my territorial instincts.

"Have you known Venetia long?" I asked. Before tonight, I had no intention of staking a claim on V, but when I saw his arm draped around her, I went a little bit insane. He wasn't nearly good enough for her. Neither was I, but at least I cared about her. One look at this guy told me everything I needed to know. He was out for one thing—a good time—and by the heat in his eyes, he planned to have it with V. *Over my dead body.*

"We have been acquainted long enough." The smug smirk on his face scraped over my nerves. "Who are you again?" He lifted an eyebrow as if he found my inquisition comical or absurd.

"I'm a—friend—of the family." I stumbled to answer the very question I'd been asking myself over and over for the past few weeks. "I'm the guy she's going home with tonight."

"Ah? Is it so?" He nodded, amusement evident in the slant of his lips. "This remains to be seen."

The direct challenge in his statement lifted the hairs on the back of my neck. Scarf-wearing, wavy-haired motherfucker. I hated the way his liquid voice slid over her name almost as much as I hated the way he saw through my bravado. I flexed my fingers into fists beneath the table until my knuckles ached.

By this time, Venetia had returned to our table. Tucker followed a few steps behind her. I'd been so intent on sizing up Guillaume, I failed to notice the cluster of Sydney's admirers until now. They turned their focus to Guillaume, extending pens and paper for autographs. He waved them off with a flick of his fingers, centering his attention on Venetia. This was war, one I had no intention of losing.

"So, I'm going," Venetia said. She looped the strap of her handbag over her shoulder. "Nice to see you all."

"Can I come with you?" Etienne shot a challenging glance in my direction, stood, and brushed his lips over the knuckles of her right hand. He leaned forward, rattling off a string of French words I didn't understand, but I recognized the meaning of his flirtatious tone. A renewed wave of jealousy constricted my chest. She smiled and answered in fluent French. They both laughed. He asked another question, voice lower and laced with innuendo. I glared at both of them. In my head, I cursed my high school guidance counselor, the one who persuaded me to take Spanish as a second language instead of French.

"No, you may not," she replied in English, leaving me to burn with curiosity over his question. "But it was nice to see you again, Etienne."

I made a mental fist-pump in the air. Take that, motherfucker.

"Suit yourself. The loss is all mine. Perhaps another time," he said. He leaned forward to kiss her on the lip, but she turned her cheek. Within seconds, he was seated at the bar next to a pretty girl in a short skirt, signing autographs for the guys he'd waved away moments earlier. Relief loosened the knotted muscles between my shoulders. Victory hovered in my corner, and it smelled sweet.

"You've got your key, right?" Venetia directed the question to Sydney, ignoring me.

"Yes, thanks. Don't wait up," Sydney said. Her eyes never left Tucker's mouth. Tucker waved a hand, eyes bright. Poor sap was head over heels for Sydney. I knew right where he was coming from. The ebb and flow of my possessiveness and jealousy for Venetia signaled a shift in my feelings for her. I was falling for her, hard and fast.

"I'll walk you out," I said to V, pushing out of my chair. I expanded my chest and squared my shoulders before taking her elbow in my hand, aware of Guillaume's eyes on us. I met his gaze. He nodded and lifted his drink in a silent toast, conceding his defeat. Score one for Beckett.

I muscled through the growing crowd, my hand on Venetia's back. I liked guiding her, taking control, protecting her. She didn't move away from my touch, and I took that as a sign of her approval. When we reached the street, I lifted a hand to wave down a taxi. The fall wind cooled my heated face and whisked away my jealousy.

"Really, Beckett?" Venetia turned to me, her voice filled with a mixture of humor and annoyance.

I couldn't look at her, afraid my emotions showed on my face, not quite ready to admit my change in feelings. "He's not good enough for you. Or our baby. No one is."

"Oh, please." She rolled her eyes. "Who are you to judge? If you ask me, there's not a whole lot of difference between the two of you."

I stepped back, wounded by her comparison and the knowledge that she was absolutely correct. The taxi pulled to the curb in front of us. I opened the door for her and followed her inside. We continued down the street in silence while I mulled over her statement. Who was I kidding? I was Etienne Guillaume. We both operated on the love-'em-and-leave-'em principle. Or at least I had. I didn't love Venetia, did I? I definitely wasn't going to leave her. Not ever. But was I going to be with her? *Be. With. Her.* The words called to me, taking on a new meaning, sounding so right it made my chest ache.

When the cab arrived at her building, I paid the driver and got out then extended a hand to help her exit, my blood heating at the touch of her fingertips to mine.

"I'm coming up," I said, eager to resolve our differences in the bedroom.

"No." She shook her head, chin lifting in a familiar gesture of defiance. "I'm sleeping alone tonight."

"What? Why?" I never considered she'd reject me. In my head, I had it all planned out. We'd fight a little, fuck a lot, and get back to the routine of our lives.

"Because I said so." The volume of her voice climbed. "I'm not your booty call, Beckett. This relationship won't work until you figure out what you want. I don't want to spend the next twenty years going back and forth with you when we have a child stuck in the middle."

"Okay." I shoved my hands into my pockets, a little bewildered and a whole lot ashamed. She made a good point. "You're not my booty call. You never were." She was much more than that, so much more.

"You said you were all in." She placed a hand on my chest, her hand a direct lifeline to my heart. My pulse escalated, thudding against her palm.

"I am," I replied, surprised by the desperation in my tone. Whenever she was around, I seemed to lose my self-control. No woman had ever affected me like this.

"I'm not sure you are." She pulled her hand away, and the connection between us snapped.

Tell her, Beckett. Tell her you care. Tell her you want more. I wanted to say the words, but my lips froze, pressing into a tight line instead. We stared at each other. Silence blanketed the street, broken by the whistle of wind around the buildings and an occasional distant car horn. I stepped closer and hunched my shoulders, shielding her from the cold wind.

"Can I call you?" I asked, feeling awkward and uncertain, hating myself for my weakness. If she said no, I'd be crushed. "Later? When I get home?"

"Yes, you can call me." She lifted to her tiptoes and brushed a dry kiss over my cheek. "But not tonight. I'm exhausted. Tomorrow."

"Guillaume's not coming over later, is he?" I asked, suddenly wary.

"Stop it." Her laughter sent red-hot heat into the tips of my ears. "You don't get to ask those kind of questions." In a swirl of delicate perfume, she moved away from me. The doorman tipped his hat to her. I stared after V, feeling like a puppy kicked out of the house in the middle of a rainstorm.

"Fine. I'll call you. Tomorrow. You can bank on it," I said to her backside. After I paid the cabbie, I walked down the street, needing the exercise and time to reflect.

I hadn't been so unsettled, so confused, since I'd fallen in love with my tutor back in elementary school. Was that the problem? Was I in love with Venetia? The idea seemed too preposterous to consider, but I couldn't find any other explanation for my need to claim and protect her. I tried to blame it on the baby, but it was so much more than that.

The next morning, I met Tucker and Sam at the gym for an early game of hoops before work. I loved the smell of sweat and adrenalin. It took me back to the good old days when my problems consisted of making grades and improving the accuracy of my free throws from the foul line. Our shoes squeaked on the gym floor as Tucker drove down the line, and I scrambled to block his shot. He brushed past me and scored an easy layup. I grimaced. I was off. My head and heart weren't in the game.

"Man, you suck this morning," Tucker teased. He dribbled the ball from right hand to left and back again as he spoke. He shot the ball to Sam with a chest pass.

"What's up with you?" Sam asked. He feinted to the left and evaded my outstretched hands easily. He launched a three-pointer from outside the circle. The ball swished through the net. Tucker raised his hand into the air, and the two men slapped a high-five. I shuddered.

"I didn't get much sleep last night," I said. In truth, I'd tossed and turned for hours. The few moments of sleep I'd managed were peppered with dreams—make that nightmares—of Venetia with Etienne Guillaume.

"Beckett's in love," Tucker said. I shot him a warning glare, and he smirked.

"Shut up," I said. I knocked the ball from his hands, drove to the basket, and slam-dunked it into the hoop.

"Really? This is news." Sam retrieved the ball and stowed it beneath his arm, bringing the game to a standstill. "Anyone I know?"

I lifted the hem of my shirt and wiped the sweat from my brow, made more profuse by this line of questioning. The nature of my relationship with Venetia weighed heavier on my conscience every day. We wouldn't be able to keep the secret much longer. Sooner or later, Sam needed to know, and the longer we waited to tell him, the more jarring the revelation would be. The idea of lying to Sam caused acid to flood my stomach. I wanted to tell him, but not yet, not until I had Venetia's permission.

"Yeah, anyone we know?" Tucker echoed Sam's inquiry. By the enormous grin on his face, he was enjoying my predicament entirely too much.

"Drop it, Tucker," I growled.

"Must be serious." Sam studied me. I avoided his gaze, choosing instead to head toward the locker room.

"I'm done," I said. "I've got to get back to work."

"Well, I'm in love," Tucker said. His admission brought my feet to a halt. Sam's jaw dropped. "And I don't care who the fuck knows."

I closed my eyes. While I preferred a more cautious approach, Tucker plunged into love like it was one of his extreme sports, with enthusiasm and a complete disregard for his personal safety. I drew in a deep breath, once again finding myself in an ethical and personal dilemma. Sydney was going to marry Alex in what her network termed a publicity coup. I'd personally handled the premarital agreement and preliminary terms for divorce. Of course, confidentiality agreements ensured my silence on the matter. The growing number of secrets threatened to drag me down into the quicksand of hell.

"I bought a ring," Tucker added. "I'm just waiting for the right time to ask her."

"Are you sure you want to do that?" I turned to face him, feeling powerless. I looked to Sam for assistance. "I mean, you don't really know Sydney that well."

"Becks has a point," Sam concurred. "Take it from me, marriage is a big deal."

185

Sam's advice echoed in my head, as much for my own sake as Tucker's. I nodded. "Divorce is a big deal. I see it every day. Marry in haste, repent in leisure."

"That's no shit," Sam said. He dropped the basketball into the equipment bin.

"I've got no doubts," Tucker said, his jaw set stubbornly. "She's the one. The only one."

In unison, we moved toward the locker room again. I was beginning to feel sick from the stress of holding my tongue. One dilemma followed another. My life seemed to be spiraling toward disaster at breakneck speed, out of my control. Inside the locker room, Sam went straight to the showers, but I paused next to Tucker.

"Be careful, man," I said. "And if you decide to do this, be sure to get a premarital agreement. You've both got a lot of assets to protect. Don't rush into anything."

"Says the guy who's got a surprise bun in the oven." Tucker rolled his eyes. "I know what I'm doing."

"I know you do. It's not you I'm worried about," I said. We stared at each for a long, hard minute.

"Unlike you, I'm not afraid to go after what I want." He pulled his shirt off over his head and tossed it onto the bench. "I'd rather take a risk and lose than sit around on my ass watching the opportunity of a lifetime pass by."

What if he was right? What if all my caution and fear led to the greatest disappointment of my life? If I hesitated with Venetia, if I chose to stay single for too long, I might lose out on a future filled with promise, a wife, and a family. An even more terrifying thought gave new shape to my misgivings. What if I missed out on *her*?

It was wrong, the way my heart skipped a beat when I saw her face. My palms dampened, and my mouth went dry. She wore a short denim skirt, an oversized knit sweater, and knee-high boots. I went instantly hard. Fucking unbelievable. Overcome with panic at the rush of need, I backpedaled toward the door. This had been a huge mistake. I wasn't ready to admit my feelings. She hadn't seen me. I could turn around and leave the furniture store before she noticed. I could send a text, leave a message, make some lame excuse for standing her up. Before I could choose an option, our gazes connected, and her big eyes sucked me into their vortex. I had no choice but to smile back and go to her.

"Hey," she said. She looked away, studying the housewares sign at my left.

"Hello." God, this was awkward. I wasn't sure where to put my hands, so I shoved them into the pockets of my jeans.

"So, let's get started." The casual tone of her voice confused me. After the way we'd parted at her apartment building, I had no idea where I stood with her. Did she feel the same conflicting emotions for me? Or had I completely lost touch of reality in this situation. I didn't want to be the fool, the sorry bastard in love with a girl who didn't love him back.

We wandered through dozens of makeshift furniture clusters. I tried to pay attention while Venetia pointed out appropriate pieces and chattered about focal points, color cues, and texture. One sofa pretty much looked like another to me. I was too distracted by the way her hair kept falling over one eye. Loose waves cascaded down her back. The next time the glossy locks went astray, I brushed them aside with a sweep of my hand. We both tensed.

"Sorry," I said and cleared my throat. My fingers tingled at the touch of her skin.

"Focus, Beckett. What do you think about this one?" She flopped back onto a leather sofa, long legs stretched in front of her, propped up on her elbows.

"It's fine." I wanted to follow her down onto the couch, part her thighs with my knees and settle against her sweet pussy. "It doesn't matter to me. I don't really care."

"If you don't want to be here, just say so," she snapped. "I'm trying to be helpful, and you're just being a dick."

If she knew the twisted, dirty thoughts running through my head, she'd turn around and run the other way. The situation was getting way out of hand. I wanted her in the worst way. She haunted my thoughts, my dreams, and my sleep. I couldn't get through the day without jacking off to a mental image of her perfect tits in that flowing blouse at the pub last week.

"Get up," I ordered. I was just about to drag her into the men's room and fuck her against the wall when my phone vibrated. Margaret's name flashed over the caller ID. Talk about a reality check. I raised a finger to Venetia and answered the call. She frowned, shook her head, and walked toward the front of the store. "Mags, can I call you back?"

"I've got the rest of Seaforth's documents," she said. My gaze followed Venetia's backside out the door. I hurried after her. "The wills for both parties and the final draft of the prenup. I need you to sign off on them."

"Sure. I'll be in Monday."

"Not Monday. Today." Margaret's tone left no room for argument. "He wants this done."

"Fine." I burst out the door to find Venetia waiting in the parking lot, arms crossed over her chest, toe tapping on the pavement. "Later, Mags." I shoved the phone in my pocket. "Come on. I'll give you a ride home."

"Go ahead. Be with her. I'm not stopping you." In spite of her cool tone, her chin quivered. If I didn't know better, I'd think she cared. The notion thrilled me.

"I told you. She's a coworker." I took her by the elbow and led her to my car.

"You're screwing her." She halted and pulled her arm from my grasp. "That's more than a coworker."

"I'm not screwing her." We glared at each other. "Not since before New Orleans." *Not since you.*

"I don't believe it." She cocked her head, the tension in her shoulders easing a tiny bit. "Once a player, always a player."

I scrubbed an exasperated hand over my face. This girl challenged me at every step, and I loved every confusing minute of it. "I need to stop by the office for a minute. You can meet her and find out for yourself."

"Really?" Her features softened. A ray of afternoon sunlight turned the color of her eyes to intense blue. I blinked at their brightness. "I'm sorry. That was out of line. I don't know what made me say that."

"It's okay." I opened the door of the Wrangler. The rusted hinges squealed in protest. I cringed. Venetia laughed.

"You're still driving this?" She bit her lower lip, cheeks flushed with mischief, the tension between us forgotten. "Seriously, Beckett."

"Don't make fun of Harriet," I said, shooting her a playful, warning glare. "She's very sensitive."

Chapter 28

Venetia

WE RODE the elevator up to his office in silence, our gazes locked. Something had changed in the way he looked at me after he met Etienne. His gaze lingered on my lips, lifted to my eyes, then back to my lips. A tremor shook my fingers. I pressed my palms against the wall behind me to hide the shaking. Our relationship changed directions with the swiftness of the wind, keeping me on edge, always uncertain.

"What?" he asked, voice textured and deep. My nipples tightened beneath my blouse. He could do that to me, turn me on with a single word or gesture.

"Nothing," I said.

His eyes narrowed. "Not nothing. It's something."

I'd never seen a man smolder before, but that was the only way I could describe the heat in his eyes. The cotton fabric of his T-shirt stretched taut over the muscles of his chest and shoulders. The scent of laundry soap hung in the air. In casual clothes and with his hair mussed, he looked younger, more dangerous.

"Why are you looking at me like that?" I asked and crossed my arms over my chest.

"How am I looking at you?" It seemed impossible, but his voice dropped lower still.

Where to begin? I felt like a mouse trapped in a cage with a hungry lion. The line of Beckett's jaw squared, and a muscle ticked beneath his cheekbone. He was a virile, sexy beast of a man, filling the confined space of the elevator car with testosterone. My hormones jumped to attention. I blamed it on the pregnancy and not the attraction pulsing between us.

"You're making me nervous," I confessed. In fact, I was nervous about meeting his Margaret. *His* Margaret. I didn't know the woman, but I already wanted to claw her eyes out.

"Why?" He took a step closer. Next to his towering tallness and his hard, flat muscles, I felt small and curvy and overtly feminine. I tipped my head back to look up at him. Dark, somber eyes stared down at me. His voice lowered to a husky caress. "Are you scared of me, baby?"

"No," I said stubbornly, but it couldn't be further from the truth. I was afraid he'd touch me, and I'd be unable to resist, unable to avoid falling under his spell. I weaved on my feet, drawn to him with a force beyond my control.

"I would never hurt you, V." The backs of his knuckles drifted over my cheek.

Everything below my waist clenched with need and wanton lust. "I know," I whispered, because I *did* know. He wasn't the kind of guy to lead me on or play with my emotions. His hand cupped the side of my face. I closed my eyes and leaned into his touch, breathless with anticipation.

Ding.

The elevator doors slid open. Beckett's hand dropped to his side. I reeled with disappointment, then his fingers threaded through mine, and a new thrill ran down my arm. He drew me forward, along the marble corridor, our footsteps echoing in the empty office. Our palms melded together.

"Piers? What are you doing here?" A silver-haired man poked his head out of a set of black double doors. Even though it was Saturday, he wore a suit and tie. His curious gaze took me in. "Who is this?"

"This is Venetia Seaforth. Venetia, this is Joseph Daniels, senior partner." Beckett's tone carried a hint of annoyance. His fingers tightened on my left hand.

"Seaforth? Any relation to Maxwell?" Daniels asked.

"Yes, I'm his daughter," I said and offered my right hand to shake. "It's a pleasure to meet you, Mr. Daniels."

"Is that so? I didn't realize he had two daughters." Daniels took my hand, his countenance warming.

"Well, he does," I replied, feeling a surge of irritation. I was getting tired of people forgetting me.

"So I see." Daniels didn't let go of my hand. Instead, he enveloped it with both of his. "And the pleasure is all mine. Piers, where have you been hiding this lovely girl?"

"Piers, there you are." A slim, dark woman exited a nearby office before Beckett could answer. She exuded confidence and capability, along with feline sexuality. She could have been the nicest person in the world, but I instantly hated her.

I pulled my hand from Daniels's grip.

Margaret smiled at Beckett, but the heat in her eyes cooled when it drifted down his arm to our clasped hands. "Oh, I'm sorry. I didn't realize you had someone with you."

"Margaret, this is Venetia. Venetia, meet Margaret." Piers waved a hand between us. Jealousy pumped through my veins. His hands had touched her body. He'd been inside her. I felt sick to my stomach.

"Nice to meet you, Venetia." She ran an assessing gaze over my face and figure. We shook hands. Her grip was firm and confident. I squeezed back. "I've heard a lot about you."

"Really? I've heard a lot about you, too," I said, letting my voice trail off, and gave Beckett a raised eyebrow. He shrugged. I ran a hand through my hair, wishing I'd touched up my makeup before meeting this beautiful woman.

"Give me a minute to take care of this, V, and we'll get out of here." He let go of my hand and took Margaret by the elbow.

"I'll watch out for her," Daniels said. He beamed at me, no doubt jazzed up by my bloodline and bank account. "Come. Have a seat in my office, Ms. Seaforth, and tell me a little about yourself. Would you like some coffee or tea, perhaps?"

As he herded me toward his office, I cast a glance over my shoulder to find Beckett's hand on the small of Margaret's back. The hair on my nape bristled. I didn't like the sight of his hand on another woman, any woman, coworker or not. By the way Margaret leaned into his touch, she still desired him. Maybe Beckett and I were only friends, and maybe we'd been forced into this relationship, but I had to face the facts. I wanted him, and maybe—just maybe—I was in love.

Inside Daniels's office, I paced the length of the room and trailed a hand over the framed artwork on the walls. Although it had pretty windows and an organized color scheme, the room lacked a focal point. His gaze followed me. I had plenty of experience with men like him. He was a parasite, quick to capitalize on the fame and fortune of the unassuming. I decided to turn the tables and use his attention to my advantage.

"And what do you do in your spare time?" Daniels asked.

"I'm an interior designer," I said, facing him with a bright smile. His eyebrows raised in surprise. He probably thought I sat around the swimming pool all day, eating truffles and drinking champagne. "This is a fantastic space. I'd love to get my hands on it."

His face flushed with pleasure. "Thank you. I've been thinking about redecorating it. What would you suggest?"

"Well—" I squinted and rotated to get a better feel for all four walls of the space. "If it was me, I'd move your desk over here." I pointed to the wall adjacent to the door. "That way you wouldn't have your back to the windows and you could see the city."

Daniels narrowed his eyes and scratched his chin. "Nice. I like that. What else?"

"I'd add pops of color. All this gray is uninspiring." I cleared my throat. "I mean, it's a very nice, but it's been proven that bright colors are stimulating for the brain and increase productivity."

"Go on." He rested a hip on one corner of his desk and folded his arms over his chest.

Buoyed by his interested, I swept an arm around the room. "I'd replace this overstuffed furniture with something clean and more modern. Like your personality." He beamed at me. "And this artwork? Too stuffy. I'd hang wall sculptures and add some lives plants or an aquarium for the corner."

"Draw something up for me, will you?" His nod of approval made me forget all my insecurities about Beckett and Margaret. "And give me a budget. If you're interested, that is."

"I'm really very busy, but I'd love that." I had nothing to do at all since I'd run out of job interviews, but he didn't need to know that. My mind began to race with possibilities. I could do this. Tomorrow, I'd look for an assistant, someone to help with the legwork and day-to-day tasks. For the first time in a long time, I had a purpose.

"V? Are you ready?" Beckett walked through the open office doors. A worried frown marred his features.

"Sure." I turned to Daniels to shake his hand. "I'll get back with you by the end of the week." Beckett led me down the hall to his office and closed the door behind us. "Is everything okay?" I asked, my previous euphoria tempered by his silence and the recollection of his hand on Margaret.

"It's fine." He gave me a reassuring smile. "What were you up to in there?"

"I'm going to redecorate his office," I said, my confidence surging once more.

"That's great. You can do mine, too." He smiled, and once again his gaze dipped to my lips. "You know, when you smile, you have a dimple right here." He touched a fingertip to my cheek. Tiny bubbles of excitement popped in my blood. Then I remembered his arrangement with Margaret and looked away.

"What about Margaret?"

"What about her?" He placed a hand against the wall behind me. "I told you we ended it a while ago. Why? Jealous?"

By the twinkle in his eyes, he was teasing me. I narrowed my focus on him, unconvinced. "You put your hand on her back."

"I did?" His brow furrowed in genuine confusion.

"Yes." I placed a hand on his chest to keep distance between us. "I didn't like it." The beat of his heart thudded against my palm. His breath hitched at my touch. The sound sizzled all the way to my core.

"We were fuck-buddies. And now we're not." The way his tongue slid over his lower lip did crazy things to my girl parts. "I don't want to be with her anymore. Do you believe me?"

"I believe you." Looking into his onyx eyes, I'd believe him if he said the sun set in the morning and cows gave chocolate milk. They were dark, infinite pools of sin surrounded by long, lacy lashes, almost too pretty for a man of his size. "But you shouldn't touch her like that. It was—" I looked away and swallowed. "It was too intimate."

"I won't do it again." His head bent closer to mine.

My life always seemed to change when I least expected it—Sam's remarriage to Dakota, hooking up with Beckett, getting pregnant. It changed in Beckett's office. I could no longer deny my feelings for him. This yearning, the undeniable need, went way beyond lust or attraction. I wasn't ready to put a name to it, but it was there.

"God, V. I know we said nothing would ever happen between us, but I really want to kiss you." His thick, deep voice curled my toes. "Tell me you want that too."

"Yes." Goodness, I wanted it in the worst way. I let my hands skate up his chest and rest on his shoulders. He was hard and lean beneath my palms.

One of his big hands rested on my hip. The other spread out over my back. He leaned forward until his mouth was level with my ear. The heat of his breath sizzled against my earlobe. "I've been dreaming about you. Every morning. Every night. I jack off to memories of fucking you, of touching this sexy body of yours."

His hand cupped my breast and lifted it, squeezing with a touch so gentle it made my knees give away. This wasn't a man groping me; this was reverent and tender. Something deep inside yearned for him, for a caress, for some show of affection. Until now, I'd had no idea how much I craved a physical connection with someone. Not anyone. Him.

"Me, too." I pressed into his body, needing to soothe an itch deep inside, one only he could scratch. "I can't stop wanting you."

"Are you wet for me?" The growl and purr of his deep voice did crazy things to my common sense.

"Yes." I arched into his touch. The space between my legs throbbed and ached.

Keeping his right hand on my breast, he slid the other one beneath my skirt to trace a finger along the lace edge of my panties. "Can I see?"

"Yes." Lord have mercy. The idea of his finger inside my panties caused my belly to flip. If he didn't do something soon, I was going to melt down.

"Very nice." I felt his smile against my ear as his finger breached the soft folds between my legs. I closed my eyes and let my head fall back against the door. "You must be the devil, because I'd sell my soul to taste you." His finger caressed and teased me. "Right here."

The heat and wetness of his mouth trailed down my neck. My eyes flew open when his mouth went lower to my breasts then lower still to my belly. Was he seriously going to go down on me in the middle of the day in his office? Beckett was one dirty boy. I bit my lower lip to hold back a surprised grin. He kneeled on the floor, lifted my skirt over my hips and hitched my left leg over his shoulder.

"Aren't you worried about someone coming in?" I managed to ask.

"No one's coming but you," he said. He tugged the lace of my panties to one side, baring me to him. The heat of his breath puffed against my delicate flesh. "Jesus, you've got a pretty pussy."

I closed my eyes again, unable to maintain intelligible speech, and waited for him to do something, anything, to relieve the agony of anticipation. The tip of his nose nudged along the apex of my thighs. I felt naughty and wanton with this virile man on his knees before me. The second his tongue flicked my clit, I choked back a cry of relief. My hands found his hair and dug in.

After a few well-placed licks, all I could think about was how good it was to have a man at my feet with his face buried between my legs. "Beckett. Beckett. Beckett." His name rolled off my tongue, over and over. "Oh, God." One of his fingers slipped inside me and curled up to tease the secret spot. My hips jerked, causing my legs to shake and my knees to dissolve. The more I squirmed, the tighter he held me, forcing me to endure the overwhelming sensations. Waves of fire undulated down my thighs.

Oh God. It hadn't been like this with Etienne. He'd been quick and rough, more focused on his own orgasm than mine. No man played my body like Beckett. He knew how to mingle pleasure with pain, nipping and sucking, walking me along the edge of overload, but always bringing me back before I imploded. While I whimpered through the last of my orgasm, he waited for my trembling to stop before he lowered my leg to the floor and stood. I let him straighten my panties and tug down my skirt before I opened my eyes. I swallowed and tried to avoid his gaze, feeling like he'd split open my chest and laid my soul bare to the world.

"Oh, no. Not now. Not when we're making progress." He placed a finger under my chin and tilted my head, forcing me to look at him. Dark eyes stared back at me, infinite and warm. He ran his tongue over his lips, tasting me. "Don't shut me out."

"I'm not." It was a bald-faced lie, but I meant for it to be the truth. My gaze drifted down to the obvious bulge behind his zipper. The sight of it resurrected my lust. I dragged a palm over his hardness. "Can I help you with this?"

One corner of his mouth lifted in amusement. "Absolutely. But not here. Not like this." He cupped my chin in his hand and swept a thumb over my lower lip. The scent of my wetness lingered on his fingers.

"Oh. Okay." Was this rejection? Every time he touched me, I went away feeling more confused than before.

"Hey, look at me." His eyes searched mine. "This was for you, not me. You think it's always about sex for me and it's not. Not with you. It's more than that." A hint of stubble had appeared on his jaw, lending to his dangerous vibe. He was probably one of those guys who had to shave a couple of times a day. "I want to do this right. Let me take you out first. On a date."

I lifted an eyebrow. "Are you feeling okay? I thought Piers Beckett didn't date."

"Better than okay," he said. "And you're wrong about that." He dropped a kiss to the tip of my nose, then his arms went around my waist, and he pulled me into a warm hug. "Piers Beckett dates you."

Our date consisted of a movie at the theater, followed by dinner at a nearby pub. We ate pizza then took a horse-drawn carriage ride to a nearby ice cream shop, where I indulged all my pregnancy cravings. Beckett held my hand, his big fingers curled around mine. My heart skipped a beat every time our eyes met. This feeling went way beyond anything I'd ever experienced. It terrified and thrilled me.

"Having fun?" The rumble of his voice reverberated in my ear when the carriage returned to its station.

"Yes."

He let go of my hand to jump out of the carriage. With his hands around my waist, he swung me to the ground. His hands lingered until I regained my balance.

When they moved away, I missed his touch. "So, what do you want to do now?" he asked as we stood by the street, waiting for a taxi.

"It's getting late," I said. A sliver of moon hovered in the black sky overhead. Even though we'd been together for hours, I dreaded leaving him.

"I suppose we should head home."

"Yes," I answered. We stared at each other. Beckett shoved his hands into his pockets and pursed his lips like he wanted to say something. I wanted to kiss that mouth, to feel his hands on me again, the weight of his body on top of mine. "When you say *home*, do you my place or yours?" He cocked an eyebrow, and the corners of his mouth curled in a sinful smile at my question. "Because I still owe you for this afternoon."

"Are you sure?" he asked. The way he was looking at me, pupils dilated and nostrils flared, sent a spear of lust straight between my legs. I didn't care where we went as long as we were together and the fire in his eyes kept burning.

"I'm sure." I slipped my hand into his and squeezed.

Back at his place, I sat on the sofa and tried to hide my amusement as he scurried around the room, hiding his dirty laundry and shoving things into the closets. He obviously hadn't intended on having company, a thought I found curiously comforting. It was good to know he didn't take us for granted.

He caught a glimpse of my smirk and stopped to grin at me. "Okay, I'm a slob. No denying it."

"It's fine. I'm a slob, too," I said, finding his embarrassment adorable. "Stop worrying about it."

He flopped onto the couch beside me. "Good to know." His rock-hard thigh pressed against mine. Awareness raced down to my toes. His arm rested on the back of the sofa behind me, proprietary and comforting. I leaned into him. He tapped the end of my nose with a fingertip. "I like learning things like that about you. What other secrets are you hiding?"

I shook my head, unable to hide a wide smile. "Oh, no. I'm not falling for that one."

"So far I know that you're a slob and a terrible driver." His dark eyes softened and focused on my mouth. "But I don't think I've ever met anyone more perfect."

A flush of hot embarrassment heated my face. "You're just saying that."

"I don't just say things, V, and you know it." He placed a finger underneath my chin, tipped my face, and brushed my lips with his.

"I know," I said on a shaky breath.

He relaxed back into the sofa, drawing me with him, snuggling me into his chest. I melted against his body, comforted by the rise and fall of his ribs, the way I fit into the nook of his shoulder. With the remote control, he turned on the television and flipped through the channels to find a movie. We sat in silence for a while, my hand on top of his thigh, his lips pressing against my temple. It felt good, right, perfect.

Before the end of the movie, my eyelids grew heavy. He was so warm, so comfortable, that I had to fight to stay awake. I yawned and covered my mouth with a hand. He shifted beneath me.

"Tired, baby?" he asked in a voice textured with tenderness.

"Yes." I hesitated to leave the sanctuary of his chest. "I suppose I should go home. Will you call me a cab?"

"You know you don't have to go." At his invitation, my insides quivered in anticipation. His tongue swept along the curve of his lower lip. "You could spend the night."

"Here? On the couch?" I lifted an eyebrow, trying to hide my excitement with humor.

"Not here. In my bed." He took my hand in his and raised it to his lips. His eyes met mine, filled with dark promise. "And just so you know, there will be nudity involved. Mine and yours."

"Well." I drew in a shuddering breath as his lips found the sensitive spot below my ear and pressed a kiss. "I thought you'd never ask."

Chapter 29

Beckett

THREE WEEKS later, I got up on Monday morning, kissed Venetia goodbye then ran four miles to sort out the kinks in my brain. We'd spent every night together, alternating apartments. I was falling in deep, so deep I knew I'd never dig myself out, but I didn't really care anymore. As I rode the elevator up to my office, I could still taste her on my tongue, hear her sweet moans when she came, and feel the velvety softness of her skin. I liked having her in my bed, spreading her legs and settling between them, watching her sleep, and waking to her disheveled beauty in the morning.

Garth met me at the door to my office. I recoiled at his harsh expression. Dark circles shaded his eyes, and a patch of stubble peppered his cheek where he'd missed a spot shaving. I lifted an eyebrow. He ignored my questioning glance and pressed a file folder into my outstretched hand. "I was up all night last night doing research on Zabbos," he said.

"Nice," I said and meant it. A smile brightened his tired features. Garth never failed to exceed my expectations. He deserved to be much more than an assistant, but I wasn't sure I could function without him. I followed him toward his desk. He looked up from his computer monitor in surprise. "Good work," I continued and wondered if I'd ever told him before how much I valued his efforts. "You're an asset. I appreciate how hard you've worked on this case." He smiled. "How's your kid?"

"He's been running a fever," Garth said, the smile slipping. "My mom's taking him to the doctor this morning."

"Why are you here?" He was the sole parent for his two-year-old son, yet he never missed a day, hadn't been late even once in two years. "Get out of here."

"No. It's fine. She'll call if it's something serious," he replied, but I could tell by the tension in his shoulders that he wanted to be there. He probably needed the income. Raising a child as a single parent couldn't be cheap, and as an hourly employee, every minute of missed work took a chunk out of his paycheck.

"Nonsense. Go. I won't die without you for one day." I picked up his phone and dialed the extension for the office supervisor. I understood the importance of family, of taking care of the ones closest to you. "Ms. Hartley, please send someone down here to cover for Garth today. He'll be taking the day off. With pay," I added.

"Mr. Beckett?" The temp stuck her head inside my office door an hour later. For some reason, she couldn't seem to figure out the intercom system. After demonstrating how to dial my office twice; my patience had thinned. "I'm sorry to bother you again."

I dragged my attention away from the computer to the nervous girl, unable to restrain the frustration in my tone. "What is it?"

"You have a delivery."

"Sign for it." I scrolled through my emails, ignoring her, but she didn't get the hint.

"He said he has to deliver it to you. Personally." The temp shifted her weight from one foot to the other, wringing her hands in front of her. She couldn't have been more than nineteen or twenty. This was probably her first job. I counted to ten inside my head.

"Fine. Send him in." I sighed and pushed back from the desk.

The man who entered wore an expensive gray suit and dropped a gold key fob on the desk in front of me.

"What's this?"

"Your keys, Mr. Beckett. To your new car." The gentleman spoke in a clipped Middle Eastern accent.

"I don't have a new car." I pushed the keys toward him.

"I beg your pardon, but you do, sir. Courtesy of Mr. Maxwell Seaforth."

Unable to believe what I was hearing, I followed the man down to the street. An Aston Martin gleamed at the curb, charcoal gray, sleek, and sparkling with chrome. I slid into the smooth leather seat and drew in a deep breath of new car scent. All my life, I'd dreamed of a car like this. For a few fleeting seconds, I imagined what it might be like to own such a piece of automotive perfection. And then I remembered the source of the gift.

"I can't take this," I said, and handed the keys back to the man.

He held up his palms in refusal. "It's already done, sir. The car is titled in your name. You'll need to take this up with Mr. Seaforth." He pivoted and disappeared into a waiting taxi before I could open my mouth to call after him.

My cell rang. Speak of the devil. I stared at the phone.

"Piers. Did you get my gift?" Seaforth's voice dripped with arrogance.

"I was just getting ready to call you about it. This is way too generous." I tried to temper my irritation and maintain professionalism.

"Consider it a little token of my appreciation. There's a lot of promise in you, son. Stick with me, and there will be a lot more than cars in your future. I can show you success and power like you never dreamed of."

The seductive tone of his voice raised my guard. I had no doubt he meant every word of what he said. He had the wealth and strength to propel my career into the stratosphere. For one nanosecond, I pictured a life filled with exotic cars, fast women, and stacks of cash. None of those things interested me. Not anymore.

"You know I can't accept this," I said. "It's against our company policy."

He laughed, the sound chilling to my ears. "We both know there are ways around policies. It's how we make our living, you and I."

"Maybe for you, but not for me." I had Venetia and our child to think about. I didn't want to spend my life bowing to the whims of a megalomaniac asshole billionaire. If I accepted this gift, I became one of his pawns. Oh. Hell. No.

"Don't be ridiculous." Steel edged his voice. "I've already cleared it with Daniels. Your partners are willing to look the other way. The car is yours. Keep it. Sell it. Hell, give it to one of your lady friends."

I pinched the bridge of my nose and let out an exasperated sigh. What I was about to say might ruin my career forever, but I wasn't going to knuckle under to his strong-arm tactics. "Here's the thing, Maxwell. It's not about your rules; it's about mine."

Chapter 30

Venetia

AFTER INTERVIEWING several people, I hired a woman named Helena as my assistant. She was in her mid-forties, divorced, and taller than my five-foot-eleven by at least two inches. Even though I'd been looking for someone young and fresh, I chose Helena because of her no-nonsense attitude. She could handle the day-to-day activities while I figured out how to start the business.

I needed the help, especially with the baby coming and my thoughts looping back to Beckett at every turn. The mere mention of his name sent my heart into palpitations. We'd spent every spare minute of every day together since the carriage ride.

"Let's get started, shall we?" Helena stared down her long nose at me and extended a hand for my notepad, bringing my wandering thoughts back to business. "Where do you want to begin?"

I handed her sketches of Daniels's office and went over my ideas. Within minutes, she was on the phone, setting up appointments to view artwork and furniture. She scheduled a dinner with a woman I'd met at the coffee bistro down the street who'd just bought a new house and was looking for an interior designer. While Helena chatted on the phone, I flipped through a book of samples. A small flutter happened low in my pelvis. It could've been nerves or indigestion, but a warm rush of emotion spread through my body. I was about four months along and my belly, although still small, was undeniably round. I placed a hand over my stomach and held my breath. Nothing happened.

"Are you okay?" Helena asked, her gray eyes filled with concern.

"Yes, I'm fine," I said, because I was. Life had taken an unexpected turn for the better over the past few weeks. The flutter happened again, a sensation like butterfly wings dancing inside my womb. "Oh," I whispered and blinked back the moisture in my eyes.

"Can I get you something? A glass of water? You're flushed." Helena set down the sample of carpet she'd been holding and rested the back of her hand on my forehead.

"No. Thank you." I steadied my nerves and raised my chin. "I'm fine. I'm just —I'm—I'm pregnant." I braced for her reaction, for the judgment I knew would follow, but she only gave me a small, soft smile. "And I think the baby moved."

"How wonderful. Congratulations." She went back to the carpet samples. "I wondered how long it was going to take before you told me."

"You knew?" It was the first time I'd admitted it to anyone other than Beckett or Sydney. The weight of secrecy lifted from my shoulders. I had no idea how good it would feel to tell someone, to share the joy.

"Of course I know." Her shrewd gaze traced my figure. "You still have a waistline, but a cute potbelly like that doesn't come from overeating. You don't look pregnant at all from the back. But you won't be able to hide it forever."

I rubbed the firm roundness. She was right. I couldn't pass it off as normal weight gain any longer. Time was rushing by. With trembling fingers, I reached for my phone to dial Beckett, needing to hear his voice and to share this latest development in our baby's life.

Chapter 31

Beckett

DANIELS AND I headed downtown to Seaforth Towers. For our higher-profile clients, we conducted business at their location. Men of Maxwell Seaforth's stature expected a certain level of privilege, and Daniels, Quaid, Beckett & Associates catered to their whims. I often enjoyed the change of scenery and looked forward to escaping the boundaries of my office, but not this time. Today, my stomach churned from too much coffee, lack of sleep, and an extreme sense of foreboding. A wise man never let his guard fall around Maxwell. He was up to something.

Once inside the lobby, an incoming call vibrated the phone in my pocket. I glanced at the caller ID. It was Venetia. *My Venetia.* My pulse skipped a ridiculous beat. I stepped aside to accept the call, palms sweating. When had a girl done this to me? The answer was never. With each passing day, she meant more to me than the day before.

"Hey," I said.

"Hi," she replied. The sound of her voice did strange things, libidinous things, to my groin. "Is it okay that I called?"

"Sure. It's fine," I said, even though I never took personal calls during work hours—unless it was Sam, Tucker or my family. But she was family now. My family. "What's up?"

"I felt it today. The baby." Wonder and awe filled her voice.

My chest constricted and stole my breath.

"Beckett?"

"Really? Are you sure?" I lingered near the elevators, not wanting to share this private moment with anyone except her.

"Yes. Pretty sure." The pitch of her voice lifted with excitement. "It's real, Beckett."

"What did it feel like?"

"Beckett, let's go." Daniels waved an impatient hand in my direction. I lifted a finger, asking him to wait a second. Nothing seemed more important than her answer.

"Kind of like a tickle, I guess." Even though I couldn't see her, I heard the smile in her words.

"Baby, that's great." I couldn't wait to check out this phenomenon for myself, but I had business to address with her father first. Every time I thought about him, about his secret, my insides twisted into knots. "Look, I'm going into a meeting. Can I call you back?"

"Sure. Wait. I have this thing to go to tonight, and I was wondering if maybe you could go with me?" The question ended in a hopeful lilt. I smiled. "I know it's last minute, but I don't want to go by myself. I meant to ask you earlier, but I forgot."

"Okay," I said, even though I had briefs and depositions backing up by the minute. "Define *thing*?"

"I need to take a potential client and her husband to dinner. It's nothing intense, just to schmooze a little." I pictured her winding a strand of hair around her index finger while she talked. "Do you have any suggestions for a restaurant?"

"Chez Renault," I offered. It had the perfect mix of coziness and elegance, and Venetia would go ape-shit over the upscale, eclectic decor. "I know the owner. I'll get us a table for, say, eight o'clock?"

"Great." I heard her sigh of relief. "Beckett, you're the best."

I wanted to be the best, her best. Not for my pride, but for her. I wanted her to look at me in a way no woman had ever looked at me before. She mattered more than work or success, and it scared the fuck out of me. "I'll pick you up at seven thirty," I said. "And I'm driving."

Daniels and I followed the receptionist down cold marble hallways to an enormous corner conference room. Two walls of windows offered the best view of the city. A mid-morning winter sun formed pools of yellow light on the charcoal tile floor. After offering us beverages and breakfast from a full buffet, she pressed a button to smoke the interior glass wall and shield the meeting from prying eyes. Five minutes later, Rayna entered the room, a flank of attorneys on her heels. We shook hands, made pleasantries, and took our places around the massive table. Twenty minutes after the proposed start time, Maxwell entered the room without apology.

"Let's get this over." He took his seat at the head of the table and twitched the knot of his tie.

I'd negotiated premarital agreements dozens of times, so I knew the drill. It was similar to buying a car, but the stakes were much higher. Both parties presented their expectations, and we haggled the details until a satisfactory resolution had been reached.

"In the event of a divorce, Rayna would like to receive a sum of ten million dollars for each year of marriage," Eckstein said. Everything about him was round, from the shape of his head to the style of his eyeglasses.

I squinted at him, blinded by the glare of overhead lights bouncing off his bald head. "Mr. Seaforth is prepared to offer five million for each year of marriage," I countered, a paltry sum considering his vast wealth. "And not a penny more."

Although the meeting consisted of standard fare, it was the ultimate lack of warmth between Rayna and Maxwell that unnerved me. Aside from their initial greeting, they hadn't spoken directly to each other. There were no covert glances, no mild flirtations, nothing at all to suggest a romantic relationship between the couple. This was a straightforward business deal. If I ever married—which would never happen, I assured myself—my relationship with my wife would be warm and caring and never negotiated by a team of strangers.

Maxwell studied me with cool green eyes. I met his stare, struck once again by the similarity of features between Sam and his father. Venetia looked so much like Sam, but nothing like Maxwell. Now that I knew why, the dissimilarity was glaring.

"And has Mr. Seaforth's will been adjusted to reflect her status as his wife?" This gem came from Coburn, the senior member of Rayna's team. He peered across the table at me, waiting for my acknowledgment. I nodded and tried not to stare at the coffee stain on his tie. "And has Mr. Seaforth provided a full and detailed disclosure of assets and liabilities including subsidiaries and satellite interests?"

"He has," I stated, knowing these questions were only a formality.

"Done." Daniels jumped in for the first time. It was well past lunch time, and I could hear his stomach growling from three feet away. "Why don't we adjourn for today?"

"Great idea." I needed time to go over Rayna's assets before the merger could be completed and a final agreement presented to both parties. "Let's reconvene next week at the same time. Does that suit everyone?"

We left the details to our assistants and shuffled out of the room.

Seaforth followed at my heels. He clapped a hand on my shoulder and pulled me to the side. "Enjoying your new car, Piers?"

"No, but I'm sure the City Center Mission is. I donated the car to the homeless shelter." I squared my shoulders and stared down at him.

His hand fell away. I might not be a billionaire, but I could be an intimidating motherfucker when I wanted. He stared at me, brows lowered. "Is that so? That's a generous donation you made." He reached past me to open the door beside us.

The office inside gleamed with brushed metal fixtures and leather upholstered furniture in a space larger than my apartment. A bank of windows overlooked the city. The wall across from the desk boasted no less than six flat screen televisions.

"This could be yours, Beckett. You and me as a team. I want you here. In this office. Leading my legal team. Think about it." He gestured to the matching desks outside the door, where two blondes dressed in sharply tailored black suits sat. "Everything your heart desires is right here waiting for you. Money, prestige, power. I'm offering you the world."

"I know what my heart desires, and it's not here with you." I shook my head. A vision of pretty blue eyes and the swell of a pregnant belly hovered in my mind's eye.

The gleam in his gaze hardened. "You never fail to surprise me, Beckett."

"I don't know why. I was up front about my ethics from the start." I turned my back and continued down the hall.

"How's Venetia?" His footsteps echoed in my wake, close enough to lift the small hairs on the back of my neck.

I recognized the edge of danger in his voice. The mere mention of Venetia's name on his lips turned my blood to ice. "She's fine. What do you care?" I stopped at the elevator bank and pressed the button, keeping my back to him.

"I don't, but you do," he said. "Why are you wasting your time with her? That girl has expensive tastes. Hell, I should now. She's out of your league."

Hatred bubbled up inside me, a feeling unlike any I'd ever known. The bastard had put a finger on my biggest weakness, my secret insecurities. I drew in a sharp breath through my nose to cool my emotions. "You're right. She's way too good for me." I stared at the numbers above the elevator door, cursing the slowness of its ascent. "But I'm sure you had nothing to do with how well she's turned out. Now, if you'll excuse me, I'm late for another meeting."

He snorted as if amused. "I had great plans for you, you know."

I remembered Sam's caution about joining the *dark side*. Nothing could ever persuade me to go against him or Venetia. "Then that was your mistake." The doors opened, and I stepped inside.

"No one walks away from me, son." When I turned to meet his gaze, he wore a smirk but his eyes were deadly. "Remember, your success is as great or as limited as I choose it to be. I own this city and everyone in it." *Including you.* He didn't say it, but I heard the inference in the silence after his words.

"Good luck with that," I said as the doors closed. Cocky bastard. He didn't even bother to veil the threat, and I didn't bother to hide that fact that I didn't care for his ultimatums.

One would think, after knowing the Seaforth family for years, I'd be accustomed to their opulent style of living. However, as I stood in Venetia's living room, the disparity of our lifestyles had never been more apparent. Maxwell had touched a nerve, stirring up my deepest insecurities. Ten years ago, a farm boy like me would never have had a chance with someone like her. The thought gave me pause. Was this where I was headed? Did I want a chance with her?

"What's wrong?" Venetia asked from beside me.

"Nothing." I turned to face her and let out a low whistle. She stood barefoot on the marble floor in a blue cocktail dress, the vision of class. The silky fabric clung to every one of her numerous curves, especially the round bubble of her belly. The neckline dipped low to hint at full breasts underneath, and the hemline was short enough to show tanned, toned thighs. By the time my eyes made it back to her face, her forehead had puckered into a scowl.

"Is this okay?" She fingered the hem in a gesture so appealing I cleared my throat to squelch a groan. "Should I change?" One of her hands swept over her stomach. "I should change. It's a little tight here."

"No. Don't change. You're perfect." My voice cracked on the last word. The sight of that small bump filled me with a rush of pride. She was utter perfection, from the top of her blond head to the tips of her red-polished toes. I couldn't wait to walk into Chez Renault with her on my arm.

"Good. I wasn't sure." She put one hand on my shoulder for balance as she slipped on her shoes.

A thrill of attraction rippled down my arm. This feeling, this yearning—it had gotten way out of control. I'd fallen in deep. My ribs felt too small to contain my lungs. I swallowed and tried to breathe through the panic. I was one hundred percent in love with her. We belonged together—her, me, the baby—the three of us.

"Are you sure you're okay?" Her hand slid down my arm in a caress while her gaze searched my face. A tiny furrow deepened between her eyes. "You're so pale."

"I'm good. Just hungry." Hell, yes, I was pale. My life was spiraling out of control. We needed to tell Sam about the pregnancy. Until we did, we couldn't move forward. Then there was the matter of Maxwell. I needed to tell her about his will. The longer I waited, the harder it was going to be. I wouldn't risk our relationship over him. Not when I had everything to lose. Better she hear the news from me, than find out by accident or from him.

"Beckett, are you listening to me?" She placed a hand on her hip and tapped a toe on the floor.

"Yes. No." I scrubbed a hand over my face. "I'm sorry. It was a rough day." Gathering my courage, I took her hands in mine, forcing her to stand still. "Look. I need to talk to you about a few things."

"Why?" A flicker of fear passed through her eyes. "You're scaring me. Is it something bad?" She swallowed. "You don't want to see me anymore?"

"Oh God, no." I pulled her into my arms and crushed her against my chest. "No way, baby." I smoothed a hand over her hair. "I adore you, and I'm not going anywhere. You're going to have to kick me out before I leave you." I felt her smile against my chest and her fingers tightened in my shirt.

"I adore you, too." She slipped her arms inside my suit jacket and around my waist, clutching me tight. Her shy confession sent my heart rocketing into the stratosphere. "I feel safe when you're here."

I held onto her, curving my body around hers, attempting to absorb her into me. Her baby bump pushed against my abdomen, safe and secure between us. I struggled to talk myself out of telling her about Maxwell. I'd do anything to protect her from that pain. Maybe she didn't need to know quite yet. Maxwell was an evil son of a bitch, and everyone knew the evil ones lived longer. He'd probably live forever or at least another thirty years, in which case I might never need to tell her at all.

"We need to make a plan to tell Sam," I said. "And there are some things I need to tell you that I haven't."

"Am I going to be upset?" she asked. Tension radiated through her shoulders.

I planted a kiss on her temple. "Probably. At least in the beginning." I pulled back enough to give her a weak smile. "But it'll be fine, I promise."

"Well, can we talk about it later?" When she looked at me with those large, bright eyes, I melted. How could I ever deny her anything? "I don't want to ruin this day. It's been perfect so far."

"Whatever you want, baby," I said, but I had the uneasy feeling I was making a mistake.

Chapter 32

Venetia

BECKETT SAID little during dinner and the drive back home. I tried to pass his silence off as fatigue. After all, he worked hard, long hours. His laptop and phone were never far from his side, and he was always texting clients or answering emails late into the night. As a child of the most successful businessman in the nation, I understood ambition and drive. They were qualities I admired in a man. Beckett possessed both, but they were tempered by an innate kindness my father had never shown to anyone.

After the meal, we said goodbye to my new client and returned to my place to celebrate the start of Venetia Designs, Inc. I watched Beckett shrug out of his jacket. His shoulders slumped as he tossed it onto a chair in my bedroom. I caught his glance. For one unguarded moment, I recognized a flash of concern in their chocolate depths. What was he worried about? Was he rethinking his part in raising this child? I knew his career was important to him. He'd have to readjust every aspect of his life to make room for the baby. His earlier reassurances did nothing to ease my insecurities.

"Beckett?" I bit my lower lip and hovered near the adjoining bathroom door. My legs ached from wearing too-high heels, and a cramp squeezed my lower back. I rubbed a hand over the curve of my spine to ease the tension. "Can you unzip my dress?"

"Sure." In one long stride, he was behind me, big hands fumbling with the tiny zipper.

I let the dress drop to the floor and turned to face him, wearing only my lacy bra and panties. His gaze drifted down my body before returning to my face, pupils large and black. His nostrils flared. We stared into each other's eyes. Unable to keep my hands off him, I cupped his face between my palms and tried to hold back the tears threatening to spill. This tall, handsome man had become my rock. He'd given me the courage and confidence to embark on a new life. The least I could do was return the favor, give him comfort and solace when he needed it. I wanted nothing more than to be there for him.

"Do you want me to rub your feet?" he asked. His concern tugged at my heart. He wrapped his arms around my waist and grabbed a handful of my bottom. My breathing quickened.

"No. That's not what I had in mind." I lifted on tiptoe to press a kiss on his lips. For once in my selfish life, I only cared about him, about making him feel better, about easing a little of the worry he carried without complaint.

"Mmmm." He groaned into my mouth as I pushed against him. When we parted, he lowered his brows. "We need to talk, baby, and if you keep doing that, it's not going to happen."

"Not tonight." He tried to protest, but I pressed two fingers to his lips. "Whatever it is, it can wait until the morning." Before he could say anything more, I placed a hand on the center of his chest and gave him a playful shove. He bounced onto the mattress behind him and lifted onto his elbows. I unhooked my bra and tossed it to the side then straddled his thighs.

"What the hell's gotten into you?" The lines around his mouth faded, replaced by the sexy grin I adored.

"You. You've gotten into me." I wrapped his necktie around my hand and gave it a jerk, pulling him into a sitting position. His hands gripped my hips and pressed me down onto the erection tenting his pants. The friction of his zipper

218

against my panties sent a surge of need into my core. "Sit back and relax while I show you a few things."

"Sounds promising." His chest rose and fell with each ragged breath as I removed his tie and unbuttoned his shirt. I slid my hands along the hard ripples of his chest and into the waistband of his pants. He hissed when I curled my fingers around his shaft and squeezed. "Damn, you make my blood boil, V."

"You haven't seen anything yet. I'm just getting started." I placed a kiss beneath his ear and dragged my lips down the column of his neck, tasting the salt of his skin.

"I can hardly wait." He gasped as I circled his nipple with my tongue and swept my hair away from my face so he could watch me kiss a trail down his belly. "How did I get so lucky?"

"I'm the lucky one." I unzipped his pants and dragged them down to his knees. His erection sprung free of his boxers and bobbed in front of me. I captured the tip in my mouth and sucked, hard enough to make him growl. I let it go with a *pop*. "You're a good man, Piers Beckett, and now it's time for your reward."

A few minutes past midnight, I awoke to unbearable warmth burning my backside. Beckett was curled around me, his chest to my back, a leg thrown over my thigh, and his hand spread wide over my belly. The coarse hairs on his chest tickled my spine as I inched away from him. I threw off the comforter and shifted, not wanting to disturb him but needing relief.

"Where are you going?" His arm tightened around my waist and his face burrowed into my neck. "Come back here," he murmured in a voice rough with sleep.

"I'm burning up," I said and tried to wriggle out of his grasp.

"Are you okay? Is something wrong?" He jerked to full consciousness, his body tensing against mine.

"I'm fine. You're like a furnace." I felt his smile curve in my hair.

"That's because you're on fire, baby." His hip pushed against me, rubbing the steel hardness of his erection against my bottom. Heat of a different kind spread over my body.

"I like having you here," I whispered and put a hand on his thigh. The muscle flexed beneath my palm.

"There's nowhere I'd rather be." His lips ghosted over my earlobe, and I shivered at the shimmer of his breath. "I want this. I want you. I want to sleep with you every night and wake up to you every morning." The hand on my belly inched lower to cup my sex. I opened my legs a few inches, enough to allow him access. He dipped a finger into the wetness there and circled along my clit. Desire built inside me. "I want to make love to you, fight with you, fuck you, own you—from the inside out."

My fingers tightened on his leg, and I squirmed backward to get closer. The thought of belonging to him made my lungs ache inside my ribs. "I want to be yours. And I want you to be mine. "

"Open up, baby. Let me inside you." The proprietary roughness of his voice raised the hairs on my arms. His cock prodded the gap between my thighs. He wedged one of his knees between mine to widen my legs and, guiding his erection with one hand, slipped inside me easily, filling me up, claiming me. We rocked in unison, letting the slow friction build between us. "God, you feel good."

The raw, ragged desire of his words split my defenses in two. I gripped his bare thigh with a hand, trying to draw him further inside me, needing him in the worst way. He adjusted, leaning over my shoulder to give me a lingering kiss. The slow, gentle thrusts of his pelvis hit the perfect spot deep inside me. His hand spread possessively over my belly.

"This is mine," he whispered, his breath tickling me ear. "You're mine."

220

"Yes," I replied. Frantic need began to build in my core.

"Say it." He stilled his thrusts, buried between my legs, and pushed hard against me until I moaned. "Say you're mine."

"I'm yours." A ripple of pleasure teased the length of my legs. He owned me, inside and out. I had his baby growing in my womb to prove it. "We are yours."

The sharp edge of his teeth nibbled the line of my jaw, sending waves of gooseflesh along my neck, puckering my nipples into peaks. They were painfully sensitive to the slightest touch. Even the sound of his voice hardened them into tight nubs. He flicked one with his thumb. I cried out at the sweet ache.

"Someday," he murmured, "when you least expect it, I'm going to ask you to make it real."

"It's real. This is real," I said, even though the night held a dreamlike quality, too perfect to be true. He started to move again, driving his cock home and dragging it back out to the tip with maddening slowness. My inner muscles clenched. I was close, so fucking close. I squeezed my eyes shut, savoring the brush of his chest hair on my shoulder blades and the flex of his leg muscles between my thighs.

"Venetia, baby, my love." His words sent me spiraling toward release. His free hand skated over my hip, along the crease of my pelvis to tease along my folds. With his middle finger, he circled my clit, rubbing with the perfect amount of pressure to send me over the edge. My orgasm broke in a series of waves and spasms around his cock. The pleasure radiated outward from my core and rippled down to my toes. Emotions tangled in my chest, making it hard to breathe. I could stay like this forever, wrapped in his strong arms, trapped against his body. Nothing had ever been so right in my life. I felt him jerk and stiffen as he came inside me. His heart pounded against my back. Endorphins rushed through my blood. He called me his love. I wanted to be his one and only, because he was mine.

In the morning, we slept through Beckett's alarm. Twenty minutes later, he leaped out of bed, ran into the shower, and jumped into his clothes. He dropped a quick peck on my nose then raced out the front door, muttering curses, phone to his ear as he called Garth. We didn't have time to talk about the night before or the pressing matter he'd mentioned earlier. I managed to shove it out of my thoughts, preferring to dwell on the euphoria of being well fucked. *My love. I adore you.* He hadn't said those three little words, *I love you*, but the implication was there. Just thinking about the way he'd claimed me and called me his made me think happy endings existed.

After he left, I lounged in bed, basking in the post-coital glow. Following a late breakfast with Helena, I headed downtown for a doctor's appointment. Beckett had promised to meet me there at eleven, but at twenty minutes past, he still hadn't shown. Unable to wait any longer, I had to go in by myself. I changed into a paper dress and sat on the table. As I waited for the doctor, I checked my phone one last time for a missed text or voicemail. Nothing. I tried not to worry but couldn't help myself. After last night, I could no longer deny it. He meant everything to me. What if he'd been in an accident? I pushed the unwelcome thought from my head. One of his meetings had probably run late. For distraction, I read the posters on the wall about sexually transmitted diseases, flu prevention, and the importance of a healthy diet.

"Hi, Venetia. How are you feeling today?" Dr. Mendenhall entered the room with a smile and gave my arm a soft pat. She was a petite woman, her face clean of makeup, brown hair pulled into a tight bun at the nape of her neck. I liked her confident air. "Any nausea or fatigue?"

"I'm doing fine. A little tired, but nothing out of the ordinary." I stared at the door. My hopes sank further with each passing minute. I tried to concentrate on her questions as she moved through the exam.

"Are you ready to find out the sex today?" While she spoke, she washed her hands at the sink then pulled on a pair of purple latex gloves.

"Sure." Disappointment tempered my excitement. I wanted to share this moment with someone. No, not anyone, only Beckett. I needed him there with me. What if something was wrong with the baby? I wasn't sure I could handle any bad news on my own. My self-confidence began to crack, the fissures widening with each passing second. I took a deep breath and tried to steady my nerves. I could do this.

"Is Daddy coming today?" she asked. Her gaze remained locked on the screen where I could see nothing but a blur of static and squiggles.

"Um, he was supposed to be here." I tried to ignore the doctor's furrowed brow. Was something wrong? My palms began to sweat.

"Have you decided if you want to know the sex?" she asked.

"No. I mean, I don't know." I bit my lower lip as she smeared cold gel over the exposed skin of my stomach. Beckett and I hadn't discussed it yet. Now, I was forced to make the decision alone.

"Well, you have plenty of time to decide." She gave me a comforting smile.

Someone knocked on the door. My hopes soared. I lifted to my elbows. A nurse entered. I swallowed back disappointment and lay back down.

"Sorry I'm late." Beckett's deep voice interrupted us. His square shoulders filled the doorway behind the nurse. I let out a tiny breath of relief, awed by the sight of him. The tailored lines of his navy blue suit emphasized his broad shoulders and narrow waist. Power and confidence swirled around his footsteps. His dark eyes found mine and sent my heart into an erratic rhythm. "Did I miss anything?"

"No. You're just in time. Come on in, Dad." Dr. Mendenhall gestured toward the chair beside the table with a jerk of her chin. She gave him an approving smile. Even doctors weren't immune to his charm. "I was just asking Venetia if you wanted to know the sex of the baby. We might be able to tell today."

"We haven't discussed it." He gave me a quick glance, one that bored into me with laser sharpness. I was certain he could see all my secrets, my faults, my weaknesses, but I wasn't afraid any longer. "You can tell already?"

"Sometimes," the doctor said. "It depends on whether or not baby wants to cooperate."

"I thought you weren't coming," I whispered, unable to quash the tremor in my voice.

He folded his tall frame onto the small chair next to me. His hand found mine, the grip warm and sure. "I'm sorry. Traffic was terrible, and I had some complications at the office. I got here as soon as I could."

"It's okay. You're here now." I squeezed his hand.

His lips curved up but the smile didn't reach his eyes. Whatever was bothering him, it hadn't disappeared overnight. "I wouldn't miss this for the world," he said and leaned forward to press a kiss to my forehead.

One kiss from him turned my world right side up. I was excited to be there and to hear our baby's heartbeat again, but most of all, I was excited to be there with him.

Chapter 33

Beckett

SWOOSH, SWOOSH, swoosh. The baby's heartbeat sounded more like a washing machine than a vital organ, but every time I heard it, I felt humbled. Tears shimmered in Venetia's blue eyes. A lump thickened in my throat. I brought her hand to my lips and kissed her knuckles. It was real. We were really going to do this thing. We were going to be parents.

"Is everything okay?" Venetia asked the doctor in a tremulous whisper.

"Everything looks great," the doctor said with a reassuring smile. "Now, do you want to know if it's a boy or a girl?"

"No. I don't," I said quickly.

Venetia's eyebrows lifted as she turned her head to me. "Are you sure?" Her forehead puckered. "It would be nice to know for decorating the nursery and buying clothes."

I shook my head. "You can if you want, but I don't want to know. It doesn't matter to me as long as it's healthy. I'd rather be surprised."

"Okay." Venetia smiled. I'd never seen her look quite so radiant. Her translucent skin glowed. I had to control the urge to kiss her on the mouth.

"I'm going to step outside and let you get dressed," Dr. Mendenhall said. "I'll come back in a few minutes, and we can talk about your next appointment."

Once the doctor shut the door behind her, Venetia swung her legs to the floor and sat up. A loopy grin widened across my face. Before I could check my actions, I swept Venetia into my arms and crushed her against my chest. With my nose buried in her hair, I drew in a deep lungful of her scent. Her hands crept up my back to fist in my shirt. I held her until she began to squirm.

"Beckett," she whispered in my ear. "I can't breathe."

"Sorry." I eased my grip but didn't let go. The need to protect her, keep her close, overwhelmed the desire to guard my heart.

"Are you okay?" Her voice shook with laughter.

"Yeah." I'd never been better. Light and happiness threatened to burst from the top of my head. The problems of my day—Maxwell, Sam, our relationship—faded away under her beautiful blue eyes. I beamed at her. "You?"

"I'm good."

Was it my imagination, or had she grown more beautiful in the last twenty minutes? Long, silky hair brushed over my hands as they rested on her back. A pink flush stained the creamy skin on her cheeks. My gaze landed on her mouth. I spread the fingers of my left hand wider over her back and pressed her against me. My right hand dropped to cup one of her buttocks. The paper gown crinkled in protest between us, reminding me of her nudity beneath the thin barrier. She tasted of bread and honey, tea and lemons. When her fingers tangled in my hair, a low growl rumbled in my chest. All I could think was *mine*. My woman. My child. Mine.

"Beckett." Venetia's hands moved to my chest. "Wait."

I pulled back, my brain fogged by desire and animal lust. My eyes couldn't tear away from her reddened lips, swollen from my kiss. I needed another taste of her. I needed more.

"Beckett," she said again, this time more firmly.

I frowned and tried to focus on her words. "What?" My voice cracked on the single word.

"Not here. The doctor's coming back in a minute." Merriment danced in her eyes. "You're acting crazy."

"I am crazy—about you." I gripped her about the waist and pulled her closer, intent on taking another kiss. "Screw the doctor."

"No, Beckett." She wriggled out of my grasp, breathless with laughter.

"Come here, woman." I reached for her.

She danced out of my reach. "Not now." Her right hand clutched the paper gown to her chest while she pointed at me with her left index finger. "Behave."

"I can't help myself." I scanned her barely hidden curves beneath the gown. "That piece of paper isn't helping matters any." I feinted to the left, pretending to lunge. She squealed and darted behind the exam table.

Someone knocked on the door.

"Give us a minute," I said, suddenly aware of the raging erection tenting my dress pants. Venetia's face flushed bright red, but she continued to smile. She stepped behind the folding screen to put on her clothes. "Do you need some help back there?" I asked.

"I'm doing just fine," she said. Her voice still brimmed with laughter. "We can continue this somewhere else."

"My place." I stated and reached down to adjust the pressure behind my fly.

"Don't you have to go back to work?" she asked amid the rustling of fabric and the growl of a zipper. I tried not to picture her nakedness, the high globes of her breasts, or the tight pink buds of her nipples above her round belly.

I was already on the phone to the office. Nothing seemed more important than spending time with Venetia, ironing out the kinks of our past and smoothing the path to our future—together. The sooner I got things off my chest about Maxwell, the better I'd feel. "Garth, clear my schedule for the rest of the day, would you?"

"I can't. Mr. Daniels and Mr. Quaid have requested a meeting with you when you get back," Garth said.

A partners' meeting? I rubbed the back of my neck, tensing with unease. "I'm sorry, baby." I covered the phone with a hand. "I have to go back to work. What about tonight? Come over, and I'll make dinner for us."

Chapter 34

Venetia

IN THE space of a baby's heartbeat, everything had changed. I felt it in the way his hand rested on the small of my back as we left the exam room. I saw it in the heat of his dark eyes when our gazes met. A charge of electricity zinged between us every time our shoulders brushed. Part of me rejoiced, while the more cautious part of me couldn't believe my good luck. I was so accustomed to being overlooked that I found it difficult to accept being the center of someone's attention.

"Don't," Beckett warned as we waited for the elevator outside the doctor's office. "You're overthinking this."

"I know." I tried and failed to smooth the wrinkle between my brows.

"What I feel for you, it's not about obligation," he said, reading my mind. He pulled me tight against his side. The heat of his breath warmed my ear as he spoke. "This is about me wanting to be with you. Just you. Not because of the baby. Not because I'm stuck with you. Because you're beautiful and sweet and the most vibrant person I've ever met." He took my chin between his thumb and forefinger, and tipped my face up to his. "Because I'm in love with you."

A tremor of excitement shivered from my chin down to my toes. He loved me. No one had ever said that to me before, and I'd underestimated the power of those five words. The way he looked at me—brown eyes black with heat, and the sweep of his tongue over his lips like he was parched for my kiss—rattled my soul. Warmth started in my chest and spread throughout my entire body. This was, by far, the happiest moment of my life. I loved him, and he loved me back. We were going to be together.

"I love you, too." I managed to get the words out a split second before the elevator doors opened and a trio of men entered the elevator. Beckett smiled and dropped his hand to his side. His fingers curled around mine, and he gave my hand a squeeze.

Once we reached the ground floor, Beckett lifted our entwined fingers to his lips and kissed the back of my hand. "It's going to be great." His eyes glittered with promise. "Just you and me and the baby." He walked backward down the sidewalk and smiled at me in a way that tied my insides in a knot. "I'll see you at my place. Text me."

He turned and headed back to work for his meeting. I watched his back until he disappeared around the next corner. Since I was headed in the opposite direction, I waited for a cab, shivering against the finger of icy wind that snaked beneath my dress. I pulled the belt of my coat tighter about my waist before scrolling through the shopping list Helena had just texted over for approval. Task lighting for Daniels's office. Carpet samples for Beckett's apartment. Just reading Beckett's name made my mouth tingle in remembrance of his kiss, the way he looked at me, his words from last night. *I want to make this real.*

"Miss Seaforth." A hand touched my forearm.

I flinched and glanced up into the face of a middle-aged man wearing a black trench coat, gloves, and a chauffeur's cap. A black Rolls Royce idled at the curb behind him.

"Excuse me, miss. Mr. Seaforth would like to speak with you."

The hairs on the back of my neck lifted. I glanced around, uncertain. Passersby gawked at the car but moved along the street. For a second, I thought maybe the driver might mean Sam, but Rockwell was Sam's only driver.

"Maxwell?" I asked.

The man nodded and gestured toward the car. "He's inside, miss," he replied with a patient smile.

Common sense told me to turn around and run like hell in the opposite direction. I studied the car. Tinted windows obscured the passenger inside. What could he possibly want? After his snub at the restaurant, I'd never expected to see or hear from him again. I glanced at the driver, needing some form of reassurance. He nodded, and I stepped toward the car. I'd always had more balls than brains. Maybe dear old Dad wanted to reconcile. Maybe he wished to apologize for his cold behavior. Maybe, just maybe, he'd had a change of heart. I was still high on Beckett, my self-confidence buoyed by his admission of love. On a day like this, anything seemed possible, and I wanted to believe good existed in everyone, even my father.

The blackout window slid silently down and Maxwell's face loomed through the opening. "Oh for God's sake, Venetia. I don't have all day. Get in the car."

At his command, the little girl inside me, the one who'd craved his approval and attention for so many years, snapped to attention. The driver opened the door, and I entered into the darkness.

I stared at the stranger—my father—across from me in his impeccable custom suit. A thrill of nerves tremored inside me. I clasped my hands in my lap to keep them from shaking. The loose folds of my trench coat hid my belly. He was on the phone, speaking in rapid-fire German, green eyes locked on mine. After an interminable minute, he ended the call and returned my stared.

My calm snapped. Enough already. I'd spent my entire life fearing this man, yearning for one word of kindness from him, anything to show he cared. By the set of his jaw and the dispassionate light in his eyes, nothing had changed.

"What's up?" I asked, my composure returning. "Why the secrecy?"

"No secrecy," he said. "Can I drop you somewhere?" Maxwell lowered the partition dividing us from the chauffeur.

"Yes. My apartment, please." After I gave my address to the driver, Maxwell lifted the partition, isolating us once more. The car pulled away from the curb. I smoothed my skirt over my legs and drew on Beckett's image to bolster my confidence. "What do you want?" Maxwell had to want something. The man didn't waste his time with anyone or anything unless he had an agenda.

"Direct." He nodded, the first approval I'd ever gotten from him. "Good." He withdrew a sheaf of folders from his briefcase and set them on the seat next to his leg. "It's come to my attention that you've reached your twenty-third birthday."

I nodded, wondering where he was headed with this line of conversation. "A few months ago. Thanks for noticing."

"Don't be snide, Venetia. It's unbecoming." He cleared his throat. "You should be in full possession of your trust and the portion of your mother's estate left to you by her will." The formality of his tone turned my blood to ice. "I need you to know that you'll no longer receive a monthly stipend from my account, and this conversation terminates my obligation to you."

"W-what?" I stammered, stunned by his statement. I didn't care about the money. Fuck the money. The blatant dismissal, however, stung like a dagger to the gut. "I don't understand."

"Your mother humiliated me with her affairs." My jaw dropped. He frowned. "I chose to look the other way most of the time, but when she got pregnant by another man, it was the last straw. I agreed to raise the child—you—as my own as long as she kept you out of my sight. My obligation to you ended when you received the full benefit of your trust."

"I don't understand. What are you saying?" Tears of betrayal and hurt blurred my vision. I blinked them back, unwilling to let him see how much he wounded me.

"I'm saying you're not a Seaforth. You're not my child. I don't have any further responsibility to you, and I'm severing our relationship." By this time, the car had reached my building. The driver eased into the drop off zone by the front door and put the car in park. Maxwell stared at me, unblinking.

"If you're not my father, who is?" I asked, still trying to wrap my mind around this painful revelation.

He shrugged. "I have no idea. For all I know, it was the gardener or maybe Rockwell. I always suspected they had a thing."

I placed a hand over my belly and tried to ignore the sting of tears. Maxwell wasn't my father. If I wasn't a Seaforth, then who was I? I felt adrift, the sudden loss of my identity a deep and penetrating blow. "Why are you telling me this? Why now?" I managed to ask.

"I had to rework my will to include Rayna." He tugged on his cuffs before adjusting his tie. "I've listed the manor house for sale. I put your mother's things in a storage building outside of town. I'll have the key sent over to you."

"Oh." I didn't know what to say. In the space of fifteen minutes, he'd stolen everything I knew about myself—my name, my heritage, and the shape of my world.

"I need your signature on these documents." He withdrew a pen from the inside pocket of his jacket and held it in front of me. I blinked. "Venetia." He wiggled the pen. "I haven't got all day."

Through the haze of shock, common sense prevailed. I shook my head. "I'm not signing anything until I have my lawyer look these over."

One corner of his mouth curled up. He nodded. "Very good. Smart girl. Have someone take a look at them and get them back to me by next Friday. If you have any questions, you can ask Beckett."

"Beckett?" My stomach turned over. "Why him?" I couldn't process his words fast enough. Beckett knew about this? He knew I wasn't Maxwell's daughter? Pain sliced through my chest, so severe I reeled back into the plush leather seat.

"Yes. He's the one who drew up the documents." Maxwell sighed, as if he'd grown weary of the effort required to speak with me. He raised a hand and rapped on the window of the limo. The chauffeur opened the door. Bright light spilled into the dark interior of the car. I sat motionless, too confused to move. Maxwell waved a hand like he was shooing a stray dog. "Go on. Hurry up. I don't have all day."

I stumbled onto the sidewalk and stood there, in the cold winter wind, clutching the damn papers until the doorman came forward and touched my arm. "Are you all right, miss?" he asked. "Can I help you upstairs?"

"No," I whispered. I wasn't sure I'd ever be all right again.

Chapter 35

Beckett

ONCE I left Venetia at the doctor's office, I floated back to work on a cloud of happiness. She loved me. *Loved* me. *Me*. In the bathroom of my office, I splashed water on my face to wipe away the goofy, lovesick grin. Sure, we had problems to resolve, but I was certain we could surmount them. I straightened my tie and left the room knowing what I needed to do. After work, I'd make a quick stop by the jewelry store. I loved her, and I needed to make her mine, officially, legally, before God and in every way that mattered. I wanted to marry her and raise a family with her. An engagement ring would show her the sincerity of my intentions.

With that out of the way, I'd move on to the less pleasant task of Maxwell. I'd tell her everything about the will and my involvement. Afterward, we'd call Sam together to tell him about the baby. At long last, the fragments of my life seemed to be falling into place.

When I entered Daniels's office, I found him seated at the mammoth desk, Quaid at his side. They spoke to each other in hushed tones, their words inaudible across the distance. A knot of unease tightened in my gut. Neither man stood when I entered the room, nor did they make eye contact.

"I didn't realize there was a partners' meeting today," I said. They ceased talking and swiveled their chairs to face me. Daniels stared at my tie. Quaid focused on a spot over my left shoulder.

"This is informal," Quaid said. He was a stout, middle-aged man, barrel-chested with sharp, uneven teeth. I rarely saw him. He spent most of his time at the Los Angeles office.

"What's going on?" I took a seat across from them, cognizant of the segregation. We were partners in the loosest sense of the term. In reality, we shared office space and little else.

"It's time to discuss your options with the firm," Daniels began.

The little shit didn't have the balls to come right out and say it, but I knew where the conversation was headed. Maxwell Seaforth had gotten to them. I fought to stay calm, to hide the shaking of my hands. The bastard hadn't wasted any time in jerking the rug out from under me.

"It's come to our attention that maybe your long-term goals aren't in alignment with ours," Quaid said. "We'd like to talk with you about dissolving our partnership."

My mind scrambled for solid ground. Not only did this affect me, it affected Venetia and the baby. I'd invested well and stockpiled funds over the years, but I didn't like proposing to her as an unemployed freeloader. Even though she had money of her own, my pride wouldn't allow her to support all of us.

The tension in the room thickened. In my most intimidating voice, I said, "Well, gentlemen, let's talk about money." I shored up my defenses and prepared to play hardball.

Chapter 36

Venetia

AN HOUR later I found myself standing outside Sam's apartment, the documents shoved beneath my arm. I pressed a hand against my heart to keep it from exploding. Maxwell's words played through my head on a loop. *You're not a Seaforth...Not my child...Not a Seaforth.* My entire life had been built around the expectations associated with the Seaforth name. If I wasn't a Seaforth, then who was I? Without a legitimate surname, I had no idea how to act. My entire identity had been erased.

The door opened. Dakota answered. She wore a pair of slim-fitting blue jeans and an oversized T-shirt spattered with paint. The smile slid from her mouth at the sight of me. I hovered in the hallway, fighting back tears, too shattered to continue the pretense of hating her.

"Is—is Sam here?" I asked. I'd been so bent on seeing him, so convinced he might have answers, that I'd failed to consider the circumstances of our relationship or that it was the middle of the day and he might be at work. "I'm sorry to barge in like this, but it's important."

"He just got here. Come in." She stepped to the side, welcoming me into their home. "Let me get your coat." Calm, gentle hands pulled my coat over my shoulders. I felt her gaze slide over my figure, lingering on my belly for a long second before pulling back to my eyes. "You're always welcome here, V. Make yourself comfortable, and I'll go get him." Just hearing the concern in her voice eased some of my panic.

"Who is it?" Sam strode out of the hallway, crisp and confident in a three-piece suit. He took one look at me and his jaw tensed. "What's wrong?"

"Dad— Maxwell." Once I opened my mouth, the words poured out in a rush. "He said he's not my father. I'm not his kid. I'm not a Seaforth. Did you know about this?"

"What? You're not making sense." He wrapped an arm around my shoulders and led me to the sofa. Tremors shook my body. "Take a deep breath and tell me again. From the beginning."

I stumbled through the story while he listened and nodded. Looking into his calm green eyes, I realized how much I missed him, how much I needed him, and vowed never to let anything come between us again. Dakota sat on the opposite side of me, took my hand in hers, and squeezed. Sandwiched between them on the sofa, I felt safe. Their show of support overwhelmed my self-control, and a tear slid down my cheek.

"I had no idea, V. This is the first I've heard about it," Sam said after a long pause. "But it does explain a lot of things." His eyes met mine, filled with sympathy and warmth. A little of my anguish dissipated. He tightened his arm around my shoulder and dropped a kiss to my temple.

"But I'm not a Seaforth," I whispered, feeling the tears building once more. "I don't know who I am."

"Doesn't matter. You're still my sister," he said, in his quiet, reassuring voice. A wicked gleam sparked in his gaze. "If it was me, I'd be glad to know I'm not one of Satan's spawn."

In spite of my distress, a laugh slipped from my lips, mingled with a hiccup. Sam always knew how to put things in perspective. "He gave me these documents to sign." The sight of Maxwell's papers brought back the sharp sting of Beckett's betrayal.

"Let me see." Sam took the documents and skimmed over them. "This looks like a release to any claims on his estate or monetary compensation. And this one is a non-disclosure agreement requesting your public silence about your parentage." He cleared his throat. "The upside is that no one's going to know you're not a Seaforth. You don't have to worry about press or negative publicity. Not that it matters."

"It doesn't change who you are as a person," Dakota said. Her worried gaze lifted to meet Sam's. The ice around my heart toward her melted. "No one can take that away from you unless you let them. And we love you no matter who you are."

"I've been awful to you both." I hung my head and studied the floor.

"Family is family, and we stick together," Sam said. "Even when I'm pissed at you, even when you're being a brat, I still care about you." He gave my shoulders an extra squeeze.

"I'm sorry," I said to Dakota. I searched her face, hoping she could read the sincerity in my eyes. "I never really gave you a chance."

"It's okay. I can't blame you. I would've felt the same way." Her smile held only sympathy and understanding. She patted my hand. "You're pale as a ghost. Let me get you something to drink." I watched her walk into the kitchen while Sam continued to peruse the documents.

"You should talk to Beckett," Sam said. "He's been handling some of Maxwell's affairs. Maybe he can shed some light on this." He reached into the interior pocket of his coat for his phone. I put a hand on his arm to stop him.

"No. I don't want to talk to him." My heart beat furiously at the mention of Beckett's name. Beckett's involvement in the situation wounded me. He'd obviously told Sam about his dealings with Maxwell, but he hadn't told me. Did he not trust me? How could he love me and withhold this vital information, knowing how it affected me?

"Why not?" Sam's eyes narrowed. "Is there something else you want to tell me?"

A hot rush of embarrassment flooded into my cheeks. In all the turmoil, I'd forgotten about the baby. I placed a protective hand on my belly. "I guess you noticed that I'm pregnant."

"It's a little difficult to ignore." A scowl darkened his blond brow. "Why didn't you tell me?"

"We weren't exactly on speaking terms." I jutted my chin stubbornly. "I knew you'd give me hell about it." My emotions bounced from one extreme to the other; hurt and anger roiled inside me.

"Damn straight I will." Sam's jaw flexed. "Who is it? Who did this to you?"

"No one did this to me." I bristled at his tone. Beckett's name hovered on my lips. We'd planned to tell Sam together. At this juncture, the last person I wanted to see was Piers Beckett. A part of me wanted to hurt him back, the way he'd hurt me by his betrayal. Tears burned in my eyes as I thought back to the previous night and how happy I'd been. I wasn't sure I could ever forgive him for lying to me. I drew in a deep breath. "It's Beckett's."

Chapter 37

Beckett

AFTER THE meeting with Daniels and Quaid, I headed back to my office. My head continued to reel from shock. Leaving the firm was only a temporary setback. It would take a few months to wrap up my current cases, giving me time to set up a new plan. The terms of my partnership agreement offered a generous buyout for my share of the business. With a little leveraging, I could walk away from Daniels, Quaid, Beckett & Associates with a lot of cash in my pocket, enough to start my own practice.

As I closed my office for the day, I pushed aside thoughts of work and concentrated on Venetia. God, I couldn't wait to see her, to take her to my bed and sink into her soft, wet heat. We had a lot to discuss and plans to be made.

My cell phone vibrated inside my pocket. Thinking it might be V, I withdrew it and frowned to see Sam's name on the screen. "Hey, man," I answered.

"I need to see you at my place. Now." Sam's voice growled over the phone

"What's up?" I tried to stay calm though my hands began to shake. Sam had a way of communicating his displeasure by tone. I'd never been on the wrong side of his temper, and I didn't want to be there now.

"Just get over here." The clipped cadence of his tone rang warning bells in my head.

"I'm supposed to meet someone." I bit the inside of my cheek, the secret of

Venetia weighing heavily on my conscience once more, and glanced at my wrist watch. "But I suppose I can swing by for a few. Or can we do it tomorrow?" By tomorrow, I'd have a plan for our future, and Venetia and I could confront Sam together.

"Venetia's here."

The simple statement turned my blood to ice. No, no, no. I shoved a hand through my hair and tried to breathe. Panic twisted my insides.

Once I got to Sam's apartment, I took one look at Venetia's face and knew shit had gone wrong in a major way. She avoided my gaze and turned her face when I tried to kiss her cheek. Acid churned in my gut.

"What's going on?" I asked, swallowing down the bile in my throat.

"That's what I'd like to know," Venetia said. The chill in her voice sent a shiver down my back. I reached out to touch her, but she shrank from my hand.

"You told him?" Relief washed over me as I tried to piece together the story, certain I could clear things up once Sam knew my feelings. "Why didn't you wait for me? I thought we were going to tell him together." A part of me felt slighted because she'd taken the initiative on her own, but I swallowed down my pride. I turned to Sam. "I'm glad you know. It's been killing me to keep this from you. We were waiting for the right time."

"Inside." Sam nodded toward his home office, jaw clenched and green eyes blazing. I followed him into the room, feeling like a third-grader on his way to the principal's office. Once inside, Sam paced the length of the room. No matter how you tried to dress it up, there was no good way to tell your best friend you'd knocked up his little sister. Venetia and the baby were my responsibilities, and I planned to take my lumps like a man. I steeled myself for a variety of responses: anger, dismay, disappointment, or betrayal.

"Want to take a poke at me?" I asked when his silence became more than I could bear. The idea of Sam's fist against my nose seemed preferable to his silence.

"How long has this been going on?" His voice sounded surprisingly calm when he stopped in front of me.

"Awhile. I don't really think you need to know the details," I said. I wanted to be honest with him but needed to keep our sex lives private. "Do you?"

"You're right. I don't want to know." He shook his head as if to clear it. A muscle twitched in his cheek. He took a step forward until less than an inch separated our noses. "So, what is she to you? One of your fuck buddies? Are you guys together now?"

The gleam in his eyes prompted me to choose my words carefully. "We're committed to raising this child together."

"But you're not a couple?" A flicker of danger sparked in his gaze.

"No. Not yet." I squared my shoulders. "We're feeling things out."

"So, basically you're screwing around with her when you feel like it." He shook his head with the slow control of a cobra about to strike.

"It's not like that." The strength ebbed from my bones. I melted into the chair across from his desk and put my head in my hands.

"Then what's it like? Make me understand." Sam took a step back and sat on the edge of the desk, arms folded over his chest. "How the fuck did this happen, Beckett?" He scrubbed both hands over his face. "I don't know whether to kick your ass or shake your hand."

"It's a mess, I know, but I'm trying to fix this." My voice cracked. The fiasco of the day crashed down on me, and my control snapped. "I love her, Sam. Venetia and the baby—they're everything to me." I stood and walked over to the window. On the street below, cars crept along the avenue, their headlights twinkling like stars in the darkness.

"If it was anyone else, I would wrap his nuts around his neck." He blew out a tired breath. "But it's not. It's you, and I trust you."

"Just not with your little sister?" I gave him a wry glance. One side of his mouth twitched as he held back a smile. Seeing the crack in his anger gave me a glimmer of hope.

"I know how you are, Becks. You've always been the player. If you're not in this for the long haul, then you need to walk away. Now." Sam scratched the stubble of beard on his chin. "Don't make promises you have no intention of keeping."

My reputation gave him every right to be concerned. I chose my next words carefully, knowing I needed him on my side, certain I could convince him of my sincerity. I walked up to him, squared my shoulders, and looked him in the eyes. Over the years, I'd given plenty of closing arguments before the courts. This was by far the most important case I'd ever pleaded.

"We've known each other a long time, Sam. You've been more of a brother to me than my own brothers. I've never willingly lied to you. I respect you too much. The only reason I didn't tell you sooner is out of respect for Venetia. She made me promise to wait until she was ready. I gave her my word, and you know when I give my word, I mean it." He watched me, face expressionless. I blundered on, determined to win him over. "I love you both, but she's a damn sight prettier than you, and I plan to be in her life for a long time. I'll do right by her and the baby. You can bank on it."

A flicker of shock flashed through Sam's eyes. He said nothing for at least five minutes. I stared back at him, bracing my feet wide apart. A bead of sweat trickled down my spine, but I refused to flinch. He needed to know I was committed, that she was more than a one-night stand, she was my life.

When he spoke, his voice was calm. "If you hurt her, I will annihilate you."

"I wouldn't expect anything less," I replied and offered my hand.

Sam pulled me into an unexpected one-shouldered hug. "Beckett, you crazy son of a bitch. I can't believe you're going to be a father." He pushed back to give me a lopsided grin. "Venetia is going to turn your hair gray. You know that, right?"

"Yeah, I know." I returned his grin. "I can't wait, man." A rush of emotion swept over me. Now that he knew, I couldn't wait to share the good news with my best friend. Keeping silent had worn on my nerves. It felt good to shed the burden of the secret after so long. It felt even better to know he was excited for me—for *us*.

"I think this deserves a drink." Sam strode over to the crystal decanter on his credenza and filled two short glasses with scotch. He turned and offered one to me. I shook my head. I needed a clear head to deal with Venetia. He cocked his head and gave me a knowing smirk. "No. Take it. You're going to need this. Venetia ran into Maxwell today, and he dumped a load on her." His shrewd eyes met mine over the rim of his glass. "Know anything about that?"

I opened my mouth to explain. Before I could get the first word out, Venetia burst into the room, and all hell broke loose.

Chapter 38

Venetia

THE DOOR closed behind Sam, and his footsteps echoed down the hall before either of us spoke. My hands trembled. I pressed my palms into my thighs to hide the shaking. From my point of view, Beckett owed me more than an apology. Once the initial shock had worn off, I was more than hurt—I was pissed.

Beckett took a step toward me, but I warded him away with a scathing glare. "How could you not tell me?"

"What's Maxwell done?" Anger rolled off him in waves. He took my chin in his fingers and tipped my face toward him. "Talk to me, V."

I told him about our conversation, about the accusations over my birthright. He listened without speaking. While I spoke, he twirled his ring around his finger. When I was done, he blinked and looked away.

"This is my fault," he said, voice low and thick, almost like he was talking to himself. "My fault."

The world stopped turning. The noise of passing cars silenced, and the sky dimmed. He knew. *He knew.* Beckett knew, and he'd said nothing while I worried and tortured myself. I pulled my arm out of his grasp.

Outside, it had begun to snow. Big, fat flakes stuck to the windows and blurred the cityscape beyond the glass. I shivered, more from distress than cold, and wrapped my arms around my waist.

"The firm has been doing some work for him." Beckett's expression tightened, and he spoke slowly, choosing his words with care. How could he be so calm when everything in my world seemed to be tumbling out of control? "His prenup. Nothing out of the ordinary."

"And you didn't think to mention it to me?" I shook my head, unable to understand.

"I wanted to tell you. I tried last night," he said. "But you wanted to wait. And then you came onto me, all doe-eyed and sexy, and I couldn't resist." I flushed at the memory of the way I'd given him head, pushing off his protests. "This morning I was late for work, so there wasn't time. I meant to tell you tonight."

"You had a hundred chances before that. A hundred different times you could've mentioned it." I took a second step back, unwilling to give in. Hurt and betrayal churned inside me. How could he not mention this? He knew how I felt about Maxwell. I'd told him everything, yet he'd failed to mention this alliance. "You said honesty. You promised to be truthful."

His jaw hardened into granite. "It's a matter of client confidentiality. I can't go telling just anyone."

"I didn't realize I was *just anyone*." The sting of betrayal stabbed me again. "You said you loved me. If you love me, how could you lie to me?"

"Goddamn it, V." Every time I took a step back, he took a step forward in an awkward, dysfunctional dance. Over the time I'd known him, I'd never heard him sound so angry or so wretched. "What do you want me to say? You know damn good and well that I can't talk about the details of client cases. I'm sorry if you're hurt, but I'm hurt too. I did the best I could under the situation."

"You could've told me. You could've trusted me."

He blew out an exasperated breath. "I do trust you, but if I'd told you, what would you have done? Would you have been able to keep something like that to yourself?"

I knew he was right, but I couldn't admit it. I'd never been able to hold in my feelings. The minute he had confided, I would have stormed over to my father's office and unleashed a tempest on him. "You should have told me," I repeated stubbornly and dropped my gaze to the floor.

"What about Sam? You made me promise not to tell him, and I kept my promise even though it was hell. I lied to my best friend for you, because I love you. For *you*." The raw texture of his voice caught me by surprise. He sounded hurt, angry—as if this was my fault instead of his. "You should've waited for me."

My heart squeezed. I wasn't sure if I wanted to throw myself into his arms, slap him, or have a good cry. He was right. I shouldn't have told Sam without him, but I couldn't admit I was wrong. I was too hurt, too confused, too overwhelmed by events of the day to think rationally. "And you should have told me about Maxwell."

"You're absolutely right. I should've told you up front, but we weren't involved then. Once I found out, I didn't want to tell you because I knew how much it would hurt you. I didn't count on loving you so much." The amount of regret in his voice shook my control. I blinked through tears to look up at him. He took one of my hands in his and kissed my knuckles. Heat darkened his brown eyes to black. "We can work this out."

"I don't know." I wanted to believe him with all my heart, but I couldn't bring myself to trust his words. How could I trust anyone anymore? My entire life had been a lie. The man who raised me hated me. I didn't even know who my real father was. Maybe Beckett was the same. Maybe I couldn't trust him either.

I turned and started walking toward the door. Sam sat at the kitchen table with Dakota. They followed me with their eyes as I passed by. I kept my chin up. "I'm leaving," I announced. "Thank you for your help today. I really appreciate it."

"Venetia, wait. You're being unreasonable." Beckett fell into step beside me. "Let's take a minute and talk about this."

"No." I tried to draw on my coat but my arm got tangled in the sleeve. Beckett grabbed the collar and helped me slip it on. My resolve cracked the tiniest bit at his thoughtfulness as I tightened the belt around my waist, walking faster. I needed to get away from him before I said something hurtful, something we'd both regret. As I passed the threshold and headed toward the elevator, I slipped on a small patch of melted snow. My arms flailed in a vain attempt to regain my balance.

Beckett lunged forward and caught my shoulders before I hit the floor. "Jesus, V." The drained color from his face. "You could've fallen. You've got to be careful."

Tears threatened to spill. I bit the inside of my cheek to hold them back. "Don't tell me to be careful. Just get away from me." With both hands on his chest, I pushed him back.

Real fear flickered in his eyes. "You can't drive like this. You're too upset. Let me take you home."

"No." The elevator arrived, and I stepped inside. He stepped inside with me.

When he spoke his voice was calm and controlled, but I felt the irritation emanating from his pores. "I'm taking you home. It's not an option."

Chapter 39

Beckett

VENETIA DIDN'T say one word on the drive to her place. Once there, I walked her to the front door, which she promptly slammed in my face. I knew without asking that I'd really fucked up this time. The pain on her face cut me to the quick. She was hurting deeply, and I wanted to be there for her. This was my doing, and even though I'd had little choice in the matter, I blamed myself. I should have refused Maxwell from the start. Greed and ambition had clouded my judgement.

On the other hand, client confidentiality was a serious matter and not one I violated lightly. Venetia needed to understand and respect the parameters of my job. If she'd given me a chance, I would've gone through the documents with her. I'd made sure the terms were fair, albeit unpleasant. And she'd broken the news to Sam without consulting me. Her utter disregard for my feelings in the matter wounded my pride. How could we raise a child as a team if we couldn't even get through the pregnancy together? The more I thought about it, the angrier I became. She didn't trust me.

At the curb outside her building, I dialed Tucker, needing to vent to someone who comprehended the predicament.

"Give her some time," he said. "You know how she is. Once she's had a chance to cool off, she'll come around."

I wasn't so sure. Venetia held a grudge better than anyone I knew. She'd gone months without speaking to Sam after his wedding. I didn't have time to waste. Our baby was due in five months, and I didn't want to miss one minute of the pregnancy. "She's a Seaforth. She can hold a grudge forever. Our kid will be out of high school before she speaks to me again." I watched the streetscape flash by in a blur of trees and cars and gray buildings.

"Then you'll just have to come up with something to change her mind," Tucker said.

Chapter 40

Venetia

A WEEK passed then two. I threw myself into work with unprecedented intensity. I took on three new clients and scored an interview in a local magazine. Beckett called or texted every day, and every day I ignored him. I didn't want to talk to him.

Sydney showed up in the nick of time to pull me out of my funk. She arrived with an extravagant baby carriage, the kind with big wheels and leather appointments. Once she'd unpacked, we sprawled on my king-sized bed, ate ice cream from the carton, and watched pay-per-view movies.

"You know what I think?" Sydney waved her ice cream spoon in the air as she spoke. "I think you should give Beckett a break. I mean, the poor guy's in love with you. You're having his baby. He's hot. What's the problem?"

I scoffed and opened a pint of cookie dough ice cream. "He lied to me. You don't lie to the people you love."

She leaned to steal a spoonful from my carton. "Tucker says—"

"You've been talking to Tucker? I thought you were going to break it off."

A flush crept up her neck and settled in her cheeks. "No. I know. I need to tell him." The sparkle in her eyes extinguished, and my heart squeezed for her. "I told the studio. My agent tried to negotiate a deal with them, but they won't drop the wedding. They've got millions of dollars invested. If I don't go through with it, they're going to sue me. The studio heads promised my career will be over." She huffed out a heavy breath, lifting her bangs.

"Syd, you've got to tell Tucker. He's going to be devastated."

"I know." A mist of tears shone in her eyes. "I'm a terrible person, aren't I?"

"You're not terrible." I pulled her into a hug, as much as I could with my baby bump between us, and rubbed circles on her back. Her tears dampened my shoulder. "But you're making a terrible mistake. I thought you loved Tucker."

"I do. Tucker's wonderful, but Alex isn't so bad either. I mean, he's hot, right? And successful. This wedding will do a lot for our careers." At the thought of her impending success, her tone brightened. "If Tucker really loves me, he'll understand."

"I don't think he will. Tucker's not like that." I stared at my friend, wondering how we'd grown so far apart. In the space of a few months, we'd taken different paths. I still loved her—would always love her—but I couldn't agree with the way she was abusing Tucker. He was a sweet guy and didn't deserve to be jerked around. I covered her hand with mine and squeezed. "Look, I'll support you in whatever you choose to do, but I can't lie to Tucker anymore. If he asks me questions, I'm going to tell him the truth."

After a long sigh, she pursed her lips and nodded. "Okay, that's cool." She rolled onto her stomach and waved her feet in the air behind her, the way she had when we were kids. It felt good to have her there, even if we were at odds. Being with her was comfortable, familiar. I smiled at her, and her eyes widened. "I think you should come with me to Cabo."

"Have you seen my belly? It's getting bigger by the minute." I rubbed my tummy and smiled at the answering kick from inside.

"Don't give me that. You're hardly showing. Besides baby bumps are all the rage right now." The movie ended, and she flicked off the TV with the remote. "Think about it. You can lounge on the beach while I film and get some good rest."

Chapter 41

Beckett

I WASN'T so sure about Tucker's advice, but when Venetia failed to return my calls, I had no choice but to give her some space. Even though I was angry with her, I was more furious with myself. This entire situation seemed pointless. We both needed time to think, but every minute away from her hurt. I worried about her. Was she feeling okay? I didn't want to lose out on the miracle of her pregnancy. I'd been forced out of her life, and I didn't like it.

A week dragged by. I spent hours going over information Garth had provided, wrapping up all the details of my open cases, anything to avoid going back to an empty apartment. It seemed dull and lifeless without Venetia there. Everything reminded me of her, of something she'd said or done. The pain grew sharper every day. I missed her smell, her warmth, the ring of her laughter, and the way her nose scrunched when I said something funny.

I reached an agreement with Daniels and Quaid and only had a few weeks left until I'd be unemployed. I received enough money from the dissolution to live comfortably for the rest of the year, but I had the baby to think about. There'd be clothing and doctor's bills, later on college. I was deep in these thoughts, when my cell phone rang, I picked up the call without checking to see who it was.

"Thanksgiving dinner. My place. Next Thursday night," Sam said, in his short, clipped tones.

Thanksgiving already? Time had become irrelevant, dragging by in slow, painful ticks. I hadn't even thought about the holidays. My parents were on a Caribbean cruise, my brothers at colleges across the country. I had nowhere to go.

"Who's cooking?" I asked. It was no secret that Dakota couldn't do much more than boil water.

His quiet chuckle made me smile for the first time in days. "I'm going to tell her you said that."

"Don't you dare. I was just wondering if I should eat first." We both laughed. I expected a lingering awkwardness in our relationship, but he didn't seem to harbor any animosity toward me. Our Wednesday morning workouts continued without incident, but I couldn't help noticing the way he avoided the subject of Venetia.

"Relax. Burgers on the grill," he said. "That's my domain."

"For Thanksgiving?"

"Hey, it's a free meal," he teased. "You got a better offer?"

"No." I hesitated. "Is Venetia going to be there?"

"No. I think she's going somewhere with Sydney," he said. I breathed a sigh of relief. "You guys still haven't made up?"

"No." My gut squeezed, the way it did every time I thought about her. "She hates me. She won't even talk to me."

"Give her time. She'll come around. Stubborn as a mule, you know?"

"Yeah, I know." God, did I ever.

"Look, dinner's at seven. We'll watch the game. Supposed to be a barn burner." Sam's words took on an impersonal precision. "Three copies, Xavier. And one for the file."

It took a second for me to recognize the name of Sam's former assistant. "Xavier's there?" After the close of our joint corporation, most of the employees had been relocated to another of Sam's many companies or given severance packages.

"Sure. The little fucker's good at what he does."

"And what, exactly, does he do?" I asked. Sam still had viable businesses, but he'd sold the more lucrative ones to make up for his personal debt.

"I'm not really sure." His throaty laugh brought a smile to my face. "But he does it well. Besides, I don't have time to train someone new."

"I thought you were belly up."

"Let's just say I've got a contingency plan." Another laugh from the other side of the phone line, this one quiet and laden with secrets. "You didn't think I'd go down without a fight, did you?"

"What are you up to, Seaforth?" I had a mental image of Sam seated behind the desk of a top-secret underground facility with his minions scurrying around him as he devised a plan to conquer the rat race.

"All in good time, my friend." His voice took on a sharper edge, the one he used for boardrooms and business. "What about you? Destroy any marriages lately?"

"Seems I'm heading into a change of career," I said. "The partners asked me to leave. I'm pretty sure Maxwell had a hand in it."

"Really?" I heard the interest in Sam's voice and gave him the short version of the events leading up to my situation. "Interesting. Look, I've got to go. Conference call from Japan in ten. But we'll talk more about this Thursday. I think I might have an opportunity for you."

Chapter 42

Venetia

IT WAS a little past noon on the following Tuesday that I found myself sandwiched between endless bolts of velvet and satin fabrics at an upscale upholstery shop on the upper east side. Helena clutched a purple throw pillow in one hand and her tablet in the other. I squinted at the pillow, the picture on the tablet, and the assortment of cloth in front of us then shook my head.

"This is impossible," I said. "We're never going to find anything to match that stupid pillow."

"You can and you will," Helena said firmly. "I've got faith in you."

Although we'd only known each other for a short time, Helena and I had fallen into an easy friendship. Before her, I'd always been the assistant, the one fetching coffee, scheduling appointments, and holding the throw pillow. It felt a little strange to be on the opposite side of the table, but Helena had immediately put me at ease.

"Whoever heard of a purple-and-green color scheme in a French chalet?" I asked Helena. She laughed and came to stand at my side. We stared at the offensive throw pillow and tilted our heads to the left in synchronicity.

"Maybe you could—" Helena's phone buzzed. She stopped mid-sentence to pull it from her handbag and frowned at the caller ID. "It's him again," she said in a stage whisper, as if whoever it was could hear her. "Hello?" Her eyes met mine.

"Yes, Mr. Beckett. I gave her your message."

I shook my head vehemently. I didn't want to talk to Beckett. The thought of him caused my chest to ache. He'd hurt me, however unintentional it might have been, and I wasn't ready to forgive him yet. She rolled her eyes but ended the call. Two seconds later, my phone vibrated in my pocket. I groaned and knew without looking it was him.

"Persistent bugger, isn't he?" Helena flashed a toothy smile. She was head-to-toe perfection in a sage green pantsuit.

"He's getting on my nerves," I said.

"Answer it, or he'll never stop." She snatched my phone out of my pocket and handed it to me.

"Fine." I yanked the phone out of her grasp. "Stop calling me, Beckett."

"Hi. Venetia? Hello." His deep, rich voice washed over me.

Tingles of attraction sparked along my nerve endings. "Hello," I replied and fell silent. Tears stung my eyes. I placed a hand over my chest. I had no idea how much I missed him, how much it would hurt to hear his voice.

"I didn't expect you to answer." I heard the slow intake of his breath while he formulated his next sentence. "How are you?"

"Fine." I dropped my gaze to a bolt of lavender damask and fingered the edge. Helena's curious stare bored into me. I turned my back to her, needing to conceal whatever emotion flashed across my face.

"Why haven't you returned any of my calls? We need to talk this out."

"You know why," I cupped a hand around the phone, not wanting Helena to hear.

He groaned. The delicious sound shimmered into my ear and dissipated in waves through the pleasure centers of my brain. "Let me make it up to you. We can start over."

"No." I continued to peruse the aisles of fabric, pretending to shop, but I saw nothing.

"Come on, V. Just one dinner. Some good food. A little conversation." Sensing my hesitation, he ramped up the charm a notch. "You know how I hate to eat alone."

"No." I wanted to go with every fiber of my being, but my obstinate nature overruled physical desire. Besides, I needed to learn a little self-restraint, and I decided to start with Beckett.

"Lunch?"

"No."

"Breakfast?"

"No." I suppressed a chuckle. I admired his persistence, but my hurt pride required more than a plate of pancakes to soothe it.

"I didn't get where I am by giving up." He fell silent, but I could hear his even breathing. "Look. I'm sorry about Maxwell. I should've told you in the beginning. I just never knew—I didn't realize—" His voice trailed off, tinged with frustration. "Hell, V. I never knew you'd come to mean so much to me. I didn't know I was going to fall in love with you."

My resolve weakened with every passing second. I closed my eyes and remembered his hot kisses along my throat, the feel of him deep inside me, riding me to a climax so mind-bending it stole away my breath. Every fiber of my being yearned for him. As if in protest, the baby shifted, stabbing one of my kidneys. I placed a hand on my stomach, easing the ache. Another uncomfortable silence ensued. When I couldn't bear it any longer, I invented an emergency. "Look, I've got to go. I'll talk to you later."

"When?" he asked. The hope in his voice brought the sting of tears to my eyes. "I miss you, V."

I swiped at my eyes with the back of my hand. "I miss you too," I whispered. His next words split my heart in two.

"Then tell me what to do, and I'll make this right."

"I can't." My throat tightened around the words. "I need time to think, to figure out who I am, and I can't do that around you. Just give me some time."

He was silent, but I heard his breathing on the other side of the call. When he spoke, pain echoed in his voice. "Do what you need to get through this, but don't take too long, okay? I don't want to miss out on one minute of having this baby with you."

Chapter 43

Venetia

FOR THE tenth time, I dumped my purse on the bed in search of my passport. I scrambled through lipsticks, packs of chewing gum, and pens. Sydney frowned from the doorway, hands on hips, a nervous glint in her eyes. As I searched, all I could think about was Beckett. Tomorrow was Thanksgiving. In my fantasies, before our falling out, I'd dreamed about our first holiday together as a couple. Knowing it wasn't going to happen left me with a dull ache that no amount of sun and surf could cure.

"Come on, V. We're going to be late," Sydney said again. "The car's downstairs waiting."

"I know. I know." I turned and, for the eleventh time, dug through the contents of my desk drawer. "It was here. I swear it."

What was Beckett doing? He probably went home to his family for the holiday. He probably wasn't even in town. My fingers curled with the urge to call his number just to hear his voice.

"Oh my God, you do this every time." Sydney gritted her teeth and slapped a hand to her forehead, drawing me back to the current dilemma.

"Crap. I'm sorry. Sorry." With an impatient groan, I squeezed my eyes shut and tried to remember the last place I'd had it. I felt curiously close to tears, my hormones swinging unpredictably. "I can't think with you talking. Just give me a minute."

"I don't know why I ever go anywhere with you," Sydney continued to grumble. She withdrew her cell from her purse and scrolled through her contacts. "I'll call my agent and tell him we're going to miss our flight."

"No, no. Don't do that." I scanned the room. "I have no idea where it's at, but I'll find it."

Sydney glanced from the clock to my face and back again. I rummaged through the desk drawers one last time, cursing myself. She grabbed my hands and pulled them together between us. "V, stop a minute. Look at me."

"What?" I frowned at the interruption to my frantic search and bit my lower lip.

"Sweetie, why are you crying?"

"I don't know." The words broke on a hiccup.

"Aw, come here." Another tear slid down my cheek. She swiped it away with her thumb and shook her head, dark hair swinging above her shoulders. "Sit down a second." She patted the bed. We sat down together, my hands still in hers. "I think that deep down, you don't really want to go."

"Sure I do," I said, but the minute the words left my lips, I recognized them for a lie.

"No, you don't." She squeezed my hands. "It's okay. I understand."

"I miss him," I said. The confession tumbled out and my tears quickened. "I don't want to have this baby without him. I need him, Syd."

"Shhhh. Hush. I know. I know." Her arms stole around my shoulders and pulled me into a warm hug. "You love him. Who am I to stand in the way of true love? Go be with him."

"I want to. I do." Another hiccup wracked my chest. "But he hurt me."

"Of course he did. That's what people do. They hurt each other." She rocked me back and forth, patting my back until I stopped sniffling. "You've got to get over this need to always be right."

"I know." We pulled apart. I studied my fingernails, embarrassed by my emotional outburst.

"So, I'm going to go, and you're going to call Beckett." Her bright smile eased my distress.

She made it sound so easy, but I didn't call him. Instead, I stared at my phone, willing it to ring. For once, it seemed Beckett had taken my advice and didn't call. My pride was going to steal the only man I'd ever loved, if I didn't do something. I decided to take the night and sleep on it. Sam and Dakota had invited me to dinner at their house. Maybe they would be able to help me mend the breach with Beckett.

On Thanksgiving day, Dakota greeted me at the door with a hug and a smile. I hugged her back, feeling awkward with my belly bumping into her. The aroma of burgers and brats wafted through the air. I drew in a deep breath and tried to think positive thoughts. I could do this. I could be nice. Drama no longer appealed to me the way it had a few months ago. I just wanted peace in my life.

"I'm so glad to see you," Dakota said. "There's way too much testosterone in here."

To prove her point, deep male voices rumbled from the other side of the apartment, where I could hear the game blaring over the TV. I followed the sounds of shouting into the living room. Sam stood in front of the flat screen, beer in hand. Tucker sprawled over a club chair by the fireplace. My heart pounded as I recognized the third person. Someone made a touchdown in the game. Beckett leaped from the couch and pumped a fist in the air.

"Yeah. That's right," he declared in his low, sexy voice. My stomach flipped. "Pay up, Seaforth."

"Game's not over yet," Sam said. The three of them turned to face me, sensing my presence. "Hey, V. Come on in."

Tucker lifted his beer in a toast. "Want a beer? Or a glass of wine? Beckett brought some great pinot."

I didn't hear the rest of what Tucker said, too busy staring at Beckett. Our gazes locked across the room. The smile left his lips. My heart pounded so hard I thought my ribs might crack. A gray Henley stretched over his broad shoulders, and black stubble dusted his square jaw. He looked tired. My fingers curled, filled with the urge to run through his hair, and smooth the worried lines from his forehead.

"No, I'm pregnant. Remember, goofball?" I managed to croak at last. "I'll have some water." I turned and made my way back to the kitchen on weak knees.

"I thought she wasn't coming," Beckett said as I left the room. His statement weakened my self-confidence. Had I waited too long? Had his feelings changed toward me?

"Her plans fell through," Sam replied, and I lost the rest of their conversation when Dakota handed me a glass of water.

I wasn't prepared for the way I felt. All of the hurt and betrayal returned in a rush. I put a hand on the breakfast bar and tried to calm my breathing.

"Are you okay?" Dakota put a reassuring hand on my back. "You don't look so good."

"I'm fine, just tired," I replied. "Can I help you with anything?" I didn't know squat about the kitchen, but then, neither did Dakota.

She gave me a smile. "Well, you could set the table, I guess."

The menial task took my mind off the men in the other room. For a minute, I considered grabbing my coat from the closet and bolting out the door, but I'd come too far to chicken out now. Like it or not, Beckett was in my life forever. Our child bound us together, for better or worse, tighter than any legal documents. I needed to find a way to get over his betrayal and my pride for the sake of the baby. We had to get along, even if it killed me to see him.

"Can I talk to you for a second?" I jumped at hearing Beckett's voice in my ear.

I placed a hand over my heart. "You scared the crap out of me."

"Sorry." The rich brown of his eyes caused a flurry of butterflies in my stomach. I saw the shadows under his eyes and felt a quick surge of protectiveness. "We can't keep going on like this." He took one of my hands in his and turned me to face him. "V, talk to me."

Hearing the texture of his voice, feeling his hand on mine, it broke me. The pain and anger I'd been harboring for the past few weeks swelled. "You hurt me." My voice cracked. "You should've told me about Maxwell. I trusted you. You should've had my back."

"Baby, I know. I'm so sorry." He brushed the hair away from my face and swept his fingertips along my jaw. "This whole deal has been a mess from the beginning, and I'm sorry. It kills me to see you unhappy like this."

I turned my face into his hand, brushing my lips against his palm. He smelled clean, like soap and fabric softener, and his skin tasted of salt.

"When Maxwell came to me for help, I had no idea you were pregnant, that I was going to fall in love with you. I got a little distracted from what was important, but it didn't take me long to figure it out." His gaze searched mine. A thrill of attraction bolted into my center. No, it was more than attraction; it was need, *desire*. "I know we got a rocky start, but we can make this work. I want to make it work with you."

The room faded around us until I saw nothing but him. Overhead lights glinted off his black hair, hair I knew felt as silky as it looked. I swallowed and looked away to keep him from seeing the emotion in my eyes. Hearing his words, I couldn't remember why I'd ever been angry with him in the first place. This was Beckett, my Beckett, the guy I'd loved from afar for half my life. Now he wanted me. *Me.* And we were having a baby together. Nothing seemed more important than being together. I'd be a fool to turn him away when he was everything I'd ever wanted.

"I want to make it work, too," I whispered and faced him. "I was wrong to tell Sam without you. I owe you an apology for that." I cupped his cheeks in my hands, feeling the scratch of his beard against my palms. "You're a good man, Beckett."

"You have to talk to me about things. We have to work at this. God knows, this isn't going to be easy, but I have faith in us." He leaned forward to press a kiss on my forehead. All of my reserve crumbled. My fingers curled into the fabric of his shirt. His arms stole around my waist and pulled me into his chest, into the curve of his neck where I belonged.

Chapter 44

Beckett

I HAD no idea how badly I wanted to hear those words from her lips until she said them. *You're a good man, Beckett.* It was all I ever wanted to be, really. For her. For the baby.

Thanks to Maxwell and the firm, my reputation had suffered a hit. I didn't care. People were fickle, and it wouldn't take long to rebuild the damage done. My stellar record spoke volumes about my work. Besides, I had a change of career in mind. Sam had something cooking. I could tell by the gleam in his eyes that he was ready to make a comeback, and I intended to be by his side.

A few days into the new year, I was about to cross the street, when V called my phone. The sight of her name on my caller ID tightened all the muscles in my groin. "Hey," I said.

"Hey, yourself." I liked the sweet, soft tone she used when it was just the two of us. "Can you stop by the store and pick up some toothpaste? I think you're out."

She stayed at my apartment almost every night these days. Once, I would've cringed at the idea of a woman in my space, but now I enjoyed the sprawl of her cosmetics on my bathroom sink and the sight of her panties in the dresser drawer next to my boxers. The lease would be up on her penthouse in a few months, and I intended to have her move in with me once the baby came.

"Yep. Be there in fifteen."

"And Beckett?"

"Yeah, baby?"

"Can you hurry?"

The hopeful tone of her voice prodded my feet to jog down the street to the nearest convenience store.

A few hours later, we were in bed, a proper bed with a frame, the one she'd purchased with my credit card a few weeks earlier. She reclined against the headboard, a copy of *Architectural Digest* propped on her knees. The sight of her in my bed, all soft curves and femininity, warmed my heart and hardened my dick.

"Did you turn off the coffee pot?" She poked me in the ribs with a fingertip. "Why are you staring at me like that?"

"Because I like you in my bed," I said. "And yes, I turned off the coffee pot."

Her blond hair was piled into a messy bun on top of her head. A few long strands escaped and hung down her back. Fresh pink polish tipped the toes of her feet and fingers and matched the flannel nightshirt outlining the prominent swell of her belly. I turned on my side and propped my head up with my elbow to see her better. The baby had grown into a round basketball over the past few weeks.

"Are you listening to me?" she asked.

"Sorry?" I took the magazine from her hands and tossed it to the floor.

"What are you doing?" She frowned, an adorable crinkle in her nose. "I was reading that."

"Come here." I tugged her down beside me.

"Beckett. You're going to smudge my nails." She wriggled in protest.

"I'll repaint them for you." My hands found purchase on her breasts and gave a gentle squeeze. She squirmed, but I kept going, if only to hear more of her laughter. The musical lilt of the sound buoyed my spirit more than a goal by my favorite team or winning any divorce case. "Just one kiss."

She pushed playfully at my chest as I attempted to pull her against me. "I know how you are. One kiss, and I'll be naked again."

"And what's so wrong with that?" Once my hand found her bottom and squeezed, she stopped protesting and melted into my chest. The baby pressed against my abs, a round, welcome intruder into our circle. Then I felt it. A gentle jab against my belly. I looked up at Venetia. Her eyes had gone misty and soft.

"Did you feel it?" she asked on an exhale.

"Yes. Was that her?" A tremor of pure excitement flooded through my core. I'd been trying for weeks to feel one of the kicks but had missed out every time.

"Or him," she said, just to tease me. "And yes. Give me your hand. Here." She pressed my palm to the left side of her belly, where I a second, confident poke prodded my hand.

"That's amazing." Our eyes met. Nothing had ever been more right or perfect in my life.

Chapter 45

Venetia

BECKETT PULLED up my nightshirt, baring the growing mound of my belly, and pressed a kiss above my navel. His big hand circled around the bump, loving and tender in its touch. The puff of his breath tickled against my skin. I bit my lower lip and squeezed my eyes shut to hold back tears of happiness.

Little by little, with Beckett's help, I'd begun to put my future together. I rented an office space in a quiet neighborhood and hired two more assistants, putting Helena in charge. I had a long way to go, but with time and effort, I felt confident I'd succeed. None of that mattered without Beckett at my side.

"You're going to be so loved, little one," Beckett whispered to my belly.

My chest constricted to hear the emotion in his voice. I ran a hand through his hair. The dark strands had gotten longer than his usual short, spiky cut, but it looked good on him. His kisses traveled farther down the slope of my stomach, nearing the patch of hair below my pelvis. He swept a hand along the bare skin of my inner thigh, pushing my legs apart to allow his mouth better access.

"Ah," I murmured as his tongue teased my clit.

He paused and lifted his head. "Still worried about your manicure? I can stop if you want."

"No. I'm good." I nudged his head down and felt his wicked smile against my thigh.

He knew exactly the places to lick, the right amount of pressure, the perfect time to slow down or speed up. The texture of his tongue on my sensitive flesh caused my legs to twitch. Tingles of pleasure radiated from my hips down my legs to my toes.

One of his fingers slipped inside me, then two. Combined with the slide and glide of his tongue, the pressure of his lips, and the heat of his breath, he undid all my self-control. I writhed against his mouth, needing more, ready to rush into climax but hoping it would never end.

The first time I met Beckett, he was the object of my teenaged fantasies. When we met in New Orleans, I had no idea how one night of passion would change both of our lives forever. During our relationship, I lost my father, but I gained a wonderful man. It was all worth it—the sleepless nights, the tears, and the uncertainty—because it led me to him.

Epilogue

Venetia

ON A cold spring day in early April, I met Beckett for lunch at the bistro near his temporary office. He planned to merge with Sam and create a new corporation. After the baby arrived, I planned to join the team as an investor and partner. Together, we'd build a new Seaforth empire. In the interim, Beckett continued his family law practice.

After a chicken pasta salad and iced tea, we walked side by side along the street, back to his building. He looked dashing in a long black trench coat with a sky-blue scarf around his neck and polished Italian shoes on his feet. The guy had a sense of style, and I was proud to be seen at his side. By the number of admiring female glances tossed his direction, I wasn't the only girl who noticed. I pulled together the lapels of my coat, conscious of the twenty pounds I'd gained over the past few months. Between water retention and a ravenous appetite, I'd gone up two dress sizes and felt like a fat cow. His gaze never wandered from the sidewalk ahead of us though, not once, not even a flicker in the direction of the smiling college girls or the model-like twin brunettes.

"Are you cold?" Beckett regarded me, concern etched in the lines around his mouth. "I'll get a cab." He raised an arm and waved at a passing taxi. The crazy spring weather had bounced between sunshine and snow for the past week. Overhead, pear and cherry trees boasted bright blossoms. Irises and hyacinths poked through the thin layer of snow that dusted the green grass.

"No. I'm fine." I caught his forearm with my hand and pulled it down to my side. "I need the exercise."

"Are you sure?" He stopped walking and turned to face me.

A shiver snaked down my spine. Not from the cold but from the heat in his eyes. No man had ever looked at me like that, only Beckett. And I realized the others no longer mattered, because he was the only man I needed in my life. I trusted him, and I knew he'd always be there for me. "Yes, I'm sure." A surge of giddiness lightened my heart.

"I can't have you catching a cold," he said and touched the tip of his finger to the end of my nose.

I savored the moment, unsure when or if the next one might appear. I needed to grab each and every instance of happiness, enjoy life, and take each moment with Beckett as a precious gift.

Several snowflakes fluttered through the air between us and spiraled to the pavement. I followed their trajectory to our feet. One of them landed on Beckett's shoe and melted. When I glanced up again, Beckett's attention had snared on a couple standing at the crosswalk. A small child, two or three years of age, was suspended between his parents, each of his little hands secured by one of theirs. The light changed, and the parents lifted the little boy into the air. His delighted squeals brought a smile to Beckett's full mouth.

"I can't wait," he said. His low, textured voice caused all the muscles below my waist to clench. "I can't wait until our little one gets here."

"Really?" I found it difficult to catch my breath with him looking at me so intently.

His smile turned his dark eyes to liquid chocolate. "You're the best thing that ever happened to me. I thank God every day for that night in New Orleans." He leaned forward and pressed a kiss to my forehead. My pulse tripled. "Our child is the best thing that ever happened to me."

"What if he's ugly? What if he has a hump on his back or three eyeballs?" I teased.

"Are you kidding me? Have you seen his mother?" Beckett wrapped an arm around my waist and began walking again with me tucked into his side. "She's gorgeous. The most beautiful woman I've ever seen." He cast a cocky sideways glance beneath his lashes. "There's no way this kid could be less than a knockout."

"I hope he looks like you," I whispered.

It all felt so right, his arm around me, the way I fit into his shoulder like I belonged there. The fullness in my chest threatened to break my ribs. I blinked back the sting of happy tears and tried to keep my feet from floating above the sidewalk. Things like this just didn't happen to me. *Me*. Venetia Seaforth. The forgotten one.

"Have you thought about names?" he asked.

"No. Have you?"

"Sure. Horatio," he said. I cringed, making him laugh. "Or Ophelia, if it's a girl."

I sucked in a horrified breath. "Are you kidding me? That's terrible." By his smirk, he was teasing. "After a lifetime of being named Venetia, I could never do that to my kid." I relaxed and smiled back. "What about something simple like Jane? Jane Seaforth," I said, testing it out.

"Don't you mean Jane Beckett?" The smile slipped from his lips. "This is my child. I want him or her to have my name."

I'd assumed our child would take the Seaforth name, my name. It never even occurred to me that Beckett might want the kid to take his name, too. Even though I wasn't a Seaforth by blood, I felt a loyalty to the name, my mother's name, Sam's name.

We stared at each other, at an impasse.

"What about Jane Beckett Seaforth?" I offered.

"Or Jane Seaforth Beckett?" he countered. By the set of his shoulders, he

277

wasn't going to budge on this point. I lifted my chin and stared back. At my gesture of defiance, he shook his head and chuckled. "There's plenty of time to discuss it. Why don't we table this for later when we've both had time to think on it?"

A strand of hair fluttered away from my temple. He tucked it behind my ear. The simple brush of his fingers on my bare skin sent tingles along my neck. "Okay. Later." I'd never been good at compromise, but I wanted to please him. His smiles did something unspeakable to my insides. I resolved to keep an open mind and at least hear him out when the time came to revisit the topic.

"Wait. Take a look at this." He changed direction suddenly and led me to a nearby storefront filled with children's toys. "I've got to buy that." He pointed toward a miniature baseball glove, no bigger than a deck of cards.

"Beckett, you can't be serious." I laughed at the bewilderment on his face. "Don't you have to go back to the office?"

"I do, but in a minute." He tucked my hand into his elbow and pressed his lips into my hair, voice insistent against my ear.

"You know I love you, right?" The glimmer in his eyes made me regret not saying it more often, for waiting too long to say it the first time.

He smiled and brushed his fingers beneath my chin then gave me a soft kiss on the corner of my mouth. Tender, loving, and gentle. "I know, baby."

Ten minutes later we resumed our walk, with Beckett's wallet a good deal lighter and my mind whirling from the frenzy I'd just witnessed. Beckett had bought so many toys, the store had offered to deliver them to his apartment.

"Where are you going to put all that stuff?" I asked, thinking about the open concept of his studio apartment.

He threaded his fingers through mine, lifted my hand and brushed his lips across my knuckles. "In our house. The one I'm going to buy." He tucked my hand into the crook of his elbow and smiled down at me. "The one you're going to live in with me after we get married."

My heart skipped a beat. "Piers Beckett. Is that your idea of a proposal?" I stopped in the street and propped my hands on my hips.

His eyes twinkled with mischief. "No." Deep laughter rumbled through his chest. "I'm just warning you. When you least expect it, I'm going to ask. And I hope you'll say yes."

"I guess you'll just have to wait and find out," I teased but I already knew my answer.

We walked on, comfortable in our silence. When we stopped at the corner to cross the street, something warm and wet trickled down my leg. A sharp, twinge followed, low in my back. I drew in a hissing breath.

"What is that?" Beckett frowned and stared at the puddle around our feet.

"I think my water just broke."

Beckett

Ten fingers. Ten toes. I counted them over and over, unable to believe the tiny miracle in my arms. She was perfect in every way from the top of her fuzzy blond head to the tips of her kicking feet. My daughter. *Mine.* I had no idea the way my world would shift with the arrival of this new bundle of life. Too many intense feelings tangled together inside me as I held my baby girl for the first time. Protectiveness. Joy. Relief. I blinked against the burn of tears, startled by the flood of emotion.

"See I told you." I turned to Venetia, angling the infant so we could both admire her cherubic face. "She's a knockout, just like her mom."

Venetia held out her arms. Her hands trembled. She was exhausted from sixteen hours of hard labor, and no wonder. The last few hours had damn near killed me, and I'd been a spectator. I placed the baby on her chest then smoothed the damp strands of hair away from her forehead. She smiled, and my heart swelled until I thought it might burst.

"Have you decided on a name yet?" one of the nurses asked.

"I was thinking about Ellen," Venetia said, casting a questioning glance at me. "If that's all right with you."

"I think it's a perfect name for a perfect baby." I bent and pressed a fierce kiss to Venetia's forehead. "Do you have any idea how much I love you? Both of you?"

She smiled, and it was the bright, brilliant smile I cherished. "I love you, too, Piers Beckett."

I kneeled down on one knee beside the bed, ignoring the hardness of the cold floor, and dug a hand into the breast pocket of my shirt where I kept the ring. I'd been carrying it around for weeks, waiting for the perfect moment. "Marry me, V. Maybe this isn't the best time, but I can't leave this hospital without knowing you're mine. Both of you."

A tear slid down her cheek and quivered on the point of her chin. "I can't think of a better time," she whispered, her voice breaking on the last word. "And the answer is yes."

--The End.

Before You Go

DID YOU ENJOY READING THIS BOOK?

If you did, please help others enjoy it, too.

Lend it.

Recommend it.

Review it at Amazon, iBooks, or Goodreads.

If you leave a review, please send me an email at jeanamann@yahoo.com or a message on Facebook so that I can thank you with a personal email.

WIN A $50 GIFT CARD!!

Monthly giveaway inside my newsletter.

Get the inside scoop on new and upcoming books, sneak peeks, sales, book signings, and giveaways!

A gift card winner will be chosen at random each month.

SIGN UP HERE!

Other books by Jeana E. Mann

Felony Romance Series

Intoxicated

Unexpected

Vindicated

Impulsive

Drift

Pretty Broken Series

Pretty Broken Girl

Pretty Filthy Lies

Pretty Dirty Secrets

Pretty Wild Thing

Pretty Broken Promises (Dec 2016)

Published by Ishkadiddle Publishing
Copyright 2016. Jeana E. Mann Author.
Cover by Ishkadiddle Publishing
Edited by Rhonda Helms

Ebook
ISBN-10: 1-943938-05-9
ISBN-13: 978-1-943938-05-6

This ebook is licensed for your personal enjoyment only. This ebook may not be resold or given away to other people. If you would like to share this book with another person, please purchase an additional copy for each person. If you're reading this book and did not purchase it, or it was not purchased for your use only, then please return it and purchase your own copy. Thank you for respecting the hard work of this author. To obtain permission to excerpt portions of the text, please contact the author at jeanamann@yahoo.com

All characters and events in this book are fiction and figments of the author's imagination. Any similarity to real persons, alive or deceased, is purely coincidental.

www.jeanaemann.net

Jeana Mann is the award-winning author of hot contemporary romance. She is a member of Romance Writers' of America (RWA).

Jeana was born and raised in Indiana where she lives today with her two crazy rat terriers Mildred and Mabel. She graduated from Indiana University with a degree in Speech and Hearing, something totally unrelated to writing. When she's not busy dreaming up steamy romance novels, she loves to travel anywhere and everywhere. Over the years she climbed the ruins of Chichen Iza in Mexico, snorkeled along the shores of Hawaii, driven the track at the Indy 500, sailed around Jamaica, ate gelato on the steps of the Pantheon in Rome, and explored the ancient city of Pompeii. More important than the places she's been are the people she has met along the way.

Be sure to connect with Jeana on Facebook or follow along on Twitter for the latest news regarding her upcoming releases.

LINKS

Website   Facebook   Twitter   Goodreads

Made in the USA
Monee, IL
03 March 2023

29122634R00164